ANGEL'S CONQUEST

A PARANORMAL ANGEL ROMANCE

ELEMENTAL ANGELS

AIMEE ROBINSON

AMR PUBLISHING LLC

Angel's Conquest

Copyright © 2024 by Aimee Robinson

Cover by Angela Haddon Book Cover Design

Edited by Sara Burgess at Telltail Editing

All rights reserved.

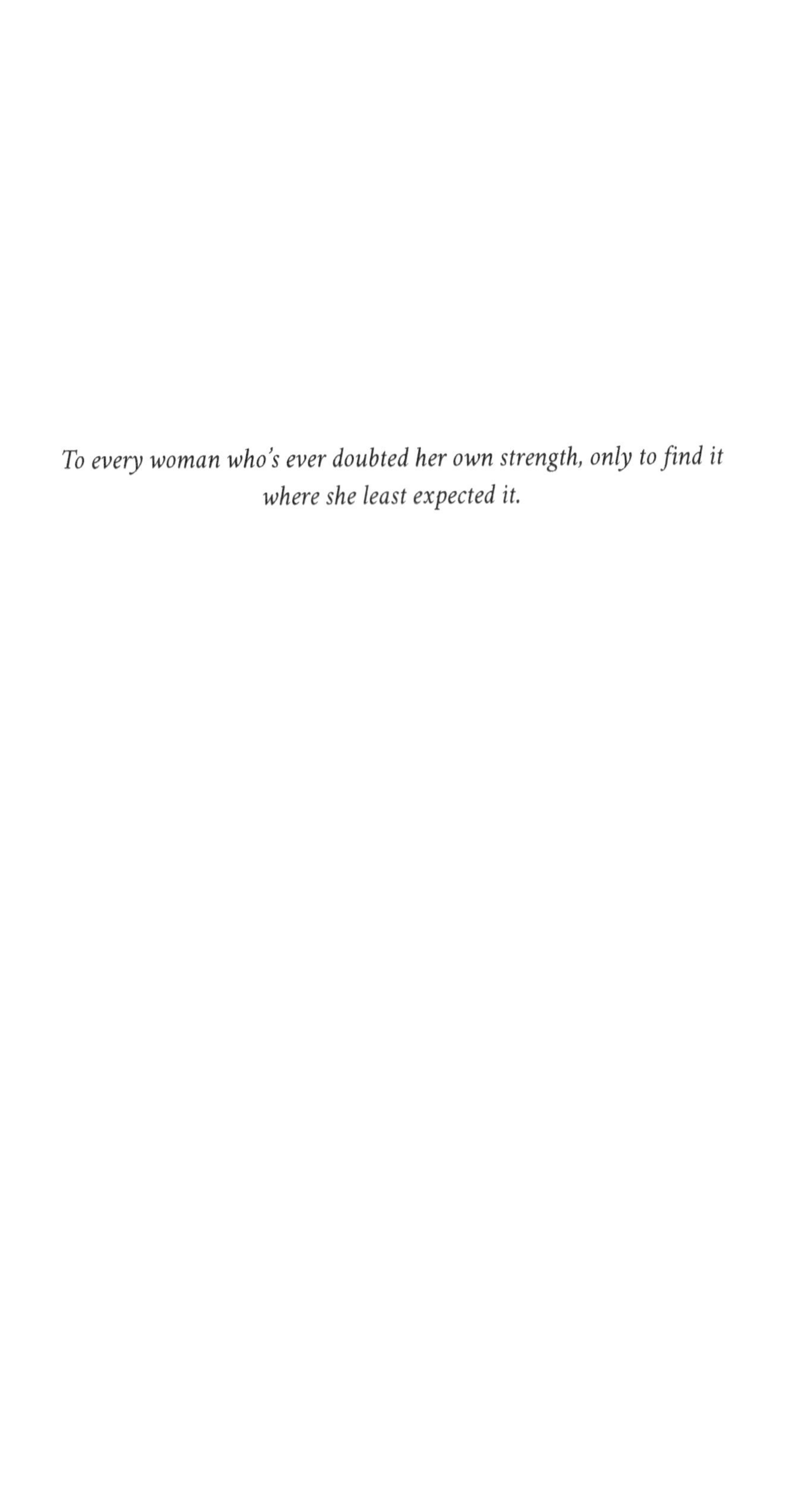

To every woman who's ever doubted her own strength, only to find it where she least expected it.

ELEMENTAL ANGELS

CHAPTER 1

An ancient oak's spindly tree branch snagged against Clara Ander's fine cloak, nearly choking off her air supply and her hasty retreat. Her preference for keeping the former alive and well was only mildly contingent on the latter succeeding.

If she failed, well . . . it wasn't something she was willing to contemplate.

She'd learned long ago that Hell wasn't simply some pit in the ground reserved for those with bad behavior and dark intentions. For Clara, it was a highly personalized and promised experience, complete with custom-measured cells and unbreakable chains, and one that was tipping closer to her defenses with each passing moon.

The cloak pulled harder against her windpipe, and pain lanced across a throat already too tight and dry from her exertions. Before the forest's darkened terrain swallowed her entirely, she managed to kick her leg out and steady herself against a moss-slicken log.

Maybe she did need a moment of rest. Just one moment, though. A slight nod of relief over not having been taken out before she'd had her first chance at freedom, and by a damned tree at that. Outside of the occasional controlled hunts her father, the king, permitted her to entertain, her wolf's reflexes had received little use as of late. Thank the Moon Mother they'd not failed her now. She'd take whatever they could offer.

Though the moon was newly high overhead, its crescent sliver was hardly enough to illuminate the slim footpaths winding across the forest floor. Clara had heard tales of passages leading away from the stronghold, ones that led to the human lands, but how the hell did she know she'd taken the right one? Surely, the merchant she'd purchased her hiking boots from hadn't lied to her, had she?

She isn't in my father's employ, not directly. Did I misjudge the old female's loyalty?

No, best not to think that way. Clara *had* to be on the right path, especially after the kind of money she'd been forced to pony up. In that line of work, a trade so reliant on favorable word of mouth, giving out poor information was bad for business.

Yes, the female had sent Clara in the right direction.

Shoring up her shaky beliefs, she clasped her cloak tighter around her shoulders and breathed in the forest around her. The slow speed at which she inhaled grated at her wolf. Patience had never been a strong suit for her lycan side, and that was a danger Clara could not afford. Yes, her wolf's sense of smell was infinitely stronger, as well as the beast's eyesight, but with Clara's luck, her wolf would veer her off in the direction of whatever late-spring game hadn't managed to hole itself up in its den this far into nightfall, and then where would she be?

Not in the direction of the human lands and definitely *not* in the more urgent direction away from the stronghold.

It was a risk she couldn't take, and the inward growls that answered made her wolf's stance perfectly known.

Great. Another thing to feel guilty about.

Putting her wolf from her mind, Clara again inhaled, this time drawing in the furtive aromas of a wood that had been just as much a garden to her as it had been a guardhouse.

Damp earth. Piquant bulbs to ward off predators. Moldy leaves, rotting bark, crisp water . . . Her eyes flew open.

"Water! Yes!" Clara bolted in the direction of the soft babbling stream, which the merchant had assured her would lead Clara safely out of lycan territory and into the human lands.

Humans.

For a race of creatures so foreign to her own, they'd certainly taken up more of her thoughts over the past several weeks than anything else. Even as she urged her exhausted body over gnarled tree roots and trained all her senses on the tinkling murmurs of the water ahead, her wolf again voiced her concern at what Clara was rushing them toward.

With each clumsy step she took away from her father's stronghold, a different weight settled within her bones, one of urgency and desperation that cocooned the one emotion she and her wolf could agree upon: hope. Clara clung to the stuff like the vital resource it was. All good things dried up eventually: wells, fossil fuels, love. Not hope. Clara would roll over and offer her wolf's belly to the earliest awaiting fangs before she'd accept that.

As if summoning the precious stuff, Clara reached beneath her leather-lined wool mantle and clasped the moonstone relic dangling from her neck. The smooth surface cooled her clammy skin where the curve of it nestled against her palm, anchoring her to the unknown path before her. When she'd taken it from the royal coffers after offering to see it safely stowed there, she had been surprised at how light it was. Topping out at no more than six inches in length, the curved fang-like stone had been shockingly easy to steal, especially for one so foreign to the act.

Yet another thought she forced herself to bury beneath her fleeing footsteps.

Please work. Please.

The boots were clunkier than she was used to, but they got the job done, propelling her faster through the woods and over the rocky terrain better acclimated for paws than rubber padding. Beneath the uncomfortably thick soles, soft well-packed earth gave way to thicker copses of overgrowth. Reedy tendril-like branches snagged at her cloak, pinching through the heavy fabric like claws yanking her back home.

"No," she breathed through heavy lungs, then shook her shoulders free of the constricting vegetation. "Almost there."

Her wolf whined as Clara pushed her legs harder, higher. They shook with the combined weight of never-been-tested endurance and the crushing load of paranoia. Thighs trembled through the sludge of what she'd left behind and how much time she had before her absence would be noticed.

Reluctantly, she let go of the relic and tucked the thing into her blouse, letting it settle comfortingly between her breasts, rocking against her skin in time with the frantic flutter of her heart. The ancient stone's steady sway was like a metronome taunting her with its incessant ticking, guiding her down a path that would only reveal itself if every step she took was correct. No lagging behind, no alteration in pace. Just keep moving.

Harder. You're almost there. You've got to be.

As Clara scrambled up a small hill that was only scantily lit by the meager moonlight, her recent machinations played out in her mind like the haunted maneuvers of another, someone more skilled in the arts of evasion. Clara's studious nature had made it impossible for her not to triple-check everything before she fled, but her solitary circumstances also punctuated the severity of her calculations. Drugging her father's guards had been surprisingly easy, but the excuses she'd made to the other household staff as to her whereabouts, however, would have no alibi.

If they looked into her story too deeply, asked the wrong person the right question . . .

"Stop it," she bit out, her breath an arid raspy plea against the new-spring mist. "It has to be just a little farther."

Within Clara's mind, her wolf howled her encouragement. Good, the she-wolf heard the water, too. With one final push, Clara heaved herself fully over the mounded earth and crested the hill by ungracefully collapsing onto a nearby boulder, hugging the thing as if it was a long-lost relative coming to greet her. Then a soft sad chuckle escaped her despite her efforts to squash all emotion. The cold stone against her heated cheek wasn't terribly far off in terms of the tenderness she was used to. The abrasive surface eerily mimicked the bristly rasp of her father's beard the few times she recalled him showing phys-ical affection when forced to do so under public scrutiny.

It was the only time he was ever forced to do anything.

The memory jolted another spike of adrenaline into her aching body. She craned her head up and over the boulder, measuring the descent of the embankment ahead as best she could.

How much farther could she run? She couldn't tell which was more tightly wound, her nerves or her muscles. Did it matter? Both screamed in anguish, but staying still was as much a death sentence as what awaited her in the stronghold.

Unless she could reach the human lands.

"Up," she barked to her straining limbs. "Onward. One foot in front of the other. The stream. We start there."

It nearly took an act of the Moon Mother herself, but Clara managed to straighten her spine and anchor herself enough to review what the merchant had told her.

"Once the stronghold fits into the L of your hand, follow the stream west until its waters churn into the river. When the runoff reaches the

stone circle, look above and find the bridge that will take you to the humans."

At the time, they'd seemed like simple enough directions. Now, however, with her paranoia poking holes in her mind's cognitive functions and her body dragging a white flag behind it, the old female's words felt as murky as the fog around her and just as aimless.

Clara lifted her gloved left hand, bit the fabric at the tip of her trembling middle finger, and yanked the garment free, lest it skew what she was looking for. Well, here goes nothing. Sinking into that eternal hope, she formed the shape of an L with her index finger and thumb and turned to the direction she'd come from. Silence met her stance, and the tension that had taken up residence in her shoulders and spine relaxed slightly. Taking advantage of the stillness and terrified of how long it would last, she shot her hand up in front of her. Once raised, her extended fingers cradled the massive stone stronghold that now appeared no larger than one of the stones she'd almost rolled her ankle on a moment earlier. The sloping roofs barely reached the tip of her index finger's fingernail, while the expansive gardens stretched no farther than the fleshy pad of her thumb.

Relief perfused her aching muscles like water through a parched sponge.

"I made it!" But the joy of solving one problem was short-lived. A low howl stretched through the dark trees, blanketing the night with an ominous warning. Foreboding tension returned, coiling around the base of her spine and tugging her into a frozen shell of herself. Her she-wolf fought and scratched at the surface of her mind, urging her to run, begging her to shift into her wolf form.

And Clara would have. On any other day, she would have given herself over to the wolf and cowered in her mind, content knowing the stronger part of her lycan makeup would carry them far away from any physical threat. However, even as the howl grew, becoming loud enough in its echoes that the stream vibrated with its own fear, it couldn't sway her. Not in this.

Clara whipped her glove back on and crouched low, ensuring the boulder blocked as much of her body and scent as possible. Then, with one unsteady foot, she tested the steepness of the embankment and nearly crumpled with exhaustion. By the moon, her thighs were shot! She had no idea how many miles she'd run. Couldn't even recount her exact progress if someone put a knife to her throat demanding the answer, which would soon wind up being a truer statement than she'd like if she didn't move fast. But she had to try, had to get her bony backside down that hill and use the water to mask her scent. They'd know she came this way, of course, but once she hit the water, all bets were off. The lapping stream would do its job of dispersing whatever descended into it. All she had to do was get there safely.

She dipped lower to the ground and gritted her teeth against the trembling in her thighs. All too quickly, her legs boycotted what she asked of them and dumped her onto her knees. The stinging pain of the impact shot through her kneecaps and wrenched her mouth wide, preparing her body to release the sharp cry that sat poised at the base of her throat. Her palm caught up her wincing sob before it was set free into the night air around her.

Shift! Shift now, before they find you!

Tears welled in the corners of her eyes, but she shook them away, wondering, not for the first time, where this surge of bravery came from. It certainly hadn't been taught to her, nor had she observed any true acts of heroism from the males in her father's employ. The most experience she had with the rebellious emotion had been the occasional time or two she'd insisted on fewer chaperones during her garden walks or, Moon Mother forbid, an extra hour's curfew extension.

Bravery was not a concept that had been readily available to her. Her flight from the stronghold had as much to do with courage as a rat's plight to the upper decks of a sinking ship had to do with wanting to get a better view of the skyline.

"No," she whispered through the pain. "I can't shift."

Her clothes, the relic, all of it would be left behind if she shifted, and she *needed* that relic. It was the only thing that would identify her as who she was. Once she reached the human lands, she'd need that relic to prove what she feared her words alone could not, which would be absolutely nothing if she didn't reach the bridge first.

Clara lifted an aching leg out from under herself and made to rise—

Her foot lost what little purchase it had against the slick leaves, dragging her down the embankment. Limbs followed her loss of balance. Arms pinwheeled out around her while frantic fingers scrambled for purchase on anything. Dirt and forest debris filled her vision before the tail of her cloak rose up and blocked what was left of the meager moonlight. Any remaining hope was tossed among the wooded detritus along with her tumbling body. The world spun out of control faster than any of the events she had set into motion, faster than the panic gripping her heart and freezing her extremities into commandless weights that whirled around her.

Useless. Everything was useless.

Icy water caught her, welcoming her into its numbing embrace. Chilling prickles nipped at her cheeks and lips while her clothes swelled with an even more exhausting weight. She thrashed and fought against the churning water, but her weak legs had already become tangled in her sopping cloak. Her wolf whined, and Clara tried to kick out again, but her jerky move-ments caused her temple to smash against a protruding rock along the stream's bed.

Her protesting mind stilled into a serene calmness before her topsy-turvy world sank into an ocean of black.

CHAPTER 2

There was something about slicing a heated blade through demon charmer bone that put an obscene amount of pep in Bronze's step.

And wasn't it a sad state of affairs that *those* were the fantasies he looked forward to as of late? Long nights on patrol with a whole lotta nothin' doin' when it came to hunting the soul-sucking bastards had given him more than enough time to analyze—and hyperfocus—on anything else other than what had been rattling around inside his brain for the past several months.

Normally, he'd be in Aurora with his brothers, volunteering for reconnaissance duty over the sleepy New Hampshire town that had no idea just how bad its demon problem had become. Charmers, despite their name, had about as much charm as a venereal disease and were about a thousand times more pervasive and exponentially more deadly.

Fortunately for Bronze, however, tonight was finally the fallen angel sentinel's lucky night, and boy, did he need it. Well, *need* was a relative term because the need to sink his halberd into a breathing demon body was as strong as a swimmer's need to claw to the surface lest their lungs give up the ghost. He couldn't even remember the last time he'd had a kill. Had it been weeks? No, a month and a half at least.

The quiet concerned them all, for one did not stay quiet if one had something to say. For all the eons Bronze had fought the demon ruler, Cyro, and his charmers, he'd always known the bastard to have far more words than good reasons to use them.

Which meant the silence was a tactical maneuver, and Bronze was *so* sick of it.

"Always with the fucking games," he muttered into the night air. "Just give me something to kill."

Because if he had a task to occupy his mind, it would push out the irreverent words of a deity who had decided to publicly take him down a notch by hitting him with one of her prophecies.

All because he'd foolishly made a joke at her expense. A joke that, regrettably, didn't go over as well as he'd hoped.

That's what I get for sassing a goddess, he thought wryly, which brought him right back to the massive problem at hand: when his body wasn't busy hacking charmers to pieces, it gave his head free rein to fuck with the rest of him. Right on cue, her words floated to the surface like a water lily parting the murky algae of his mind.

"Not all curses are created equal, sentinel. Some require more skill than luck to defeat them. One day soon, you shall meet a woman to challenge you in this regard."

At that, his eyes lit up. "A woman, eh?"

"Yes. I wish you luck. Lycans are so very fond of their games."

So, yeah, he *really* hated playing games.

Bronze twisted on his perch and was surprised that his ass hadn't fallen asleep yet. The branch he'd chosen wasn't particularly wide, but it was broad enough to ensure neither ass cheek fell asleep on the job. Only mildly proud of himself for selecting a halfway decent tree to scout from, Bronze took in the abandoned textile and cotton mill that protruded from the ground below in all its decrepit glory.

The former mid-eighteen-hundreds four-story brick building—former, because the poor thing had been relieved of a story or two thanks to some angelic fire power—abutted the Ellis River and had once been a hotbed of charmer activity. With all the recent demonic trails having gone cold, the sentinels had been forced to retrace their steps and ensure the rats hadn't scurried back to their initial home once the predators had fixated on prey elsewhere.

If there had been a shittier place for the demon ruler to establish his original base of operations, Bronze couldn't think of one. That had been the fucking point and the reason he was going to have to shave down his palm with a rasp later just to get the dump truck's worth of splinters out of his skin. After driving Cyro and his forces from every pimple they'd sprouted from recently, the sentinels didn't put it past the bastard to make what was once old new again, especially if Cyro thought it would be the last place they'd look for him. Lucky for Bronze, he'd drawn the short straw that evening, which left him scratching his ass and surveilling an old hideaway that likely wouldn't—

The faint, rhythmic whirring was all that preceded the shuriken's arrival. Bronze jerked his head to the left just in time to absorb the throwing star's vibrations from the tree trunk it sank into behind him. Gleaming silver winked from a honed point three inches from his chin, nearly turning his goatee into a one-sided walrus mustache that had looked good on no man ever, let alone the gingers.

But the thrill . . . Oh, the thrill that pumped through him as he eyed the deadly edges so clearly meant for one of his more vital bits was the drug he'd been too long without.

Sweeter than sex and just as addicting.

Tracking the trajectory of the weapon had been the work of a moment. There, on the far side of the building, settled on the north bank of the river, a pair of gold eyes flashed beneath the mill's ancient wheel before descending back into the shadows.

That dangerous pleasure pumped into Bronze's limbs until they were full to bursting, awakening what had always been poised at the ready. Mages, he lived for this. The chase, the capture. It wasn't that he was a sadistic fuck who liked to toy with his prey, it was just that— Aw, hell, maybe he *was* exactly that. The problem was, after living as long as he had, there was little to recommend him for taking the high road. He'd seen just how brutally agonizing it was when a charmer unraveled a soul from its mortal, the flailing body, its limbs slowly dying one by one . . .

And then there were the other tactics employed by the demons that hit far too close to home. Intimately so. Rather than shirking the terrors, he draped those horrifying memories around him like a warrior's cape and let them coax his celestial fire from his depths like a brutal lover only called upon to slake darker urges.

No. I'm not above anything my power wishes to take from them. Let's have our dance.

Bronze leaped from the tree he'd perched in and flung his arms wide, chest parallel to the floor in the ultimate swan dive. Before gravity got it in its head to pull on his strings, he freed his power and his wings. Twin condor-length panels of shingled bronze feathers rippled from his back and caught the wind like a fighter jet, narrowing him toward a target that had no hope of hiding.

If Bronze had been anything like the majority of his brothers, he'd have palmed his firearms and shot the charmer full of angel-fire-fueled bullets. Sure, it was effective, as the sentinels' fire was the only thing that could kill a charmer, but where was the fun in long-range combat, especially after one of those fuckers had tried to give him an even closer shave?

Nah. Not his style.

Bronze reached around to the small of his back and gripped his sickle sword. The blade itched to sink its edge into some demon flesh, or perhaps it was just the power of Bronze's anticipation that set his weapon to humming in concert. A blur whipped along the river's edge, then there was nothing save for the sparse patch of reeds that swayed in the opposite direction of the vegetation around it. Bronze banked hard, his angel fire curling up his spine and threatening to punch through the first meaty demonic thing it could. His power not only had teeth but a tightly coiled tension that couldn't wait to spring. The heat of his celestial fire was a comforting heaviness around his soul, one he savored and acknowledged every time he called upon it.

For it never lasted nearly as long as he wanted it to. Not anymore. Unfortunately, his most formidable weapon was the sole celestial power that remained after he and his brothers fell from the Empyrean, Heaven's highest realm.

A sharp whizzing rent the night air, buzzing along Bronze's flesh in skittering tremors. Another shuriken. Bronze rippled into his metallic skin and angled sharply to the right. Sparks flared brightly in the inky darkness as his sword sliced three throwing stars out of the sky. As he batted the last weapon away, the charmer sprang up from his crouched position and beat feet along the river's edge.

"Hey, where ya going? I haven't given you your goody bag yet. You can't invite me out and not let me return the favor. Bad form, my dude. Bad form." Bronze dove low, recalled his wings when he was mere feet above the demon's head, and dropped onto the charmer right as it got to the bridge above where the large wastewater pipe fed into the Ellis. The dilapidated overpass' cobblestones had no problem showing off their age, giving Bronze a marvelous cheese grater-like surface to ground pound the charmer into. The demon collapsed under Bronze's weight and skidded to a halt facedown against the brick.

Well, facedown with an angel sitting on his back, his head cranked toward the sky, and a sword kissing his exposed throat.

Bronze squeezed his thighs around the demon's neck, making sure to hammer down on that carotid good and tight while leaving those pale ears free and clear. Mages, he missed this. The strain of holding his power back against his enemy when his angel fire was near to bursting through his muscles was the ultimate erotic act. Knowing he could smear the charmer writhing beneath him into a soot stain with no more than a thought was its own type of power. The endgame orgasm. The kind of high that elite athletes would sell their souls to achieve, just for the chance to chase the feeling down and lick its heels if they ever got close enough.

They would never be so lucky, of course.

Because they weren't him.

"Uh-uh, if you try to fire up your portal magic, mystic, you might hurt my feelings. Make me think you don't like my company." Bronze slowly recalled his metal skin and was afforded a much better view of the scum beneath him. Teal and gold tattoos painted the thing's face, outlining its golden eyes, and even swirled above the single gold band around the charmer's neck, which signified its class as a mystic—a magic user.

The thing spat its defiance across the cobblestones, slickening the poor hunks of granite in its black blood. Bronze smiled. Good. He'd nicked something important in the takedown, then. Always a boon.

Through the struggle, the charmer managed to twist as much of its head upward as it could, doing its best to address its captor. Once that golden gaze was pegged on Bronze, the earlier familiar thrill caused him to puff out his chest again. It didn't matter how many times he looked into those fuckers' gazes. The stare-down was always what did it for him. Power recognized power, after all, and among immortals, a clash of the eyes was akin to a battle cry.

"We are many," the mystic wheezed out. "And you are not."

Bronze leaned forward, yanked the thing's forehead back so the blade bit in harder to the soft flesh at its throat, and hissed, "Please let that be a threat. Oh, pretty pretty please with a cherry on top."

"Facts are not threats. They just are."

The thing was taunting him, playing with him like *he* was the damn fish on the hook with the boning knife at *his* throat.

Bronze's fire punched through his core and raced along the edge of his sword in a sheet of blue flames. The instant the fire touched the charmer's skin, the demon screamed and bucked against Bronze's hold.

"Are you not reading the room, my man?" Bronze bit out over the wails. "I know where you all are now. I know you'll return here. And I sure as shit know how big of a hard-on I'll be sporting when every single one of you assholes is howling in such agony that you'll be begging to suck down my fire just to end the suffering."

The feel of the charmer's neck against Bronze's sword was far too comfortable, so much so that Bronze feared the sensation would evaporate before his power even had a taste of what it remembered the kill to be like. After all, there were nostalgic experiences, and then there were addictions.

With Bronze's angel fire left to operate on a shift worker's schedule, the line between nostalgia and addiction was fucking clear as mud.

He needed to drag this out, needed this kill to last as long as his power could hold out, because come morning, without recharging his energies, his fire would have no more strength than the shit stain on the cobblestones the sun would make of the demon if Bronze let him live long enough to see it.

Guess he might as well stretch out the intermission on the torture dinner theater—

A pale green swirl flared to life out of the corner of Bronze's eye. A twisting flick of the charmer's fingers, murmured words Bronze hadn't caught before he put the blade to its throat, and a bolt of vile magic that arced from the demon's hand, cracking Bronze in the ribs.

The sickle sword sliced across the charmer's throat in time with Bronze's bellow. An underhanded blow, he had to admit, but an effective one, if somewhat uninspired.

Too bad the fucker wouldn't stick around to blow out the candles and make a final wish.

With one hand pressed against his ribs and practiced boredom slowing the rest of him, Bronze stood and peeled his long legs away from the charmer. The thing flopped around like a fish on a boat deck as blue flames worked their way southward from its gaping neck wound and incinerated everything below it in a slow hungry sweep. Blackened ash painted the vintage granite with stucco-studded character, but Bronze wouldn't stick around to see the final product.

He turned away from the light show, not the least bit interested in the finale, and inspected his side. Blood seeped from a gash that would take more than a few hours to heal fully, but if he got himself underground within the next hour, he should be good enough. Damn, that final hit was a bitch. Not unexpected, but like pain gave a shit whether the end user saw it coming or not?

Once the pile of demon detritus stopped smoldering and Bronze was finally able to inhale without his ribs sputtering in crimson protest, he dispersed the debris over the bridge with the sweep of his boots. He was just gearing up for a second pile to be shuffled overboard when a parched white swath of something floated along the riverbank. The sliver of pale moonlight offered a scant peek at the thing before it stole back its beams and plunged the water's edge into darkness.

"What the hell is that?"

Sheathing his sword but double-checking that all daggers were present and accounted for in his chest holster, Bronze leaped down and trudged toward the shadowy space along the river that, once again, flashed a bleached wink at him before being swallowed up by the darkness.

He didn't have time for this shit. He was bleeding all over his favorite graphic tee, and as the hour had just plunged past two in the morning, he needed to get underground and start the healing process. The minerals and elements imbued in the great mountain he and his brothers dwelled beneath were the literal lifeline for recharging his elemental energies and healing small wounds. If he left now, he could get in maybe three good hours of rest before the sun was up and at 'em again.

His boots stayed put, and try as he might, he couldn't pull his eyes away from that shadowy copse near the water.

"Fuck," he breathed out, already regretting how the rest of his night was going to shape up.

Curiosity dragged him along like a toddler wearing one of those leash backpacks mortals put on their kids. As he drifted closer, his responsible brain screamed at him to get the hell back to the den and recharge his power. Screamed, stomped its feet, even did one of those *I'm warning you* finger-pointing maneuvers. He now had confirmation—fucking *confirmation*—that Cyro and his boys were showing their assess around their old stomping grounds, and what was he doing with this information? Socking it away in his cranial palace while he, of the injured and weakened state, went to go what? Turn over rocks to check for bioluminescent algae or some shit?

Bronze slowed his pace, grateful that there must still be at least one station for his logic train to pull into, but instead of turning around, he came to a halt not three feet from where he thought he saw . . . whatever it was he thought he saw.

There! The white swath appeared before him again, stealing away some of the shadows at his feet, along with his breath.

He hadn't known what to expect, but he sure as shit couldn't have predicted the cascading fall of white hair floating in the shallow water along the river's edge, nor the unconscious woman attached to it.

CHAPTER 3

The smell of the woman's blood mobilized Bronze's ass faster than any throwing star aimed at his throat. He surged toward her and was ready to pitch himself into the water over how he'd missed the still form sprawled out before him. Her long white hair swirled on the water's surface in lazy waves while her equally pale face was stretched toward the shy moon. Her closed eyelids sported dusty shadows similar to the ashen hue that painted her slightly parted lips. Since it was clear that even the moon had little interest in offering up its spotlight services to help him, he couldn't see the rest of her.

What he did see, however, was a whole lot of stillness.

Not good.

His legs hit the water a breath later, and his arms were under her shoulders before he even had time to register the chilliness of the water. With one hand supporting her slight weight, he lightly but insistently tapped at her cheek with the other. Cold. Mages, she was so cold. How long had she been out there?

"Miss! Can you hear me? Miss!" When nothing but silence greeted his efforts, he surged to his feet and attempted to pull her up the riverbank and out of the water. A firm resistance stalled him out, and he slipped, landing ass-first on a protruding rock. "Fuck! Mages dammit."

He'd managed to slide himself beneath her in the fall at least, ensuring she didn't sink farther into the water. But why the hell was she stuck in the water? When he pulled her again, the fabric wrapped around her tightened against her throat, as if it was snagged somewhere and used its counterforce to choke the woman's lovely neck in protest to being disturbed.

Cursing, Bronze released one of his chest daggers and sliced the ties from her neck. The dark fabric relinquished its captive and lurked back into a billowing pile below the water's surface. But it wasn't quite the win he'd hoped for. The woman's feet were still hidden beneath the river muck, which had left her lower half solidly suspended underwater while the rest of her, thank the mages, had bobbed above the surface. The boulder jutting from the riverbank had been a stroke of luck for both of them, as it created a makeshift enclave that effectively prevented her from drifting farther upriver.

Securing her against him more tightly, Bronze got good and personal with a whole lot of cold and wet crud and reached down to shimmy her stuck feet until they were free. The water released her willingly this time, and Bronze hefted her out of the river. Curses flew freely as he laid her out on the forest floor and searched his brain for what to do next.

As if in answer to his prayers, a sliver of moonlight poked its way through the dark blue cirrus clouds gathering overhead, shining its guiding beam down on the very last thing commanding his attention . . . until now.

Breasts.

Free of the metric fuckton of fabric he'd cut off her and left as an offering to the river monsters, he noticed what had been concealed underneath. Below her abundance of soaking white hair, a dark green leather-lined half-cape thing with a slit down the middle had capped off her upper half. Lying on her back, however, caused the center flaps to fall open and reveal the sheerest frilly white blouse he'd ever seen.

A white blouse that was pasted with papier-mâché precision to breasts that pooled in perfect mounds tucked above what his brain could only describe as a . . . was that a half corset? One of those waist-cincher things? Whatever it was, it offered up the poor woman's flesh to the elements like cooling carrion.

And why the fuck was he thinking about her breasts? The woman was motionless. The only rush of color anywhere near her was the smear of blood at her temple staining her hairline, which had somehow escaped the river's cleansing.

Shaking himself to get with the program, Bronze cradled her jaw while his fingers worked around the back of her neck, poking and prodding for signs of cervical fracture. Something hard and curved bumped his knuckles, tugging slightly at the thin leather cord that hugged the base of her throat. A necklace of some sort, with a pendant that must have gotten whipped around behind her.

To hell with the jewelry. What he was looking for was of the spine-deforming variety. Notches of vertebra out of place, pinched discs, spinal column bones feeling like anything other than neatly organized ridges . . .

He worked faster, terrified he'd find something. His maneuvers lifted her mouth higher toward his and brought the rest of her features into view beneath the scant moonlight. The white hair was not a wig, nor was it, he suspected after studying her scalp's middle part, some dye job aimed at jumping the gun on the whole aging gracefully bit. Matching eyelashes fanned out in sweeping waves over lushly rounded cheeks that were far too pale and would have looked lovely cradling a smile. The rounded exuberance of her youthful beauty hinted at her being in her twenties, but the furrows between her brows, even relaxed as they were, mirrored the stony set to her chin and suggested a stoic regalness often afforded to women who'd seen too much and had been help-less for too long.

In other words, he had a gorgeous unconscious woman on his hands who could be anywhere north of twenty, south of forty, and heading further south real fast if he couldn't jump-start her engine.

"Miss. C'mon, wake up. Wake up, dammit!" Bronze pulled one hand away from the back of her neck and pressed it against the center of her chest. "Breathe, baby. One breath. That's all I'm asking."

He had never been the praying type, especially since he had no idea whether the prime mages could even hear his prayers from the mortal realm, but he offered them regardless. Seemed like the least he could do, since his particular set of skills was far better at serving the mages in other more lethal capacities. He opened his mouth to offer more words—

And the woman's chest rose against his palm.

Relief walloped him so hard, he nearly stumbled backward and silently cursed himself for not checking her airway first. His experience with mortals injured in this fashion was limited, and breathing wasn't necessarily a concern for him when he was in his metal skin.

"Yes! Yes, that's it. Again, breathe for me. Can you do that?"

Those frosted lashes fluttered wildly against her cheeks before the timer ran out on the moon's good graces and pulled the woman's face back into shadow.

"No!"

Without the benefit of light, he focused on his hand again and the feel of her cold, wet body against his palm. Her chest rose but not enough. Not nearly deep enough. She was breathing but far too shallowly and certainly not with any sort of repetition that could be compatible with mortal life.

Shit!

Out of light, warmth, and options, he used the only tools at his disposal. With one hand still at the back of her throat, he positioned her neck so her airway was as wide open as it could possibly be, pinched her nose, and brought his mouth to hers.

<hr>

THE WARMTH on Clara's lips was no more than a slight press of heat, a candle flickering in the aftermath of an avalanche. It had little impact on the foggy weight of her mind or the stillness the rest of her seemed to float aimlessly through.

By the moon, she was cold! And every limb throbbed with a soreness she imagined one might experience if their body had been tossed on the rocks upon which the angry sea crashed.

Was that what had happened to her? Had she finally been thrown aside, discarded like the refuse she had long been treated as?

But then where was that warmth coming from?

Clara leaned into the flush of heat that was gently parting her lips. Her wolf even whined with warmth against the onslaught of sweet breath that fluttered over her teeth, across her tongue, and cascaded down the back of her throat in a rush. And wasn't that just wonderful? The heaviness that had pummeled her chest a moment ago suddenly lifted away, and that sweet intoxicating flood of air filled her most intimately . . .

It was a dream she never wished to surface from. Even after her lungs deflated on a sigh, the warm flow of air filled her chest again, invigorating parts of her that had borne a deathlike stillness. And the scent . . . it was almost heady in its heat. A campfire smokiness that unfurled nature's secret spices and lured not only her wolf but every sleepy cell in her body.

Clara clung to the scent hard, chasing after it with a desperate curiosity when it would ebb away from her. Gosh, why was she doing that? Where had this need come from? As soon as the question hit her, it was accompanied by a nagging prick that tickled the corners of her mind. She was forgetting something, but what?

When she arched her back through the next onslaught of air, her shoulder blades pressed into something hard. Long, curved, pointed at the tip . . .

The moonstone relic!

Clara's eyes winged open, and fear froze what little motion remained in her numb body. Someone was on top of her, pinning her into the damp earth. Darkness dressed the figure in shadows, blocking out any light that may have illuminated her circumstances. But that heat, the seductive heat that lingered in her lungs and under her skin, still swirled above her and everywhere their bodies touched.

Fingers cradling her jaw, lips warming her own, a slight rasp of a beard jerking her free of the fog.

And then the scent hit her. Smoky. Spicy.

Not lycan.

A human! A human was kissing her!

With floundering strength, her shaky hands heaved against his strong shoulders. To her great surprise, she needn't have bothered. The human tore his mouth from hers and flung himself off with a speed to rival any hunting wolf. Though there was no shortage of nearby boulders along the riverbank, he'd chosen the farthest one, it seemed, to enmesh himself against. He held up his long arms, all fingers extended high toward the moon, and stayed in a crouched position, as if in defense of a circumstance both out of his control and in need of dire explanation.

"I wasn't trying anything, I promise. I saw you floating in the river unconscious, and when I pulled you to shore, you weren't breathing well enough on your own."

Clara's head slowly fell to the side as she studied him, and instantly her cheeks warmed with that seductive heat from earlier. Was this what all humans looked like? Even clouded in shadows as he was, she could still make out the rich auburn hair that hung in loose waves about his chin as he shook the emphasis of truth into his words. A beard of similar color framed his mouth in a neat gathering, though the hairs didn't extend along the rest of his jawline like the beards of most lycan males.

Males . . . she was with a male.

Thoughts of her kind awakened her realization of the compromised state she found herself in, and she quickly tried not to let her gaze linger too long on that beard or, more particularly, his mouth. But damn her, she couldn't resist the urge to see more of him.

A human. A real human! She'd done it!

But her soft elation was quickly quelled when she spied the chest holster fitted against his toned frame. Blade hilts sat in neat little rows snugly along his ribcage, hugging his chest like an unbreachable wall. Straps of what looked to be leather criss-crossed over his trapezius muscles as well, which drew her eyes to land on a handle poking out from above a tense shoulder. She didn't need to see more to know what that handle was likely attached to and what a male with as much strength as the one before her could do with a simple reach behind himself.

It was that awareness that brought back every ounce of cold her body had, for some reason, forgotten to shiver through. Clara gripped her dripping mantle tight around her shoulders and risked a glance at the surrounding forest floor for her cloak.

"It's in the water," the human male replied. "I had to cut it off to free you."

That certainly got her attention. Free her? Free her from—Oh, God. The relic. It had been tied around her neck. Had her father's guards found her? She opened her mouth to speak when a comfortable and familiar weight pressed against her upper back.

No, I didn't lose it. It's here.

As discreetly as possible, Clara gripped the leather strap cinching her throat and twisted the relic so it rested comfortably between her breasts, then stowed it safely beneath her blouse.

Her wolf's low growl of warning rattled through her now-shivering muscles, a silent reminder that safety was not assured. Clara quickly rose to her feet, and the human's hands flew up in front of him.

"Whoa! Slow it down, there. I just pulled you from that river not two minutes ago. There's still water running off you, and you're a far cry from being high and dry." The male kept his hands raised but took two steps closer, his gaze assessing her hairline where her temple throbbed. "You've got quite the head wound, and I have no idea how long you've been soaking up more than your share of the Ellis, so we've got to take care of things before any blood still in you decides to evacuate."

How strangely he spoke. Oh, she was able to gather his meaning about her injuries, but his vernacular was so odd. "The . . . Ellis? What is that?"

He gestured toward the river. "The waterway that runs through this part of the White Mountains. Feeds into all sorts of treatment plants in and around Aurora, including the town's reservoir. The treated wastewater dumps out at this part of it, so the rapids can seem a little edgier at the base here."

Clara followed the nod of his chin toward the bridge that loomed above the churning waters and had to stifle her gasp. The small archway was crafted from the smoothest stones she'd ever seen, which glowed nearly alabaster against the barest light of the moon. None of the architecture in her father's stronghold could ever have been so fine. She was almost tempted, despite the unknown danger of the male before her and the risk to her relic, to shift into her wolf form just so the she-wolf's enhanced eyesight could be her own. The masonry of the work alone was astonishing. She could barely make out any mortar that didn't appear as smooth as her own skin. And the curve of the bridge itself! So flawless she couldn't imagine mortal hands possibly crafting something that contained zero traces of embellishments or protrusions. Her gaze drifted lower, drawn toward the rush of water tunneling out of a circular enclosure that was still mostly shrouded in shadow.

Holy mother . . .

Churning water. A river reaching a stone circle. The bridge.

She was in the human lands. She'd made it.

She inhaled sharply and looked to the sky. The blanket of stars was no longer visible as they had been when she'd first fled, but even through the thin clouds, she was able to note their positions in relation to the waning moon.

She'd been gone an hour or two at most.

And then it all came back to her. The howls chasing her, the slide down the embankment, the horrid crash into the frigid water. The rock meeting her temple and the darkness that consumed her after.

Clara whipped toward the human male, who still hadn't moved from his position near her, nor had he lowered his hands. He merely stared at her with a worried sort of wonder, as if she were a skittish creature who would either bite him or bay at the moon for help.

She did neither. Instead, she called on the inner strength of her wolf and used what little they both could muster to throw herself at the male. Once she had her nails firmly embedded into the meat of his biceps, she hung on, forcing all her desperation into her weight, and cast pleading eyes up at him.

"Compete for me."

He tried to hold her upright, while still keeping her at arm's length. The shock of both her strength and her words quickly twisted the male's face with additional alarm. "I'm sorry, what?"

"My hand," she hurried out. "Compete for me. It will be yours, for surely, you can win." She squeezed the toned muscles of his upper arms tighter in a harried attempt to convey her point. Though most of him was cold and damp like her, his body did not shiver against the elements. There was a quiet fortification to his powerful frame. Slight, yet unsuspecting.

Yes, he could be her champion. The others would overlook him, dismiss him, but she alone would know—

"Win what? Lady, your head . . . you've been through a heck of a—"

"You have no idea what I have been through, human," she gritted out, her voice elevating to levels she'd never dared to use against other males. "But it will be nothing should you refuse to compete for my hand in marriage."

They both stilled as the word landed at their feet with the weight of a fallen oak.

"Marriage?" he asked in disbelief as he tried to steady her, seemingly no longer realizing that she had already stopped moving. Then a drawbridge of concern slammed over his stern brow. "Are you in trouble?"

There it was. The very question she had prepared herself to answer, the one whose response she'd rehearsed a thousand times on her journey from the stronghold. The calculated message, the specific words, the exchanges, the agreements.

But when the time finally came, to her great horror, what came out instead was the truth. Simple words to a simple question that revealed more shame than salvation, but she couldn't bring herself to care anymore.

She was cold, and she was here. She'd found him, and that had to be enough for now.

"Yes," she breathed with a relief so strong it lightened more than her lungs. "We all are." And then she did the one thing she'd promised herself she'd never do again.

She begged.

"Please."

There weren't many words in any of the myriad of languages Bronze knew that had the power to knock him on his ass, but *marriage* was certainly one of them. Add to that the fact that it was spoken by a beautiful—and formerly unconscious—woman he'd just pulled out of the river and he would have thought the prime mages had it out for him, worse than they no doubt already did.

Marriage?

"Look, I know my gender tends to encompass the majority of mouth breathers on this rock who have *so* not earned the right to say this, but please, calm down."

Aaand, as expected, the panicked pools of brown staring back at him flattened under the hazy annoyance of every female creature who had reluctantly been pushed back into a box by someone who had no business doing the pushing.

Shit.

"Let's start over. Please, you're bleeding and inching closer toward hypothermia the longer we don't get you dry and warm." Which was definitely the largest of his concerns at the moment. Given her sodden clothing, head wound, and the odd state of her mind upon coming out of her little river respite, Bronze had to do a little triage. The bleeding had largely slowed, and there'd be time to parse out whatever she was talking about, but in his experience, body temperature didn't exactly wait around for all parties involved to get their acts together before it decided to crash.

Given that *she* had grabbed onto *him*, he figured there was some measure of safety in continuing that physical connection if he could escort her to the flat rock beneath the large spruce that was a safer distance away from the water. But fuck, the charmers! Those things could be as prevalent as alley piss. And now that he had as much proof as he was going to get that they were lurking in this area, safety was not guaranteed.

Once Bronze settled the woman onto the rock, it was blatantly obvious that time was not on her side either. That ashen tinge to her lips had yet to fade, nor had the shadowed creases beneath her eyes. Fucking hell, how was she even upright and talking, let alone coming at him like a pass rusher in overtime?

He took a deep breath, tried to still his racing mind, and focused on what he needed to. Black and white biology first. Heat he could do, and she needed a metric ton of the stuff in short order or he'd never get to the question portion of the show.

Bronze squatted down in front of her and rested her back against the tree when she began to lilt to the side. "Stay here. I'll get you warm in a bit, but I need to get something first. Are you able to sit upright for a moment?"

Her head bobbed heavily on her slim neck. The movement didn't exactly inspire confidence and was a far cry from the ambushing power she'd exhibited earlier, but what choice did he have? Clearly, whatever reserved energy that had surged to the surface moments before had been quickly spent, and he'd have to make do with the leftovers.

"Okay. Yeah, that's it," he whispered softly, encouraging her despite his reservations. "Just"—he looked around for something she could use for protection, then settled on his vest—"here, take my dirk. Pointy end goes into anyone who's not me. No exceptions. I need two minutes tops, and I'll be able to hear anyone who gets within a mile of you before then."

The woman nodded again and gripped the hilt, though she hardly had the strength to keep the blade pointed anywhere but at her feet.

Right. Perfect. Exactly who he should give a weapon to.

Fuck.

Before Bronze could grapple with the urge to grab her and fly her out of there or, at the very least, fix her damn grip on the weapon, he bolted toward the river's edge and found her cape. The thing was a sodden mess and was giving off more of a Salem witch hunt fashion sense than anything sold in those fancy Aurora boutiques, but like he was one to judge? She was cold, nearly losing heat faster than he had time to replenish it, and with the charmers' ability to fucking portal anywhere, he had to make this quick.

Despite the embankment blocking her view from him, he still turned his back to her direction before he let his power free. A few quick pulses of his celestial fire's energy were all it took for the garment to dry completely. He was already halfway up the rocky hill when what he saw nearly made him wipe out on a patch of damp leaves not twenty feet in front of her.

The woman—fuck, did he even know her name?—was exactly as he left her, propped against the crumbling bark of a tree, looking like death warmed over.

Except death, as far as he knew, didn't make a habit of licking its fingers before swiping them across bloody head wounds.

Bronze crested the rest of the hill and continued toward her but slowed way the hell down as what he was seeing became clearer. Even in the dim moonlight, he could make out the swipe of her pink tongue as she brought it daintily across the pads of her index and middle fingers. After two licks, she lifted her hand to the cut at her hairline. She did it once, twice, then again, all the while keeping her eyes closed, as if she were concentrating on something wholly more important than what simple vision could detect. The deep grooves between her brows still hadn't lessened and were clearly working overtime on something that didn't concern him. But then she took one more moistened swipe at her forehead and—

"Holy shit," he whispered, sharpening his celestial senses to make sure he was actually seeing what he was seeing.

Faster than it had any right to move, the skin along her hairline stitched together starting from where the gash began at her ear. Another brush of her damp fingers and the two inches of raw flesh above her left eyebrow turned the pale pink of a fresh scar. One more sweep and all the blood was gone. A final pat at her brow was the last ministration before even the deepest part of the laceration in the center of her forehead right above her nose melded together into a seamless ivory canvas.

The woman had yet to open her eyes. She just rested her hand on her brow and hung her head forward as though she was fighting off the migraine to end all migraines. As though she hadn't just sewn her skin together with literal spit and determination.

It wasn't until she finally lowered her hand that many of the facts floating around Bronze's orbit decided to land in congruous shapes his brain could finally process.

With stark unease, he realized this hadn't been the first time he'd seen a creature heal in such a way. He'd known it to be done several times. Felines came to mind first because of their fastidious nature, but it was the canine imagery that stayed locked in good and tight inside his brain. Dogs, wolves, didn't they all have some sort of antiseptic properties in their paw pads? Wasn't that how they aided in healing themselves when they got nicked?

Bronze sharpened his celestial senses even further and took more of the woman in than just what he had previously focused on to assess for injuries. The white hair, the tawny-brown eyes . . . not a usual color combination for human mortals, especially not for those still in their youth. It was a much more sympathetic color scheme for an animal, specifically one adapted to polar climates or one uniquely hued young out of a litter. Not entirely uncommon.

Again, for animals.

Bronze's palms turned sweaty, and he had to throw her garment over his shoulder lest he inadvertently scorch the thing. He rubbed at a spot in the center of his chest where a tightening pressure had begun to take hold.

Exhaustion was very close to claiming its due from both of them. But as the woman's head fell to the side at a sharp angle and the curtain of her damp hair draped across her face in heavy clumps, other images smacked him across the face.

When she'd first seen him after regaining consciousness, she didn't speak, not at first, but her neck had tilted to the side in the same jarring manner. Not slow and assessing, but quick and cunningly, like a wolf might if it only had mere moments to assess its situation before making a move.

Then the freight train of reality barreled toward Bronze, and he hadn't even realized he'd stepped onto the tracks.

Her surges of strength, her eyes looking to the moon for guidance and awareness . . .

"By the mages . . ."

She wasn't a human. She was a lycan.

CHAPTER 5

Never in her entire life had Clara endured something so equally demeaning and exhilarating as being blindfolded. Perhaps it also had something to do with the surprising warmth of the human holding her throughout their short journey, or the agonizingly unusual slowness with which her body tried to heal itself, but one thing was for certain: no amount of secret archival studying or silently purchased missives from merchants could have prepared her for where she'd landed.

And landed she had.

Her human escort hadn't said much on the brief excursion he'd insisted she accompany him on, which only added to the myriad of worries stacking up inside her. After he returned from fetching her cloak, which had somehow been dried out and warmed enough to take the edge off her shivering, an equally chilling silence had fallen between them. And wasn't that the strangest thing? The male was, after all, merely a stranger, and, well, she *had* thrown herself at him like a rabid soaked animal spouting what she was sure he thought of as all sorts of nonsense, but for the brief moments he'd spoken to her after she awoke, he had been . . . kind.

That she hadn't expected the human male to show such concern was, strangely, the largest shocker of the many shocking things that had assaulted her since she fled the stronghold. For the umpteenth time in her life, she cursed her father's name and every vile prejudiced dogma he'd worked so hard to indoctrinate her with.

This human male was far from the creatures she was afraid she'd encounter, and perhaps that was another reason for her worry entirely. If humans didn't behave as she'd always been taught, then what other falsehoods had also been painted as truths?

Goodness, it was too much to sort out, and her head hadn't stopped spinning since she'd awoken beneath that . . . Come to think of it, he hadn't even told her his name yet, and she, likewise, hadn't shared hers. She'd just been so relieved to have found him. And to have that male be so well-suited for her cause and clearly honorable enough that he would surely aid her? It had all been so fortuitous, so she'd only bothered with the most pressing details while she still had the strength to declare them.

Her body jostled in his arms when the male turned her to the side as if to fit through a doorway. The blindfold had been a requirement of his aid, he'd said. While her wolf fiercely whined her protestations against having one of her senses taken away, what choice did Clara have? Whatever adrenaline had bolstered her awake from the river had long since left her. She could barely sit up on her own, let alone make the journey back to her stronghold. Yes, Clara may have been brash to flee as she had, but she wasn't so entirely stupid to refuse help, especially when the one doing the offering held far more cards in his hands than she hers, at least until she could get her strength back.

Behind the torn strip of her cloak that was now a makeshift

blindfold he'd fastened around her eyes, a light flared, poking through the tiny holes in the fibers. Her heart kicked up a strange beat, and she realized that disappointment had begun to pour into her on the heels of whatever light had been ignited around them.

Yes, there was a certain exhilaration that came with being blindfolded. Because, as the human settled her on top of a strange bed and gently removed the cloth from her eyes, the familiar dismay that had chased her into the forest in the first place returned to cast its pall over her circumstances.

"Where have you taken me?" She winced at the obvious weakness in her voice and was surprised her words managed to carry to the stranger at all. Judging by his expression, he'd heard her just fine.

Had that squeaky rasp really come from her? Gosh, she could barely lift her limbs and use her hands to accentuate her words, as was a habit of hers when she was nervous. Even the slight blanket that the male had settled around her shoulders felt as if it weighed as much as the mountains around them.

"Someplace to get you healed up enough so we can have a conversation."

Clara looked around and squinted through the harsh light of the compact room she found herself in. The bed was small and caged by bracketing arms that the human drew up and locked into place. Beyond the bed, along the walls, were counters and cabinets made of highly polished materials that looked nothing like the marble, wood, and stone she was used to seeing when it came to that type of carpentry. Small glass jars sat in neat rows along the far edge of one counter, while a strange pole with hooks stood erect in the corner at the foot of the bed. A fresh pile of white and cream linens rested on top of a nearby chair. The human grabbed a second blanket from the stack and laid this one across her.

Heated. Oh, Moon Mother, the blanket was *heated.*

Clara and her wolf sank into the warmth that had been wrapped around her as though it was the softest cotton imaginable. She could have fallen asleep right there had it not been for the heavy steps that followed the male into the room.

Good Lord, there were more of them. And they were huge! Three males as large as any of her father's private guards filled out the small room so immensely, she worried whether there'd be enough air to go around.

The first male sported a russet-brown beard as thick as his shoulders and as coarse as the expression twisting his face. Hair of equal thickness and surprising length was pulled into a knot at the back of his head. Deep red and green flannel covered his mountainous body, though, oddly, the sleeves were rolled to the elbows, revealing two wide brown leather cuffs bracketing each wrist like bracers. There was little comfort in his countenance, which caused Clara to shift uneasily beneath the blanket. He didn't simply acknowledge her. No, his stare was deeper, more insistent, as if he was marking her, tracking her.

The other male behind him was equally tall but far leaner and lighter in physique and coloring. Blond hair so pale it nearly matched her own stood in short sweeping waves down the middle, while the sides were closely shorn. His umber gaze settled upon her, and though the first male's dual-colored eyes stayed pinned to her like the intruder she was, the second human's expression was softer, painted with what she might call a sad recognition of sorts. He even offered her a small smile as he looked around the room with what she could only describe as resigned familiarity.

Then the third human stepped over the threshold and stole what little breath remained in her tired lungs. He prowled into the room with enough self-assurance and sense of command to convince even the ocean to shift its tides if he asked it to do so. Honeyed blond hair dusted the tips of his powerful shoulders and the others moved to the side to make way for him.

This was a king. Clara had no idea how she knew it, but her whole body vibrated with the knowledge that she was in the presence of absolute authority. Should she bow? No, a curtsy was more appropriate, but he wore no rings to kiss, nor any outward symbols of his position, though it was clear just from being near him that he was someone of importance. She fidgeted, urging her weak body to rise from the bed so she could search for a way to pay her respect to a foreign leader and plead for further aid, but the auburn-haired male who had brought her there simply settled his hands on her shoulders and urged her back down.

"You're not ready for prime time yet. Sit back, sip on this *slowly*," he warned her with more than words as he handed her a small bottle of water, "and I'll make introductions." He eased to his full height and nodded around the room with a casualness that would have garnered severe repercussions had they been back in her father's territory. "These are some of my brothers and extended family. The one with the ugly face and uglier attitude is Iron, Rhode's the sun-starved blond, and the big guy in the middle with a conditioner fetish is Tungsten."

Clara froze, uncertain how to behave following that caliber of introduction. Surely, they were aristocracy or esteemed guardians of some sort, or likely both. But the way he mentioned their odd names, it was as if they were at schoolyard recess. Were the upper echelon of humans always so informal?

At a loss for how to behave and what to do, she smiled and dipped her head, hoping that, if it was not the appropriate response, she would at least be forgiven for her actions, as they could be attributed to her weakness.

"And you, warrior?" She whispered the question, taking a chance that her assumptions were correct. "That is what you are, is it not? A warrior of the human race? What is your name?" She winced at her directness, then lifted the water to her mouth lest any more inappropriate questions come flying out of it.

A few coughs bounced around the room, and a deep flush colored the male's cheeks. He glared back at the humans behind him before turning to her. "I'm Bronze. Yes to the first part." Then he paused for a moment and trained his hard eyes on her as he said, "No to the second."

Clara slowly lowered the water from her mouth. "I'm sorry?" Surely, she hadn't heard him right.

The blond leader took that opportunity to step forward. "And what may we call you? I gather you are not entirely human yourself. Before you answer," he said, holding up his hand, "know that no harm will come to you here, provided you mean none to us."

"H-harm?" Oh, no, what had she walked into? "I, uh, would never harm anyone," she tried to shout in a defensive tone that would have been more effective if her lungs hadn't been doing their utmost just to gather breath into her chest. "You mean you are not humans? Are these not the human lands?"

Worried glances bounced from male to male, and her heart sputtered warning beats within her chest. Her wolf growled against her bones, pressing her harder and harder to shift, to flee. It was only the growing chaos in her mind that kept her from focusing on the change.

"No. No, this can't be right," she breathed out shakily. "The merchant said to search for the stone circle. Find the stone circle, and I'll find the human lands." Clara squeezed her eyes shut and tried to recall the exact words.

"Once the stronghold fits into the L of your hand, follow the stream west until its waters churn into the river. When the runoff reaches the stone circle, look above and find the bridge that will take you to the humans."

She'd done that. She'd reached all those markers, had seen every one of them. She should have made it. Had she taken a wrong turn? But, no, she awoke beneath the stone circle, and the river . . .

Tungsten stepped forward next to the male at her side, until her bed was blocked in by a wall of male shoulders even her wolf at full strength had no hope of fighting through.

"Your name, miss," Tungsten's deep voice bellowed, though his tone seemed to skirt the edge between calmly authoritative and demanding. "I will have it now."

She looked to Bronze, who, with his arms folded across his chest, stared back with an unreadable expression. Likewise, the other two males eyed her with curious intent, though, with every passing moment, the encroaching panic crept higher, tightening around her and drawing all her air into a vacuum she had no hope of surviving.

She was going to die. She had made a terrible choice in leaving, and she would now pay for it. By the mark of her own stupidity and carelessness, she would pay for it.

"Tungsten, Bronze, back away. Now," the blond one said.

Clara threw her head from side to side as the hyperventilating kicked in. "This can't be happening. I found the stone circle, the bridge. I did everything I was supposed to do."

"Shit, she's going into shock." The large one, Iron, barked orders and ran toward the bed. Large hands yanked the blanket off her. "Why the hell does she still have damp clothes on? Get one of the mates in here now."

Rough hands pressed against the pulse points at her throat and wrists. Her sleeve was shoved up high on her arm, then something sharp pricked the skin at the crux of her elbow. Her wolf snarled, but even her beast had weakened too much. More shouting, drawers opening, footsteps banging down the hall, heading toward the room. A woman's voice. Then more yelling.

"No . . . no . . ." She had worked so hard, covered her tracks, learned everything she could before she planned her escape, and it still hadn't been enough. Anything she did would never be enough.

A heavy pall pulled her further into the hysteria, until all she could do was embrace the darkness that rose up to claim her.

But before her mind was pulled from consciousness entirely, she caught a few mumbled words from the male who'd brought her there. Bronze, she dimly remembered. His name was Bronze.

"Not a human . . . a lycan . . . some sort of trouble."

Her final thought left her in a whisper of despair and regret.

She would truly die this day, but that didn't crush her nearly as hard as the weight of her failure.

CHAPTER 6

Thirty minutes later, Rhode and Drea—his care provider and soul bond to Bronze's other brother Chrome—walked out of the sick bay where Clara was being seen. Bronze barely let Drea's purple nitrile gloves hit the waste bin before he rushed over to both of them. But before his first question could leave his lips, Rhode pegged him with a warning look that said far more than any expression had any right to.

All's good. Settle. And then finally . . . *We've got a lot to talk about.*

Drea squeezed on a few pumps of hand sanitizer from the wall unit outside the patient room, gave her hands a few good hearty shakes to hasten the drying and dispense with some of the alcoholic fumes, and dug around in her lab coat for her always-present bottle of lily-scented moisturizer. Mages, even in the middle of the night, the woman stuck to a personal care routine with enough diligence to make the Armed Forces seem like they were slacking in the scheduled efficiency department. Figured it made sense, given that she *chose* to have ass-length hair and all the maintenance that came with it and had *still* managed to patch up their boy Rhode after his captivity far better than any of the sentinels ever could.

Not for the first time, Bronze wondered why more mortal civilizations weren't matriarchies. Shit made sense, even if he *was* a millisecond away from the vein in his temple exploding and taking him into aneurysm territory over the woman's dallying.

With painfully slow movements, Drea finally finished her mile-freaking-long skin care routine and gave them both a reassuring smile.

"She's sleeping now. Fluids are dripping into her just fine, and all her vitals are steadily creeping toward normal. Whoever she is, she's damn lucky you found her when you did."

Bronze nodded and did his best to keep from not so slowly escorting his brother's mate way the heck out of earshot so he could get to the bottom of whatever Rhode had managed to discover. The former seraphim commander of Chrome's intelligence unit may have been out of the game and stuck in the mortal realm like the rest of the sentinels, but old habits didn't just die hard with that one. They were pulverized into atomic ash and cast to the wind along with the dead secrets of his enemies.

Efficient, that one.

In other words, the dude also knew stuff. And, yeah, Bronze *really* needed to know what he knew.

"Appreciate the help," Bronze said before placing a hand on the small of Drea's back and urging her down the hallway toward her and her mate's living quarters. No easy feat, given that the woman was nearly as tall as he was and had a backbone stronger than most suspension bridge cables.

Her long blonde braid, a bit mussed from its hasty middle-of-the-night erection but still just as heavy, smacked him in the chin on the back spin as she whipped out of his hold. The look in her violet eyes promised a certain kind of punishment that made even Bronze's balls tense up on alert. "Um, *no*. You do *not* get to wake me up before the ass crack of dawn, have me explain to Chrome why I'm being forced to put work clothes on, drop me in front of some poor injured woman and say, 'Here, fix her,' without providing me details." Her insistent finger found the precise spot on his chest that had zero padding and abysmal pain tolerance, and she rage-poked the shit out of him. "I'm here, and thanks to me, so is she, so start talking. I want deets."

"Ouch! Fine, okay? Fine." Bronze murmured his agitation, grabbed up her hands and, with a show of caring patience worthy of a goddamned Academy Award, slowly placed them at her sides. But because he wasn't born yesterday, he strategically moved his grip to her shoulders lest she get any more bright ideas for sudden movements or finger jabs.

Her mouth, however, he couldn't do anything about.

"I'm serious, Bronze. Just what the hell did I walk into here?" Some of the fire had extinguished from her plea and had been replaced with the compassion and concern that made Chrome and the others love her and allowed Rhode to trust her implicitly with his care following his captivity in Cyro's camp, despite the seraph's well-guarded secrets.

Right on cue, the seraphim commander sidled over to Drea and replaced Bronze's hands with his own, then turned her to face him. "You are, by far, the greatest asset to any of us, and to me, especially."

A subtle flush darkened Drea's already heated cheeks. Mages, the woman cranked out BTUs like a frickin' fighter jet engine when she sank her teeth into something. But the tells of exhaustion were there for those who knew to look for them. Despite the calculating questions running behind her eyes, the shadows beneath them told a different story, as did the way her shoulders sagged into Rhode's far gentler hold.

Girl was as ferocious and determined as a honey badger but

had a paltry amount of experience exerting her dominance when she was bone tired. Who could blame her?

"Right now, you know what we know. It does none of us any good to conjecture on speculation, especially not at this late hour. As you said, she's sleeping, so there will be no further answers for any of us tonight. I suggest you take the opportunity to return to Chrome. He's wired the sick bay to alert you instantly if a patient even snores funny. At the first sign of a change, you'll be the first to hear of it, I promise. Please, Drea. Go rest. You'll be a better help to her if you're not using every spare amount of energy to keep yourself from getting annoyed at Bronze. *That* is a feat that can tax even the strongest warrior." He winked at her.

"Asshole," Bronze muttered.

Drea shuffled her feet and let the seraph kiss her on her forehead. "Fine. But the second she's up, I'll be here, and I want answers." The look she threw Bronze over her shoulder could have melted whatever poor stubborn polar ice caps still remained.

Message received.

Bronze nodded his thanks and hefted as much appreciation as possible into the grin he volleyed back. "You're the best, as always. Get some rest."

"Don't"—her jaw cracked on a yawn she was too slow to cover up—"tell me what to do."

"Wouldn't dream of it."

Once her footsteps turned into nothing more than retreating echoes, Bronze stood next to Rhode. "She's going to kill you for lying to her. You know that, right?"

"Who said I lied?"

"Drea does *not* know what we know, because I saw the way your eyes settled on the lycan woman's belongings before Drea stuffed them into a plastic bag. You know something, or at least some part of you recognized something of hers."

Bronze let the note of challenge settle around the hallway. When it hit the floor unanswered, a different kind of unease reverberated back at him through the quiet, and he cursed inwardly.

It was a dangerous thing to tear secrets out of spies. But to attempt to unearth them from a former spy who'd been tortured, lost to time, experimented on, and rescued with no knowledge of what happened or whether the celestial powers stolen from him would ever return?

Forget honey badgers. Bronze had just poked an unstable atomic bomb held together by secrets and seclusion.

Despite the cold warning swirling in Rhode's eyes, Bronze never bristled. He had too many questions about the lycan woman, and the memories of how he found her, coupled with the remnants of the sun deity's little lycan prophecy where he was concerned, only made him twitchier.

Rhode let his chest fall and directed Bronze to another empty patient room across the hall. "Let's talk."

THE IDENTICAL FOUR WALLS, beige cabinetry, and jars containing every possible size of sterile-wrapped gauze under the sun made for a terrible audience to what Bronze needed to both say and hear.

After he spent so many eons cracking jokes and lightening the mood at the expense of his brothers, the ironic change of spotlight that was only enhanced by the sterile glow of all that medical shit was an oddly hollow experience. His past was so riddled with sunken holes and buried promises, he sometimes wondered whether there was anything of worth to find there at all. When Saulé, the celestial goddess with the supremely unhelpful lycan premonition, cast down her beam of light on him, he'd half expected it to bounce around an empty tunnel shrouded with nothing but cobwebs that shielded up his trap doors.

He should have known someone would eventually test the load-bearing qualities of his past to see just how swiftly those in his life would fall through.

Rhode strode into the room after him with a large plastic bag in his hand.

Bronze lifted a brow. "It's a little late for takeout, but I can always eat."

Once the door shut them into the small space, Rhode placed the bag on top of the counter, and the familiar garments the lycan woman had worn when Bronze had found her were pulled out in a neatly folded pile. Everything had been dried and folded into a succinct little bundle, and Bronze tried not to look too closely at the loose white blouse that sat on top. If he stared at the fabric with the same intensity the damn thing called to him with, the conjured image of a pair of perfect breasts molded with the stuff would distract him away from the answers he intended to throttle out of Rhode.

Bronze swallowed hard and sliced his gaze away, instead focusing on the peculiar necklace Rhode had grabbed that had been tucked beneath the woman's outerwear.

The thing kind of looked like a cross between a large fang and a small horn of some kind, though why the woman would wear it was beyond even his wildest fashion sense, which wasn't saying a whole lot considering he pretty much vacillated between graphic tees, various leather chest holsters and baldrics, and full-body metallic armor.

"What's that?" he asked. "Something of hers?"

Rhode took the necklace—for it was a necklace, judging by the thin strap of leather Bronze now recognized from when he'd examined her neck for injury—and placed it by itself on the counter, far away from everything else. Though the seraph held the object with great care, he also wasted no time releasing the thing. Once his fingers were free and clear of what looked like bone matter, he breathed a soft sigh of relief and collapsed onto the small nearby stool. Even though he had been rescued from captivity the better part of a year ago, he was still occasionally plagued by bouts of exhaustion and weakness. Damn, it hurt to see, but Bronze wouldn't belittle the angel's progress or pride by looking away.

"I've seen something like this before," Rhode said calmly once he'd regained more control of himself.

"You have? Where?"

There was a long pause where those umber eyes of his seemed to glaze over with some distant memories before returning to the present. "At Cyro's grotto."

Every molecule in Bronze's body stood up and took notice.

"What?" Bronze dropped his arms and pushed away from the counter he'd taken a lean-to on. He had half a mind to charge at the seraph and shake more words out of him, but that faraway haze returned again and, with it, an eerie sense that what Rhode was about to reveal was just as much for his benefit as Bronze's.

"Cyro referred to it as a relic."

Huh. Interesting.

Bronze's voice gentled. "When did you see it?" Careful. He had to be very careful here, but shit, he wasn't skilled with the whole patiently diplomatic routine.

"The better part of a century ago, we were located in a different underground location from where Drea and Chrome found me. One time, when Cyro visited my cell, he didn't come to me right away but instead stopped to converse with an apex about something. It was unusual for him to hold such a conversation in front of me, though perhaps he thought I was not capable of listening. Most of the time, he was right. That time, however, I had a brief respite of a more lucid moment. I heard every whispered word."

Bronze let the seraph's mind wander where it needed to go, though every instinct burned with fury at the mention of Rhode's time there, of what the angel must have endured, especially with an apex charmer—the highest class of charmer and the most ruthlessly powerful—as a jailer. More than once, Bronze had thought it was a blessing from the prime mages that Rhode didn't and wouldn't remember his time there. Now, after witnessing firsthand the angel's glassy eyes and haunted visage whenever the past came upon him, he wasn't so sure.

Rhode spoke idly, seemingly unfazed by the memories that tumbled out, as if used to the dull blankness. "The relic holds dormant celestial magic."

Bronze stiffened. "How is that possible? What would Cyro want with it, and why the hell would a female like her be found wearing it?"

"Cyro was convinced it was the key to entering the Empyrean somehow. He never mentioned specifics, but he believed it contained a core component capable of opening up the gates again, so that he might finally have the means to enter and lay siege to Heaven's highest realm."

The room, small as it was, got about a thousand times smaller under the weight of Rhode's revelation. "What are you saying? That this horn thing has magic that can get us home?"

Home. By the mages, how long had that word sat like a lead weight on his chest making each breath that much harder to punch out? Yes, it had been right, what he and his brothers had done. Sealing off the gates of Heaven so the Empyrean and all the souls in it would be forever free from Cyro's tyranny and invasion, even if it meant Bronze and the sentinels might never hope to see the realm's light again.

For Bronze, however, it wasn't just about the homecoming that had made his eons in the mortal realm particularly painful. It wasn't just the wasted years or the endless battles or the daily depletion of his celestial powers.

It was about who he'd left behind and the sacred vow he'd sworn to uphold that had been forever lost to him.

Polina.

"Can we get back?" Bronze asked through a tight throat. "Can that thing get us back?"

Rhode blinked away the fog that had settled over his expression, and familiar clarity once again returned to his features. "I don't know, but I *do* know that Cyro has a relic identical to what your lycan female was wearing around her neck."

Bronze's enthusiasm stalled out at that. There was a *second* relic? "How do you know it's not the same one?"

Rhode shook his head. "I thought it was the same one at first, but after I examined it more closely, I noticed a crack at the base of this one. I removed the fastener to get a better look, and I was correct. The one Cyro had was pristine. I remember how strong the glare of its pure opalescence was compared to the dinginess of the grotto and how I winced when I looked at it. The relic was pristine but also, somehow, incomplete. The base of it was shorn and jagged, while the rest of its curvature was unblemished. Cyro had made a point of saying so. This one, however," he said, pointing to the fang-like bit of stone that sat so unassumingly on the counter, "is flawed, though only slightly, and when you remove its fastener, the base is cut in a similar way as to fit together with what I've seen before. I believe it is the other half of what Cyro has."

"The other half . . ." Bronze trailed off, giving his thoughts free rein to thoroughly freak the fuck out.

The Empyrean. Dormant magic.

Was he really facing down an item that could return them all to their home? And more to the point, what the hell was a half-dead lycan female doing with the damn thing wrapped around her neck?

"Why would—" Insistent alarms sounded out from the room across the hall. He'd heard them before. They were the sounds of steady rhythmic vital signs kicking into healthier, higher gears when someone returned to the land of the living. But for the first time, those sounds took on a different cadence. One of desperate questions, worried outcomes, and . . . hope.

Rhode got to his feet and opened the door. "Let us see what she can answer."

CHAPTER 7

The clock on the wall had just crept past three thirty, and Clara hoped her internal timepiece wasn't lying to her, though she couldn't blame it if it was. Good Lord, her head hurt. If every hunger headache she'd ever experienced had all been rolled into a cumulative ball and squatted on her frontal lobe, it *might* come close to the pain she was feeling now.

Thank goodness the lights were dim. The even dullness of the glow was a bit unnerving, however. She knew humans had other means of illuminating their buildings than the fire lamps she was used to, but did the light have to be so flat and uniform? Never in a million years did she think she'd miss the sway and temperament of a simple flame.

Please still be night. Please still be night.

If it was night, that meant her chances of returning before her father noticed her absence were significantly slimmer. Oh, who was she kidding? The only reason he would notice her missing was if one of the wealthy males vying for her hand—and her father's power—inquired after her whereabouts and she was nowhere to be found. Her father had only ever expressed as much interest in her well-being insofar as her ability to breed and how her unique pedigree would benefit him in gaining more players on his political chess board.

Pedigree. If she had to hear that word one more time, she was liable to shave the hair off her head and hang herself with the length of it. It was a stark reminder of just how dire her desperation had been of late and what had driven her into the woods in the first place.

Driven her to the human lands. To that male . . .

Wondering whether he'd return to her, Clara inched herself higher against the pillow and frowned. What on earth was she wearing? A pale blue dotted gown of some sort covered her from shoulders to shins. When she lifted the blanket on top of her to inspect further, she gasped.

Holy mother, she was naked beneath that gown! Just who had changed her into this? And where were her clothes? Oh God, the relic!

Clara pushed through her throbbing temples and tried to extricate herself from the linens. By the time her bare feet hit the cold floor, the door to her room swung open.

As before, Bronze was the first one to greet her, followed by Rhode and another female in a white coat who had blonde hair that seemed almost as long as hers, though the braid made it difficult to discern in the low light. Damn, where the heck were her clothes? Was she really to meet a stranger—another woman of the same class as these guardians, no less—wearing what amounted to little more than a sheet? Her wolf's low rumble echoed her worry.

Then she remembered that these were not humans.

Bronze stepped forward, his presence every bit as commanding despite the jovial nature she'd caught glimpses of here and there. She didn't quite know how she knew it, but his casual manner, especially how he'd acted with her, suggested an innate comfort with more lighthearted tactics. Oh, yes, he was no stranger to laughter. Quite often, too, if the smile lines at the corners of his mouth and eyes were any indication. The prospect certainly made her original proposal to him more appealing.

If a male made room for joy in his life, then, surely, there was less room for the darker urges of cruelty.

Clara let some of the anxiety ease from her body. *Yes, I was right. He will do. He has to.*

"Glad to see you're awake," Bronze said. "How are you feeling?"

"I have a bit of a headache, but I am otherwise myself."

The blonde female stepped forward and checked the remnants of a clear plastic bag that hung from a metal pole near Clara's bed. "If you didn't have a headache, I'd say you weren't human. That head injury must have been ugly when it happened, especially after being pulled out of the river."

A heavy weight of anticipation filled the room, and Bronze looked at Clara with an almost rapt sort of hunger, as if he was on the verge of uncovering a secret but was being forced to quell his suspicions. *Oh, he doesn't like that one bit.*

The female, seemingly unconcerned, continued, "The gash on your forehead healed up nicely, and this IV bag is good and empty. Perfect. Fluids are definitely your friend. You're looking much better."

"Fluids?"

"Yeah, in your arm. I have to say, I don't know many people who can suck down saline so quickly and bounce back after only a few hours. Most humans would take twenty-four hours, at least. I'm Drea, by the way. I was the one who got you all cleaned up."

The female had gone and said that word again. *Humans.*

Wait . . .

Clara tracked the clear tube that extended from the metal pole straight into—

"Oh my God, get it out! Get it out now!" Clara's wolf snarled as she clawed at the plastic tubing that was fastened into the crook of her elbow and extended *inside her.*

"Whoa! Easy! Hang on, I'll get the IV out, just sit tight for a moment." Drea quickly plucked the plastic out of her, and Clara shivered at the foreign matter's removal.

"What did you put inside me? And where are my clothes?"

"Here. All your effects are in this bag." Rhode placed her belongings at the edge of her bed where her feet had been, making sure she knew he was careful not to touch her. Again, she cursed her skittish ways and wished that particular flaw wasn't so obvious in her demeanor. "You were severely dehydrated when you arrived," he added. "We had to administer fluids intravenously. That is all we did, I swear. Now, we'll leave the room while you get dressed. I'm sure you have a lot of questions."

"And we do as well," Bronze tacked on pointedly, though still with a kind understanding. "Back in five."

Once the door closed and Clara was again alone with her thoughts, her wolf managed to calm down also.

Deep breaths. You can do this. You made the decision, and now you must follow through with the plan.

A few minutes later, dressed in her own clothes and with the relic safely tucked against her chest, she heard a soft rap at the door. *Wow. Five minutes exactly.* "You may enter."

Bronze, again, was the first to push through the door, followed by Rhode. The female—Drea, was it?—was noticeably absent. It was also obvious that whatever unassuming hospitality these males had extended toward her had quickly come to an end. Her hosts' rigid stances and stiff shoulders set the tone for how the line of questioning would go. They would ask the questions, and she would be expected to answer them. Business had clearly replaced altruism.

Right, then. If that's the case, it's best to cut them off at the pass. You have your own business here as well.

She wiped her palms on her leather trousers and cringed when a shiny streak of sweat winked back at her. Wonderful. "My name is Clara," she said clearly, with her chin raised so she might address each of them equally. "Clara Ander. I—"

"Nice to meet you, Clara Ander." Bronze pegged her with a smirk that belied his tough appearance. Folded arms and a tense frame or no, he still attempted to put her at some modicum of ease. "Officially, that is."

Not knowing what to make of that, she returned his greeting with a small nod. "I—"

He stepped to the side, revealing the wide open door to the hallway. Strange how she hadn't noticed before, but neither of these males had shut her in, and the subtle shift in Bronze's position had been a way to let her know that. She wasn't a prisoner, nor were they her jailors. She could go. At any time, she imagined she could rise from the bed, walk out that door, and she'd be free to do so.

This was nothing more than a simple conversation, something she'd done countless times with numerous strangers. Yes, she could do this.

"I have come seeking a male from the human lands, but as you said, I have mistakenly arrived elsewhere." There, that wasn't so hard, was it?

"Plenty of humans walking this earth, Clara. They're not hard to find. Shit, there are so damn many of them, you can hardly sneeze without goobering at least a couple."

"Bronze," Rhode warned.

The male cleared his throat. "I simply meant to convey the scope of the species. What I'd like to know is how the hell a female lycan makes it to however many years you have and not encountered any humans before. This is the mortal realm, after all. The *mortal* realm."

Well, that certainly caught her off guard. Oh boy. How to respond. Clara was not at all prepared for Bronze to identify her species so casually, nor for her worldly ignorance to be spotlighted so fully, and in front of an audience, no less.

Honesty would have to be the best policy for now.

"Yes, I am a lycan and the daughter of King Halpin." Clara stared at the floor and waited for the recognition to flood the room. When no further comments were made, she looked up. Both males simply stared at her with expectant expressions, as if she hadn't just revealed herself to be of royal blood. As if they had no interest in her lineage or understanding of her father's holdings.

And then it dawned on her. *They truly don't know who I am.*

"You are a princess, then?" Rhode asked.

She blinked, then stammered a moment, never having been asked the question in her life. Gosh, how did she even answer that? "Yes, I am. And that is the reason why I have come searching outside my father's lands."

"Searching for what?" Bronze asked.

"A, uh . . . a male who is willing to compete for my hand in marriage." Clara cringed. Just saying her plight out loud cast a heavy shroud of desperation over her shoulders. What if it didn't work? What if this male said no? What if—

"I'll admit, none of us even knew lycans existed until a few months ago, and even then, it wasn't through witnessed events. We've no knowledge of your father, of any royal lycan lines, where you live, how you're governed, or even your physiology," Rhode clarified. "But it's clear you know something about humans. I take it your people are good at staying hidden?"

"Yes, quite so. My father's stronghold is located a couple of hours from where Bronze found me."

"How is that possible? We would have known about you," Bronze replied.

Clara shook her head. "No, you wouldn't have. Our lands are protected and well hidden."

The scoff that echoed through the tiny room was loud enough to rattle the glass jars on the counter, as well as her nerves. "We've been stuck in the mortal realm since before the White Mountains were pimples on the butt of Pangea. You expect us to believe a secret race of lycans managed to just sprout up, establish a whole civilization, and stay tucked in the corner out of sight like a clump of dust bunnies?"

"And yet, your friend admits you had not heard of my kind before a few months ago. I assure you, we are well hidden and have always been." Clara's quiet rebuff sucked the air right out of the room, leaving her flailing behind to figure out how to cover her gaffe.

Oh, precious Moon Mother. Had those words really just tumbled out of her stupid mouth? "Uh, that is to say, we—"

Rhode chuckled softly. "You don't need to apologize. In fact, you've presented the perfect opportunity for my kin here to share our own nature with you. You must be just as curious, I imagine."

Embarrassed, she nodded.

"Bronze?"

The male leered at Rhode before acquiescing to the request. "We're angels. Warrior sentinels of the Empyrean, Heaven's highest realm. We've been living among the mortals for, as I said, a good long while."

It was Clara's turn to eye them suspiciously, which would have been a heck of a lot easier to do if she could remember to blink. "Angels? With wings and such?"

Bronze smiled, clearly enjoying her renewed sense of discomfort. "And such."

It was on the tip of her tongue to state the obvious, but no, she couldn't. Could she?

Well, since they had established an open level of honesty, surely she could ask—

"The wings come and go," Bronze cut in. "Can't have 'em out all the time. Huge nightmare to keep clean. Air pollution doesn't just affect the lungs. The tarnish and buildup from that stuff is killer. Besides, they get annoying to maneuver with when you're trying to eat a meal or go for a swim. Hell of a way to get around, though."

Many questions popped into Clara's mind and fought for first place. Angels? Real angels? And she was sitting a few feet away from them?

As if sensing her mind spinning out of control, Rhode lifted his hand. "Forgive me. I'm sure you have a multitude of questions about our kind, and we'll be happy to answer them, but I find your own story quite interesting as well. Why are you looking for a mate to compete for your hand? Do you not have eligible lycan males to choose from in your lands?"

Hesitation gripped her, jarring her back to the matter in front of her. "I do. No, that's not correct. My father does, and he has already made his choice."

Clara risked a glance at Bronze and was bolstered by the sharpened heat in his hazel eyes. "The male I have been promised to is, for lack of a more appropriate descriptor, a tyrant. He would be better off mating my father directly and leaving me out of the whole business altogether," she griped, "but that is not possible."

"So you ran away," Bronze stated.

"Yes."

"Because the guy your father wants you to marry is an asshole."

"Yes," she said quietly.

It sounded so silly when spoken aloud, especially when distilled down to the sum of its parts by such a formidable male.

She needed to make him see the severity of what would pass should her union come to fruition.

"You must understand, my father is not himself a good ruler. There is no kindness left in him. Fear is his most commanding motivator, as well as his power. He is the leader of the north-eastern lycan territories and is liable to either destroy all that remains of our monarchy and people or expand his holdings through an advantageous match with a neighboring territory's warlord. He craves legacy, and the only way he seeks to gain that is through unabashed might. My people suffer as a result. More and more are fleeing the lycan lands, but there's nowhere for them to go. Some assimilate into human culture, but that is not easy or desirable long term. The warlord to the west, the one my father has chosen for me, has been moving closer, and if a deal is struck between my father and that brute for my hand in marriage, there will be no stopping the empire that will result. The prospect of that empire," she added for emphasis, "is what I believe keeps my father rising each morning. It's certainly not his love for me, if it ever existed. He . . . he wishes to see lycans live beyond our confines and has come to believe, corruptly so, that humans should no longer be allowed to have the run of the lands. He believes that their time as the dominant species is closely coming to an end."

Clara lifted her hands to her chest. Through her mantle, she pressed the relic's warm weight closer against her breastbone, right above her heart. Bronze tracked the movement but didn't speak. Slowly, she lifted the moonstone fang free of its confines and held it gently in her hands. Though the weight was slight for its size, it may as well have been the moon itself. Such was the burden she carried.

"This is my people's moonstone relic. It is the symbol of our lycan monarchy." Clara held it out expectantly, feeling not a whit lighter despite hefting the thing off her neck. When neither male took what she offered and merely exchanged indiscernible glances, she lowered the relic, and her heart sank right along with it.

They didn't recognize it at all. Not even a flicker of awareness had flashed in either of their intent gazes. And then an extremely humbling realization dawned on her. Of *course* they didn't recognize it. Her people had done far too good of a job remaining hidden all these centuries, passing for humans when they needed to, but living largely apart from them. So, why would these males—no, *angels*—know the significance of what she offered them?

Shame crept up her cheeks. God, she was such a fool, wasn't she? To think she'd thought herself clever, daring even, for stealing the relic in the first place, thinking it would be the one thing to prove her story. The one thing that would identify her as who she was. And what was she, exactly? A princess in title only, to be doled out as a broodmare in a game of land ownership and power moves. A foolish, *foolish* female who hadn't the cunning or brutality to maneuver through the world in the way that would garner her half the benefits it would her father.

At a loss for not only words but a plan of action, Clara floundered for how to proceed. She knew nothing of where she found herself, and the males before her clearly knew nothing of her. If she returned home now, it would still be night. Perhaps she could convince her father she had been kidnapped or maybe there was an intrusion in the keep? A threat? Or possibly—

Bronze's gruff voice broke the silence. "You said 'compete.'"

Clara's worried frenzy ground to a halt by the tether of his tone. "Forgive me. What?"

"When you spoke to me near the river, the first lucid words out of your mouth were, 'Compete for me.'"

A strange clarity filled up the holes of the sieve in her mind, redirecting her focus to the male before her, who had taken a step closer but still did not crowd her. "I did. Yes."

"You asked me to compete for your hand in marriage. I've

gotta confess, dragging a nearly drowned woman out of the river and getting a marriage proposal for my troubles isn't the oddest thing that's happened to me, but I haven't had time to examine that list in a while. Care to elaborate?"

Clara fiddled with the leather strap around her neck. Oh, gosh. Where to begin? "I do not wish to marry just to further propel my father's machinations into motion. The warlord he has chosen is, well, not one I wish to be tied to for the rest of my life. I do not agree with my father's view of the world, and though I may not have as many avenues available to stop what's coming, as the sole lycan princess in our monarchy, I do have one. Among my people, it is known as the Betrothal Games. In essence, if I object to the male my father has chosen for me, a series of games may be enacted wherein several competitors engage in events that advance them through a tournament. The winner shall earn my hand in marriage and all that comes with it."

Bronze's eyes narrowed. "And when you say 'all that comes with it,' you mean any connections to your father's holdings, alliances, money . . ."

"Yes. Traditionally, and for my father, it is a power play that would allow him to unite with the strongest proven male competitor in lieu of his own original choice. For me, I fled hoping to find a competitor unlike those my father would choose. Someone not of my world who is kind and just. Powerful in strength, yes, but also a warrior in his own mind. One who would champion far more than just the desire for a land grab or legacy." She lifted her eyes to his and was momentarily stunned by the earnestness there. She studied him further and detected no hint of the craving for power she was so accustomed to being around. There was something else instead, something far more intriguing and just . . . old. Ancient. Mature, even. It sent hopeful urges fluttering around her heart that he would help her, or at the very least, once they were mated, she could work to convince him of what she needed him to do to help her people. He would be malleable, dependable.

Yes. He's the one. He has to be.

"I suppose I had hoped to find someone," she continued, quietly stressing her words, "who *would* pull a nearly drowned princess out of a river and offer her aid without ever knowing one thing about her."

Her final words were a challenge, and she watched the angel intently to see whether he would engage. Again, that pressing silence made the air in their small room nearly unbearable, but she wouldn't look away, no matter how devastating his hazel stare became. She was a lycan princess, an heir, a leader to her people.

And he was the warrior angel who'd rescued her. The one she believed the Moon Mother had sent her to find.

More of those meaningful looks were exchanged between the two males, and Clara had the feeling entire conversations were taking place in the span of their silent thoughts. Were they reading each other's minds? Could angels do that?

Oh, boy, she had a lot to learn, and the pounding in her head was doing its level best to make holding herself together a near impossibility. God, she was exhausted. Mentally, physically, emotionally. If this angel rejected her, she wasn't sure there was much left in her that could withstand the hit.

Then Bronze looked at her and sealed her fate with two simple words. "I accept."

CHAPTER 8

There weren't a lot of things in the world that gave Bronze any true semblance of serenity. In his experience, cheerful clouds and happy birds on branches always preceded an ass-kicker of a storm. Even the quiet hush of crowds in stadiums was really just another omen to what was coming: a brutal tackle, a homerun, a kick to the shins when the refs weren't looking. There was always some sort of tell that shit was about to get real big real fast.

The knock-him-to-his-knees smile that stretched across Clara's face after he accepted the oddest proposal of his life would forever sit at the top of that list. Stange how an almost sort of desperate gratitude seemed to shine up at him from those wide eyes, a reaction that had seemed so far outside what he would consider the normal realm of appreciation given her rescue. He'd saved her life, sure, but who wouldn't have, given the circumstances? When she'd smiled up at him in that moment, though, something in her pained expression and eager eyes gutted him.

"Dammit," he muttered as he swiped a hand down his tired face. No matter how earnestly he'd tried to garner a few hours of shut-eye, Bronze hadn't managed to escape the female's gaze as it wormed its way into his dreams. A gaze alight with eyes so soothing, they'd begun to remind him of gingerbread, of all things. Not the stale shit from the box mortals made houses out of, but the kind swirled together with real earthy blackstrap molasses and kissed with the spicy warmth of Chinese ginger.

A strangely comforting confection for a male who'd never had much of a sweet tooth.

Top it all off with a crown of hair that swirled around her like the most decadent white frosting and Bronze could hardly figure out whether to get out of the way of what was about to tackle him or take the hit and pick the pieces up later.

Luckily, he'd always been good at two things: taking punches and solving puzzles. That female, Clara, would have him checking both boxes before the upcoming days were through, he had no doubt of it.

After her big reveal and Bronze's even bigger response, much to everyone's surprise, Rhode had thankfully taken over the speaking parts and declared that it would be best for everyone to get whatever hours of sleep they could before Bronze escorted Clara back to her home midmorning.

And that was how Bronze found himself in the great hall of the den, running on little more than adrenaline and two sixteen-ouncers of French press coffee, with every ax, sword, spear, dagger, and firearm he could carry spread out on the farmhouse table. He'd even asked his brother Titan whether he could borrow one of the dude's mini crossbows before the angel, who was infuriatingly too smart for his own damn good, pointed out that it might be unwise to carry the small arsenal Bronze had been intending to tow with him. After all, the trip was about a two-hour walk, according to Clara, and Mr. Second-in-Command Boy Wonder had oh-so helpfully made Bronze aware that carrying all his shit, including Clara, while flying would likely be a no-go.

Ass.

So hoof it they would, unfortunately, but Bronze would be damned if he didn't have a special dagger with her father's name on it tucked right along his ribs. Mages, he'd never wanted to measure the depth of a man's chest by how far his blade sank in or test the tensile strength of his garrote, which he casually tucked into his pack next to some spare socks, more than when Clara had described the sort of ass boil dear old daddy had shaped up to be.

As Bronze organized his weapons for maximum storage efficiency and began zipping them into his pack and stowing them into the various holsters he wore, he couldn't help but think how surreal Clara's story still seemed, despite all the truths that had smacked him upside the head. Sure, he was a fallen angel, and by mortal standards, that came with its own sort of paranormal spooks, but oddly enough, the fact that she was a lycan, and lycan royalty no less, was the most normal part about her, if he could even risk using such a word to describe the woman. In his eons-long lifetime of dealing with mages, messengers, demon-manipulated mortals, and goddesses-turned-monsters, little about the various species he'd met surprised him anymore.

What *had* surprised him was Clara's speech, her manner of dress, and how she described her world, which he clearly knew bupkis about. And he, an immortal angel! Knower of old shit and mountains of magic! The enormity of scale with which she spoke of the lycans had been the most alarming, and not just because it stung his ego every time he came up short with the requisite knowledge. Rival kingdoms, monarchies, warlords, strongholds? These were concepts that, while still understandable by modern standards, certainly took on an air of the past. After all, what use was a warlord when a national government and united military holdings made those aggressive commanders all but obsolete? Even if one such commander *did* have a healthy arsenal at his beck and call, it was kind of hard to show up with the threat of laying down the *pew-pew* against the powerful holdings Clara described her father possessing.

And speaking of which, in the past century, Bronze could count on one hand the number of times he'd heard the words *stronghold* and *keep* in relation to a living, breathing building at the center of a community. If her father was truly as influential as she claimed, why go the fortified-castle route instead of a normal building with a shit ton of alarms, armed security guards, and quick and convenient access to more of the same should things get out of hand?

It all made about as much sense as vegan meatballs.

Footsteps echoed up from the nearby staircase that led down to the armory, and Tungsten and Iron surfaced. They both took in Bronze's stuffed-to-the-gill rucksack as it swallowed up the last of his weapons.

Tungsten folded his arms and was the first to comment, but if Bronze knew either of them, Iron would be the one to get in the final jab. "That's quite a lot of artillery."

"A manageable amount," Bronze added.

Iron stepped forward and tucked the hilt of a dagger that had come loose more firmly into Bronze's back holster. "Considering you have no idea what you're walking into, I'd be more concerned with the artillery you *can't* see."

Ah, there it was. Right on cue.

"I'm as prepared as I can be. Why?" Bronze's head snapped up, and he threw as much charm as possible into the grin that had earned him more punches than pleasantries among his brothers. "Annoyed that Army green isn't your color? Not everyone can pull off my particular shade of auburn. Hey, while I'm gone, I better not find out you've been rifling through my hair products again."

But while Bronze waited for the volleying jibe that Iron always threw his way, none arrived. Instead, mirrored stern expressions from both of them pinned Bronze's boots to the floor. His brother, one of the largest, grumpiest uglies this side of the mortal realm, simply stared back at him with unwavering calm. Unshakable as always, the guy was like the unflappable and majestic tip of an age-old iceberg. Problem was, only a select few knew what had been brewing below the surface all those years, and every now and then, Bronze was not-so-subtly reminded of the male's limits and what Iron was truly capable of.

Some wars went on for years, others eternities. Behind Iron's rugged beard and tense mismatched eyes, a battle still waged, and hell if Bronze knew when the final body would hit the ground or whose it would be.

Bronze quickly cleared his throat and changed the topic. "Rhode seems to believe that Clara honestly holds the relic around her neck as a symbol of her monarchy and nothing more."

Tungsten lifted a skeptical brow but never unfolded his arms. "Truly?"

"Yeah. When he asked about any other articles like it, she said she didn't know of any, nor did she think that what she wore around her neck had any special properties beyond being a cherished gift her people believe was bestowed upon them long ago from their deity. The Moon Mother, Clara calls her."

"What about these other lycan territories? Didn't she mention this warlord she's supposed to marry as occupying the west? West of what, exactly? Are we talking the West Coast?" Iron asked.

Bronze shook his head. "No clue, but I'll find out more on the way. Rhode was also careful to question her without mentioning Cyro or his charmers specifically. It's clear the female, sorry, *princess*, has no knowledge beyond what she shared. I mean, she could hardly figure out how to work the overhead lights in her room, which is another piece of the puzzle I'm adding to the list of weird shit that doesn't make any fucking sense."

"Like how the hell there exists an entire lycan kingdom, presumably with full-blown royals, and not a single one of us has gotten wind of it in all the years since we've landed here?"

Yeah, that too.

In a span of a few hours, Bronze had been hit with a veritable oil tanker's worth of puzzle pieces that he was beginning to suspect didn't all go to the same puzzle. About the only thing he could take to any sort of proverbial bank at the moment was that relic around Clara's neck, and Rhode's bone-deep assertion that it had some connection to Cyro.

To possibly, one day, return to the Empyrean.

"Are you prepared to do this, then?" Tungsten asked.

Bronze swept an elaborate hand out to model his precision-perfect packing skills. "Have you not seen the number of blades I stuffed in here?" Again, he was met with a look so dry and void of amusement, he wondered whether they had all been created by the same prime mages.

Questionable, that.

"Are you prepared to enter these games under the farce we've constructed?" Tungsten added wearily. "I'll not lie to you. The stakes are rather high. If what Rhode suspects has even a modicum of truth to it, it's an assertion that may—"

"Just get us home," Iron finished.

It was the one whisper that all the sentinels, even those who had become happily mated to their soul bonds, still offered up to the prime mages. Some habits die hard. Though Bronze had always wondered what would happen should a time arise when that choice had to be made for his brothers. Most of the mated soul bonds were mortal and could not follow the angels to the Empyrean. And not surprisingly, no one had ever given an actual voice to the circumstance. Why should they, when their other halves had been discovered in the mortal realm and the promise of return had gone so long unfulfilled?

He got it. He truly did. Should the day ever come, he'd weep and mourn along with his brothers for the agony of the choice they'd face. But for him, home had an entirely different set of implications, ones that started and ended as a final oath on a battlefield and had haunted him ever since.

A promise made in blood can only be broken by blood.

Of course, when Bronze had made that pact and spoken those words, neither party involved had had the foresight to consider the only other thing that could strip a vow of its power, even when sworn to by one of the Empyrean's sentinels: banishment.

"I know what's at stake," Bronze said. "I'll get in, play some games, learn what I can, nab the relic, and leave. Honestly, I'm looking forward to it. Haven't booked a vacation with an excursion package in quite some time. Should be fun."

Bronze threw the final zipper home on his rucksack and stormed over to the kitchen to load up on far tastier travel provisions. They had another thirty minutes before he and Clara were due to head out, and if his hands couldn't wrap around the handle of his halberd, they were better off doing what damage they could to the food stores.

But even as he rummaged through produce and protein bars, two phrases from two different females, one a plea and one a warning, ran roughshod over his otherwise calculated selection process.

"Compete for me."

"Lycans are so very fond of their games."

Bronze couldn't remember tossing the gingerbread cookies into his pack, but their spice lingered on his skin long after he closed the bag.

CHAPTER 9

"So, what do people address you as where you're from? Your Majesty? No, wait, that's usually a king and queen thing, right? Princes and princesses, at least in the Western mortal monarchies, get served up with the 'Your Highness' stuff instead, if I remember. Or should I be calling you something else?"

Clara lowered the canteen of water from her mouth and did her best to hide her coughing fit behind the back of her hand. Goodness. They had only been walking for a little less than an hour, and already she'd been so churned up by his tales of the human lands and what lay ahead for them that she'd nearly spilled water on herself three times, almost rolled her ankle twice, and had been smacked in the forehead by a low branch she was convinced must have jumped out of nowhere.

The only small mercy granted was Bronze's insistence that he walk in front of her. A bit silly since *she* was serving as *his* guide, but the energy it would have taken to argue was far better spent figuring out just what the hell she'd do once they arrived back at her home.

"Clara is fine when it is just us in conversation. Otherwise, most call me 'lady.'"

Bronze hung back a bit and waited for her to ascend the small hill he'd already scaled so she wouldn't have to shout. "My lady or Lady Ander? You explained how lycan females take their surnames from the mother's line, but didn't go into how you use it."

"No, just 'lady.'"

When Clara finally reached the top, she handed him back the canteen. He took it, but when he didn't immediately stow it or continue walking, she stopped as well. He simply held the canteen, which was significantly lighter than when he'd offered it to her.

A tremulous sense of dread poked at her midsection. Had she drank too much? Were they to share one canteen each, or had she just imbibed far more than her fair portion, leaving him with very little water for the journey? Gosh, she hadn't a clue. They hadn't spoken of it. All that occurred earlier were a few small coughs on her part, which she'd covered with her mantle as best she could. By the time the fit had subsided and the dry dirt on their path had settled a bit, Bronze had already thrust the canteen beneath her nose, urging her to drink, so she did.

But, oh, he did not look happy. Dappled sunlight pierced through whatever openings in the tree cover it could find, casting Bronze's features in slashes of highlighted brilliance, as well as revealing a sour look of consternation.

"Your people just call you 'lady?'" he said dourly. "As in, 'hey, lady'? Like they're calling a dog or screaming at an irate shopper or something?"

The tone in his voice caught her off guard, and again, she worried she'd done something terribly wrong.

Perfect. Just perfect, Clara.

God, she was making such a muck of this already. If she

couldn't manage a simple conversation with the male, a task that had been quite easy since he'd done most of the talking, how on earth was she supposed to navigate their interactions when they got to her home?

"Does my title offend you somehow?" she offered hastily. "As I said, you may call me by my given name in private."

The crude manner with which the angel shook his head sharply was a jarring upheaval of his otherwise delightful nature. Dismissive almost, and it unnerved her. He seemed to mutter something under his breath before addressing her more fully. "I'll play along and do what you need."

"Thank you." Though she had no idea what she was thanking him for, exactly.

They walked in silence for a few moments, and the short respite was painstakingly needed. Clara brought her hands to the relic and fiddled with the fang's tip while she sorted out the next phase of what she hoped would change the course of the rest of her and her people's lives.

She thought back to the moment this entire odyssey of an idea had first occurred to her. The moment when her father's actions had solidified into so much more than the base manipulations only he and other select males in the stronghold seemed to excel in.

The argument she'd witnessed had been between two rival farmers, both of whom maintained properties on the outskirts of her father's lands. One was a dairy farmer, while the other operated an apple orchard, and both had solid footing in the human lands as well as the lycan territories, as dairy products and apples were among the top five commodities for the region regardless of species.

Traditionally, Clara had never been called on to hear civilian disputes, as the judgment from the king was all that mattered. However, she had already been speaking to her father about another subject. Once the king's appointment to hear the farmers' dispute arrived, he'd forgotten about her entirely, as was sometimes his way, and failed to dismiss her.

The doors to King Halpin's receiving room remained open, despite the two males who had requested a private appointment with the king. Clara gripped the paper her father had signed after he'd flippantly tossed it her way. She'd managed to catch it before it soared into the fireplace behind them, thankfully. She didn't want to examine the outcome if she'd been too slow.

Her frustration was quickly growing from a measured simmer to a full-blown boil, but when the two males stepped forward, her curiosity, both at not being immediately dismissed and why the doors had yet to be closed, intrigued her more than her anger distracted her.

The king jotted down some notes in a ledger but never looked up. "What is your complaint, Mr. McCready? I read something about fences being destroyed and losing some of your herd."

The older dairy farmer ripped his flat cap from his balding head and crushed it nervously in his hands. "Yes, Your Majesty. You see, Mr. Blankenship has not been mending his orchard's wooden fences, allowing the coyotes to get through to my farm and kill my dairy calves. Our families had an agreement some years back where we'd split the cost of fencing the perimeters where our properties joined. I've kept up with my half, but Mr. Blankenship has not held up his side of the bargain."

"Your bargain was with my father, old man, not with me." The satisfied smirk on the younger farmer's face echoed the arrogance in his stance, his bony shoulders pushed back with a bravado his lanky frame could otherwise never fully muster.

"You are his pup," the older farmer shouted, pointing a gnarled finger in the young man's direction. "Why take on your father's legacy after he died if you're just going to see it ruined? You have a responsibility to your pack, to your—"

When her father's fist hit the desk, Clara shrank back farther against the tapestry on the wall. Still, he didn't look at them and continued to scribble his notes, effecting a bored tone. "Tell me something, Mr. McCready. Can an apple harm a cow?"

The old male's jowls wobbled as he shook his head in confusion. "Um, no, Your Majesty."

"And do your cows harm Mr. Blankenship's apples?" The king turned a page. More scribbling.

"No. I don't feed my livestock apples. It bloats them up terribly, especially the Jersey cows."

"Do coyotes eat apples?"

The old farmer's face fell. "I couldn't say, Your Majesty. I suppose they could."

The young male chimed in. "I've secured all my trees in the orchard with tighter, more restrictive stone fences. Whatever Mr. McCready is referring to is obsolete for my uses. Any bargain he struck with my father was verbal only. I have no need for his fences."

"We had an agreement," the old farmer whined, the shock of where the conversation was heading dragging down his features further. "The cost was too high for both of us," he said, his faraway eyes slipping into the past. "The acreage alone meant—"

"Fix your own fences and don't waste my time again."

The two farmers were immediately dismissed, but before Clara could sneak out of the room as well, her heart heavier than the stones brushing along her palm that she held out for support, she caught her father's final words to his chief of arms.

"Double your lycans next time. Blankenship provided me with his shipping receipts as proof of my earlier request of his farm and, as such, has officially cut business ties with the humans. He serves only us now. Our message to McCready was not strong enough, however. When he delivers his next dairy shipment to the human lands, have your males take out half his herd the following night. That should readjust loyalties quite nicely."

A blurry palm waved across Clara's vision, blending the

helplessness of her memories with that of her present. She blinked and looked up.

"Hey, she's back! Good. I got worried for a second. Thought I'd lost you. *Again.*" Bronze dropped his hand and smiled delicately at her, though it was clearly more for her reassurance than his own.

Had she just been . . . daydreaming? Where in the mother's name was her wolf? She'd been overcome by more distractions in the past week than in her entire life. So much for her keen lycan senses.

Clara reached inward and immediately relaxed when the familiar canine whine rose up through her mind. Weaker, though. Much, much weaker.

How long had it been since she'd shifted? A few days, at least. No wonder her she-wolf was getting quieter. Clara had not let her roam in some time. Wonderful. A new guilt to add to her ever-growing pile.

"I was just, um, thinking about preparing you for when we return to my home."

"Please, enlighten me. I've been gabbing for ages, and I'm quite sick of hearing my own voice."

She gasped when he cupped her elbow through her cloak and helped her over a large tree root, then released her as if he'd done little more than brush off road dust.

"Besides, there's only so much I can say about cars, video games, and social media. Tell me more about what I'll be walking into, at least. These games . . . what can I expect?"

You can expect to win them all and marry me, so I might have at least one male I can convince to speak on behalf of my people and overrule my father.

And there it was. Her remaining worries rang loud and clear through her consciousness, except even in her thoughts, she wasn't entirely truthful. One only had to spend five minutes in

Bronze's presence to know the male couldn't be convinced of anything he wasn't inclined to agree upon first.

No, her ploy wasn't about convincing him of anything but manipulating him into letting her rule the way her people deserved. The way she *could* rule them if her father was finally forced to stand down.

"Well, there are usually three tasks, one to represent the three different credos of our monarchy," she offered, keeping her eyes firmly on the path before her and not on the male at her side, who'd resumed his stride to match hers. As he drew nearer, a trickle of sweat teased her hairline at the base of her neck, despite the late-spring's cool breeze.

"And what would those be?"

Clara took a deep breath and recited the words that were as dear to her as her own name. "With power, we run. With strength, we capture. With the moon's senses, we detect and safeguard."

If Bronze held any opinions on what she'd revealed, he kept his own counsel on the subject. "I take it you're not going to tell me what those particular games entail?"

"I would if I could, but they are created by the king. Each trial pays tribute to a different credo. How they are constructed and what is involved is unknown to all except the monarch."

"Have these games ever been rigged?"

She paused and looked up at him. "Rigged?"

"Fixed. Predetermined."

"No. Not that I know of, at least, though the last games happened before my time. But when I was researching the histories in the annex, there was no mention of anything dishonest ever occurring."

Bronze softened his gaze and offered her a simple smile. Her heart sank and nearly dropped clear through to the soles of her boots. She knew that look all too well. It was the look of an adult breaking hard news to a fanciful child.

"History's usually written by the winners, Clara. I can't imagine that's different from one culture to another. If things did go south or there was ever any tampering evident, I doubt your historians would have been allowed to paint the truth of the picture, even if they were inclined to do so, especially in a monarchy."

She flinched, and the veracity of his words pricked like freezing rain on heated skin. Hot shame flooded her cheeks, and she shrank deeper into her hood. Of course he would think her naïve. Not only had she foolishly landed herself in the exact wrong company she was searching for but now the very male who stood a chance at helping her maneuver this ridiculous deception saw her as no more than a silly female. One he needed to coddle like a child to help her understand the hard truths of the world.

Because her truths hadn't been hard enough, apparently.

Stupid, Clara. So utterly stupid you are.

"Yes, I realize that," she said softly, hoping to keep the stinging pain out of her voice. "Still, I must believe it would be highly unlikely for that to occur. It is in the king's best interest—"

"Here, warm this up for me."

He dropped a small circular object, heavy for its size, into the center of her palm. Before she could question him further, he dropped to his knee to retie his bootlace. Left with no other alternative, she examined what he'd given her.

A compass. Yes, that's what it was. She'd heard that some of the human traders used them when navigating the White Mountains. Lycans had no use for them, of course, what with their acute senses and deep connection to the moon, but she was not so ignorant as to not know what one was. A guide of sorts, if she recalled correctly. The minuscule N, S, E, and W stood out in emerald green against a backdrop of black, while tiny white dashes punctuated what she assumed were different degrees of measurement between the letters.

Wait, what had he just said? Warm it up? How on earth was she supposed to do that? Was it something to do with its functionality? Well, she certainly didn't want to give him any more cause to think she was dull-witted. She was aware of the object's general uses, after all.

At a loss for clarity but determined to prove competency, she covered the compass with her palms, rubbed her hands briskly, began blowing warm breath into the small opening she made, then held it out to him, quite satisfied with her work.

Bronze didn't look up, however, and instead started plucking the laces from his other book, retightening those to match.

Damn. Had she not warmed it up enough? She snatched it back quickly before he could notice and resumed stroking the thing.

"Why don't we *not* talk about what's in the king's best interest," Bronze said, addressing her earlier comments, "because if that was even remotely high on your priority list, you wouldn't have almost died looking for someone to champion you in a marriage competition, which, by the way, we haven't yet ironed out all the particulars of."

Seriously, did this male have the longest bootlaces on the continent? Clara's skin was nearly being rubbed raw at that point.

"Yes, there is much more we need to discuss," she conceded. "But that's not likely to happen while your nose is to the ground and I'm expending all my energy warming up this thing. Surely this is sufficiently heated by now. I trust it'll work properly. When can I let go of it?"

Bronze shot to his feet in a burst of energy common among pups and patrol guards, grabbed the compass from her, and tossed it into the bottom of his pack with no care whatsoever. "It doesn't need to be warmed up to work. I just couldn't have you shitting all over your confidence when you've got a handsome angel like me to marry. Figured it was best to keep your hands busy before that little fact dawned on you and you got it in your head to wrap those pretty fingers around my throat. And," he added, adjusting the pack higher on his shoulders, "before we make it back to dear old dad's, I think we better talk about the endgame here."

Clara blinked, her palm still frozen in midair, and blinked again. In the span of a swift breeze through the trees, she'd been simultaneously tricked, understood, comforted, and, most peculiar of all, dismissed for not having the foresight to commit bodily harm to the male who . . . had rescued her? If she wasn't barreling toward the biggest fight of her life once she returned home, she wasn't entirely certain she could make it another step without drawing blood.

Of all the strangest, most frustrating, *obnoxious*—

"No one has *ever* spoken to me that way," she said icily.

"Yeah, I got that, and let me tell you I'm quite honored to be the first."

Clara shook her head. "You're unbelievable. Where I come from males don't joke in such a manner, and females certainly—"

"Don't laugh quite as much as they should. I can tell. Now, we've got another hour or so, and I need to know one very important thing before we get there."

"And what is that?" she said, snapping her fists to her hips.

Oh, her wolf was fuming. As weak as the poor thing was, it wouldn't take much for her to shift and have her other half bound down on him with the force of a forest-leveling hurricane. Hell, Clara might even let her wolf get a few good bites in before she lessened—not halted—the assault.

Might lessen.

She was about to tell him as much when he stepped closer,

chasing away whatever brave chilly spring breezes had dared to linger in his wake.

"What I need to know, princess, and what you've conveniently left out of your tale so far, is what comes *after* the wedding vows. I know my own reasons for why I'm agreeing to marry a beautiful woman and escort her back to her piece-of-shit father who made her run away in the first place. Now it's time to tell me yours."

CHAPTER 10

Clara could have sworn she'd passed the same tree three times now were it not for the slight difference in placement of the knots along the trunk. That and the hyper-focused intent with which she observed—and efficiently stepped over sans Bronze's help—the tree roots punching up through the ground at varying angles. She would *not* study the male at her side, who didn't even have the common decency to give a female her bit of space when asking after her private reasoning.

Was he entitled to the truth of it? She supposed he was. A little. But then so much of what she'd endured would have been for naught!

Clara chewed the inside of her lip, fully aware that the angel was being beyond patient in waiting for her answer. Males, in her experience, had not been blessed with such a constitution. If they had, she might not have needed to go to the lengths she had.

Discreetly, she risked a peek at him. That olive-green rucksack still sat high on his shoulders in the exact same manner as when he'd first slung it on. She had no idea what was in it, but it looked heavy enough to sever the exposed tree roots beneath him if he dropped it in the right place. The angle of her cloak's hood obscured much of him beneath the pack, but it did nothing, thankfully, to hide Bronze's shock of auburn hair that curled around his ears and neck. It was her favorite bit of chaos about him, and there certainly had been much to choose from. A part of her wondered what his hair would feel like between her fingers, whether it would be silky or coarse, whether it would spiral around the cylinder of her pinky or go its separate way.

Such thoughts were certainly unbecoming of an unmated female. A *mated* female, however, could fantasize about such things, could she not? And as he'd so confidently and bluntly pointed out, mated they would soon be.

Clara cleared her throat, finally dissolving the silence between them. "My father is not a kind man."

He snorted. "Yeah. I got that."

"It bears repeating." She kicked a stone in front of her, measuring its skips until it settled into a puddle with a satisfying *plunk*. "My people deserve far more than to suffer at the hands of a tyrant, whether that be my father or one chosen by him to engage in practices similar to his own. There are many lycans who, as we speak, are fighting to break free and establish their own autonomy, but ruling pressure has been making it increasingly impossible to do so. The king has been crippling hybrid businesses that, for centuries, have served both the human and lycan lands, forcing them instead to cut their earnings by having the monarchy and its subjects as their sole customers. Our lands are well hidden, as I've mentioned, but many lycans believe a society cannot thrive without expansion. There are ways to safely navigate human interactions, and those lycans who had figured out how to do so over the years have enjoyed great prosperity for not only their families but their communities. My father, as I've mentioned, also believes in expansion but is much more narrow-minded in who he prefers to deal with. Where I see potential for growth and development, he sees only scarcity and what the humans have that we do not."

"You mentioned hybrid businesses that had served both lands for centuries. How old are you, exactly?"

"Ninety-four. My father has been ruling in his seat for close to three hundred years but was only able to sire one offspring with my mother before she died." A familiar tightness that always plagued her whenever she thought of her mother threatened to slow the momentum of her words, forcing her to clear her throat and fight through the pain, as she always did. Clara braced for his muttered condolences and had already curled her lips into the slight smile she often gave to soothe others' acknowledgment of her grief, but Bronze never looked up at her. He just kept his head down, his steps measured, like the path before them would last exactly as long as it needed for her to continue her story.

His silence, for sure, meant she *should* continue. Right?

Goodness, he was so difficult to read. And that coming from *her*! A cloistered royal who'd spent a lifetime doing little more than people watching!

Then another thought struck her. One so obvious in its intentions it was no wonder he remained quiet.

He's not interested in coddling you. He asked for the purpose of the marriage and has been waiting patiently for you to get to the point.

With how heavily her foolishness sat on her chest, it was a wonder she hadn't sunk to the bottom of that blasted river to begin with. And even more perplexing, why the hell did she feel the need to drag out her answer to his question into some magnum opus? She had a friend or two, staff, others in her life who knew her history as well as that of her mother. It was clear from the set of his shoulders and the insistent pace he maintained that sob stories would go about as far with him as they'd gotten her. Nowhere.

Business, Clara. This is business.

"As I've said, the king has been in his seat for quite some time, and through the Betrothal Games, I hope to change that."

There. That certainly steered the conversation back into calmer waters. No matter that there was a prickling urge to tell him more, to expand and compound on not just the role he'd volunteered for but the role she'd enact from him once he took the throne.

Gosh, she felt grimy, the kind of oiliness that didn't just coat the skin but tainted everything it came into contact with, staining whatever good it touched just for the benefit of getting to touch it in the first place.

Guilt was funny like that.

"I need a monarch," she breathed out, and dammit, she hated how strong the defeat came through in her statement, as if she'd lost before she'd even played her hand. But thankfully, her desperation, far more than her despair, was a damn good motivator. "The lycans need a ruler who will support them in how *they* wish to thrive, not trample them for refusing to fall in line. If you prosper in the games, my father will have no choice but to acknowledge you as the winner and next in line to the throne upon our mating. It is my hope that after we are married, you will see what must be done and rule in a just and fitting manner."

"Whoa. Those are a lot of big heavy words you're throwing at me, princess."

"Lady. Or Clara, if you prefer," she reminded him. Best get him in the habit of properly addressing her before they arrived.

The heat of his unexpected smile was enough to cause her cheeks to warm further.

"Oh, I didn't forget. I just find it pleasing."

She squirmed and pulled her cloak more tightly around her. "What is pleasing?"

"The way your color rises whenever my compliments land."

"You didn't offer me any compliments."

"I didn't need to." He shrugged. "You seemed to like it just fine when I smiled at you, so I'll make sure to do it more often. It's always the simple things, am I right?"

"That is highly inappropriate," she murmured.

"The jury's still out on that one. Speaking of simple, though, there are two things that don't make sense to me about this whole mating thing."

Clara threw her shoulders back, attempting to shake off his, well, whatever his comments were. They certainly weren't compliments. Jests at her expense, more like. "Yes?"

"What happens to your father in this little fairy tale?"

Ah, yes, that was *the* question, wasn't it?

Careful, Clara. Tread lightly.

"It is true he will remain in rule even once we are mated, but it is my hope that, with you being in a position of power, perhaps you may make decisions or recommendations that would . . . ease his command. Take some of the governing weight off his shoulders or persuade him not to pursue such ruthless tactics. Or maybe—"

"Why don't I just kill him and leave your people to you?"

There wasn't a force on earth that would have pried her feet from where they'd been glued to the ground. The whole of the forest could have split open, swallowed up every tree and root in sight, and Clara would have happily stood there soaking in this stranger's words.

Words that had mimicked her own shameful thoughts time and time again for as long as she could remember.

"I-I cannot recommend . . . That is, it would never be possible . . . How could I . . ."

"*You* couldn't, or you would have offed the male already instead of nearly running yourself into a watery grave."

Clara swallowed down the hard truth, wishing again that her foolishness wasn't painted so boldly in every one of her actions and words. Out of reflex, she reached for her people's relic, needing to hold it tighter against her, to feel its connection to her goals anchored more deeply within her, but even that simple act of self-comfort didn't escape the angel's notice, so she quickly lowered her hand.

"Which brings me to my second question," he added. "Let's say, for argument's sake, that the king *was* no longer in the picture."

Only in her most private thoughts could she even bring herself to imagine such a future, and there they were, boldly discussing her father's death as if it was no more significant than a routine summer thunderstorm. Just the idea set her skin to trembling and had that secret starved part inside her eyeing the temptation with rapt hunger.

"I get the patriarchal society bit, and the need for you to break out of whatever cage the asshole's put you in—"

"He is the king," she said in rote defense.

"And that means fuck all to me. He's not *my* king, and from what you've told me, it sounds like you have some pretty determined ideas to overrule the bastard and right the ship before he ties you and your people to a proverbial anchor and tosses you all overboard so he can steer the thing toward whatever greatness the fool thinks he's earned."

"That is not—"

"Princess." The word was a smooth stroke down her skin. "I know the game you're playing."

She froze, then forced out the most juvenile response her addled mind could offer. "I am not playing a game, angel." Mother, could he really know? A fear like none she'd felt before gripped her heart, and her circumstances came into crisp clean focus. Her wolf whined and crawled beneath her skin, for she, too, felt the danger this male represented.

He can't know. It's impossible.

The corners of Bronze's mouth lifted, taking his goatee with it and curling his usually charming smile into something preda-torial. "You need a mate."

She nodded woodenly, half surprised her spine didn't crack with the force of the abrupt gesture.

"And you need daddy out of the picture."

Again, slower, she gave him another nod.

"So that the new monarch can right the ship."

The potency in his stare raised the goose bumps from her skin and tightened her nipples, even beneath her heavy cloak.

"Yes," she breathed.

Clara didn't remember when her steps slowed or when their little traveling party of two had morphed into something alto-gether significant. There was a weight to the hidden tenderness lurking beneath Bronze's stance and statements. Even the after-noon sun poking through the treetops knew it was there, quietly illuminating what Clara suspected the angel didn't wish to broadcast. The way his fingers loosely curled and didn't tense around the rucksack strap where it fell over his collarbone, revealing no true abhorrence to the dark things she'd confessed. The flecks of olive green in his eyes that seemed to grow more vibrant when his levity connected with its target and he successfully coaxed a smile from her, despite her need to main-tain propriety. It was almost freeing, in a sense, and she wondered what other sorts of surprises lurked within the angel.

If she wasn't careful, his sly promise of such things would entice her to do far more than simply confess her true motives.

Not good, Clara. Not good at all.

She threw her shoulders back and continued walking, resuming her steady pace. "A matriarchy has its challenges among the lycans. My people have lived under my father's rule, and his father before him, for many centuries. There are few alive who even remember a female monarch. And while, yes, I, one day, hope to change that, that day will not be today. Time and trust are the currency of any good monarchy, and I fear my father's line has done much to manipulate and abuse that trust. If you succeed, however, assuming the throne as a male will not be difficult for you. I know it may sound unconventional, but the lycans in my father's court are far more likely to put their faith in an outsider who won the crown by proving himself through demonstration of our core credos than a female who would have no hope of such practical applications of strength, even for one born into the monarchy. At least," she hurried when he opened his mouth with what she assumed was an objection, "for now."

"For now. Fine," he ground out as he walked alongside her, though the edge to his words had been rounded off somehow, as if he was holding something back.

"Besides, it is not uncommon for monarchs to take consorts, even the females, from what I was able to learn. You shall not be questioned over much, I imagine. Among the lycans, strength recognizes strength." She risked a peek at him, and her stomach fluttered. Golden sparks flared in his gaze in time with the pulsating tendon along his neck. Oh dear, had she angered him?

"What else?" he demanded.

"Well, I imagine it will take some time to establish a new way of doing things. You wouldn't have to be in attendance except for a few occasions. Select public appearances, signing certain documents, and such." Then she stopped and gripped his shoulder. "I am not asking you to give up your life, warrior. In return for what you offer, you would still have complete autonomy to be with your brothers, live as you always have, and, of course, be awarded unbridled access to any royal coffers, services, and properties. If you win the Betrothal Games," she implored, "what is ours will be yours. I ask for no more than what you've already offered."

The quiet sounds of the forest rose up around them, becoming a cacophony to the worried thump of her heart banging against her chest. She'd never thought in a million years she'd so desperately wish for a male to speak. Quite frankly, very little good had ever come from the phenomenon, but she was beginning to worry all her air would seep out of her lungs and abandon her entirely if he didn't say *something*. Those worries were more than dangerous, because each time he studied her in that silent, stoic manner, the habit was beginning to mean something, as if he was collecting quiet pieces of her she hadn't meant for him to see.

Or anyone else, for that matter.

"Do you find me pleasing, Lady Clara?"

His question stunned her, as did the spark of citrine flaring in his eyes again. "It's just lady," she whispered as she struggled to find her strength. "And why would you ask such a question?"

"It's a fair question to ask a female, especially one who will soon be my mate."

"You must win first," she reminded him.

He dismissed her concern with a cocksure smile and lifted her hand from his shoulder.

Before she could pull her arm free, her skin had already begun to bloom with warmth beneath the surprising kiss he bestowed on her knuckles. Every muscle in her body tightened.

He held her hand for a heartbeat longer, then let it fall to her side. "Okay. Assume, rightly so, that I do win. Do you find me pleasing?"

Oh, this was a dangerous road to navigate. Denying him would be like denying the sun its heat, but encouraging him would only fan the flames of a different sort of fever.

It wasn't a real kiss. Be on your guard.

"What if I said no? What if I said I preferred males with shorter hair or no hair?"

"Then I'd cut it all off, and the goatee to boot."

"You would not," she asserted.

Those dark promises from earlier lurked behind a screen of hazel. "We have not yet learned what each other is truly capable of, princess. As for what lies ahead, I can assure you I have no interest in ruling anyone, let alone a race of people who are not my own. I've got enough headaches just trying to have a say in the kinds of snacks that get stocked in our kitchen back home."

"Then why agree to any of this? Why accompany me back to my home and volunteer to aid me? You mentioned before that you have your own reasons for attending me and not dismissing me outright, but you never clarified them. I should like your explanation now, warrior."

Bronze retreated a step and focused his attention on a patch of moss that had overtaken a nearby tree trunk. His features took on the faraway indifference of a ghost. "It didn't sit well with me, how I found you. Part of me still can't believe you're here walking and talking, let alone asking me for the kind of help you need." He gently toed the velvet greenery, careful not to disturb it. "I'm a sentinel. Or was at one point. Mages know what I am anymore. Regardless, let's just say innocents suffering are the kinds of things that can keep a male like me up at night." The citrine in his gaze darkened until it had been overcome by the forest's dusty green. "And when you live for-fucking-ever, you've got a lot of nights to contemplate the ones that got away."

Bronze's head snapped up before Clara had an opportunity to ask what he'd meant. "As I said, I have no interest in ruling. That's all up to you. I haven't the head for it. But I'll help you get there and attend or sign whatever crap I need to until the boat's going the right way down the river. With you *on* the damn thing this time." He winked, and just like that, the light returned to his countenance.

"But what of my father? The other suitors and competing warlords?"

"I'll take care of 'em."

"So simply? Just like that? You don't even know how many there are!"

"As I said, just like that."

"How?" She could hardly keep the amazement out of her voice, or her enthusiasm.

"I've got some tricks you haven't seen yet, princess, and some that'll no doubt be making an appearance shortly." He patted the side of his rucksack with a wistful sort of fondness.

Just what on earth had he packed in there? Oh, hell, did it matter? He would help her, and he would win. She was sure of it.

This was happening. This was really happening. She'd done it!

A curious effervescence prickled beneath her skin, making her feel lighter than she'd ever hoped to feel. The weight of it all —her foolishness, her people's disappointment if she failed, her fear of manipulating a male who had only shown her kindness —floated away, allowing her lungs to fill with their first full, easy breath in months.

Was this what it felt like to be lucky? She'd never known luck. Such a concept had always been reserved for children's stories. But she did have perseverance and preparation on her side, as well as timing. Was that, in and of itself, her own sort of crafted luck? And would it only hold out so long as she learned to trust this male rather than carefully maneuver him through her world the way she'd originally intended?

Yes, she decided with a finality to rival her death, if it came to such a thing. Yes, she would trust him.

The moonstone relic was a warm and comforting weight against her heart. This was the right path, she was sure of it. This path, with this male, at this time.

She'd done what she could and nearly died in the process. Not only had the Moon Mother, in all her wisdom, not abandoned her, but the goddess had sent her a warrior to aid in her plight.

An angel. A sentinel.

Clara's cheeks pinched with the force of her smile. It had

been so long since she'd fully used the thing that the muscles were out of practice. But her wolf still knew how to rejoice. Oh, did she ever. A joyful canine whine vibrated through her and shook the forest floor with the force of its emotion.

Bronze's features tightened, and the outline of his biceps sharpened beneath his shirt with readied tension.

Confused, Clara tilted her head to the side. Had he heard her wolf? How was that possible? Her mouth fell open to ask him when they both heard the sound again.

Not a whine this time. A growl. A warning, one that always came seconds before the bite.

Clara risked a slow glance back at the path they'd just traveled and stared into the gaping maw of a snarling coyote.

CHAPTER 11

Bronze took advantage of Clara's immobilizing fear and flung her behind him. A quick shift of his shoulders had his pack free and anchored like a boulder in front of the female. Before her shock had cleared enough to register the threat, he already had his sickle sword in hand.

"Lower your eyes, princess," he said. The voice that left him was wholly of a different being. Thick, dark, and possessing a quality that, had it come from another, would have lifted the hairs from his body.

He didn't have time to check whether she obeyed. A flash of brown and gray blurred from hilltop to boulder and leaped through the air with blinding speed. Bronze pivoted and called on his metallic skin, but the animal's teeth connected with the meat of his shoulder moments before his power had fully armored him.

Bronze grunted through the bite and tucked them into a roll that would bring them a good distance away from Clara. The coyote thrashed through the tumult and only removed its jaw when the curve of Bronze's blade met the underside of the beast's tail, precariously close to the canine's twig and berries.

Bronze had never been opposed to fighting dirty, especially when the universal rules of *he started it* rang true across all species.

Plus, hello, balls.

The coyote's sharp whelp rang out beneath Bronze, robbing his attention from the powerful hind legs that kicked him in the stomach. Now freed, the beast pounded through the forest on the heels of its earlier echoing cry. Not wanting to risk another altercation, Bronze bounded after the coyote. Where there was one, there was often more, and given his luck, the *more* in question would likely include a well-structured family unit with a mama, an aunt or two, a host of pups, zero patience for intruders, and no interest in an uninvited lunch guest.

Just *who* would be the guest at and for said lunch was a debate Bronze needed to stomp out right the fuck now.

Bronze beat feet through the forest, urging every ounce of his celestial strength into his metallic frame. With each stride, however, his breaths became harder to rake in. Even the weight of his sword was proving too much for him. He had to tighten his grasp where the hilt met the blade just to maintain his hold. His lack of speed was a worry he hadn't expected, but one he had no time to examine. He quickly pushed the thought from his mind and propelled himself harder, skidding around a rocky bend where the coyote's tracks led him.

There was no warning that time. No growl or paws padding in his direction. Only the surprise lunges of three different coyotes blocking out the sun as they leaped at him high up from boulders that snaked northward on the forested hillside. Teeth came next, then claws and bite after bite of ruthless determination.

Guess I found their den. Wonderful.

And, yes, they were females.

His sword was quickly lost to the attacking bodies above him, so fists and feet took over, but it wasn't enough. As soon as he managed to kick one coyote off, another regained ground just as fast.

Bronze gritted his teeth when a pair of fangs punctured his calf. What the fuck? To his horror, his bronze armor had begun to recede, leaving a whole lot of cotton-wrapped mortal rawhide for some very hungry ladies.

"Shit!"

One coyote adjusted their bite and clamped down harder. Fangs scraped across bone again, and it was the literal gut punch he needed to summon his celestial fire. Bronze connected with his core power and dragged it from his center, but not before one of the coyotes lunged for his throat.

A massive white blur swept across his field of vision, blanketing his surroundings in a whirlwind of ghostly ivory. And fur.

The weight of the coyotes left his chest in an instant, and Bronze scrambled back on all fours. Before him, a white wolf almost twice the size of the coyotes tackled all three of the canines to the ground. As soon as one rose up, it was immediately met with the business end of a maw more ferocious and deadly than anything that had been using him as a chew toy earlier. And the wolf didn't go for the legs or tails.

Oh, no. It was cold, cunning, ruthless.

With a feint to the left, the wolf's mouth connected with the spine of one coyote, while it swiped a thickly padded paw at the remaining two. A sharp jerk of its head brought the wounded coyote to the ground in a cry of howling pain. Taking the hint, the other two backed away slowly. Only when there was enough distance between the downed dog and the others did the white wolf release its grip.

But it didn't back away. The growl that came next wasn't just a warning but a statement. A veritable *back the fuck off* loud enough to shake leaves from trees and confidence from predators. Sure as shit, the coyotes, even the injured one, wasted no time and scurried away with whatever remained of their tales nestled firmly between bloodied legs.

If Bronze had been a smarter male, he'd have turned tail along with the coyotes. But as any of his brothers could attest on more than one occasion, his stupid bucket was just filled too damn high. And now was one of those times.

Bronze lay there, chest heaving and, yeah, parts of him still oozing that he'd prefer didn't, and just stared at the creature before him. Seemed like the best thing to do when words failed a fella.

A powder-white pelt as thick as any snow bank flowed in sleek, strong lines around the most magnificent wolf he'd ever seen. The creature didn't have the arrogant presence of the gray wolves common among the White Mountains, and it was clear why. Arrogance had no place where majesty reigned, and boy, was he looking at it. Everything, from the more delicate snout and ears to the longer, leaner legs, drew him in like a siren's song.

Then it tilted its head toward him, and he locked gazes with familiar tawny-brown eyes.

Clara?

The wolf dipped its head to the ground and slowly, as if it was a random Tuesday and the thing hadn't just frightened off three coyotes, settled the rest of its lithe body on the forest floor. Seconds turned to centuries as that glorious white pelt morphed into the long wavy locks Bronze had first seen floating on the surface of the Ellis River. Bones lengthened and claws rounded out into perfect sets of toes and fingers.

It was over before it started, and yet Bronze would have bet his favorite Ducati that he'd been sitting there long enough for primer and a good two layers of that fancy eggshell-coated paint to dry.

Intellectually, he knew Clara was a lycan and what that

entailed. Seeing it in action, however, even as one who could transform his own skin into bronze?

Breathtaking. Miraculous.

Beautiful.

But it wasn't until Clara lay on the forest floor fully human —and fully naked—did he realize the severity of what he'd gotten himself into.

And what he feared he could no longer turn back from.

THE SHIFT to her mortal form was much harder that time, owing, no doubt, to how long she'd gone placating her wolf into remaining so. But every creature had its limits, and as she'd caught up to Bronze and witnessed those coyotes sink their teeth into his no-longer-metallic flesh, her she-wolf had had enough.

As grateful as Clara was to her wolf, the need to speak and inspect Bronze's injuries currently outweighed the need to let the creature roam free.

Sorry, girl, but he needs us.

Clara lay hunched on the ground in the manner in which her wolf had left her, belly down, knees tucked beneath her, arms folded at the elbows and forearms extended toward Bronze. Her eyes barely had time to focus before his legs, bloody and torn, appeared before her. He squatted, and she got a precursory eyeful of the damage, but he was careful to keep the pain from registering on his soil-smudged face.

A face that had been solid metal a few short moments ago.

"Let me see. How bad is it?" Clara pushed off the ground in a hurry, then slowed when his gaze dropped to her exposed breasts.

Crap. She'd never shifted in front of males before, and for this very reason. While nudity was a natural inevitability of lycanthropic heritage, that did not automatically equate with a lack of modesty.

Or, for that matter, how males from outside her race might view her body.

"A moment, please," she pleaded when he didn't move. Clara searched around frantically for her traveling cloak, which she had managed to throw off and save, along with the relic, before her wolf shifted. The rest of her clothes were most likely tattered shreds, unfortunately, but there was nothing to be done about it.

When she didn't immediately see her garment and Bronze still hadn't moved, a new worry bloomed within her chest. In this part of the forest, following that commotion, they were exposed, and she more so. They were not far from her father's lands, from other lycans who could stumble upon them and surmise a different sort of picture from what had actually happened.

Any onlookers would simply see a bloodied male hovering above a naked lycan princess. In the forest. Alone.

All it would take was for one of her father's guards to patrol just a hair outside their jurisdiction, or a merchant firmly in the king's pockets to see what they didn't understand and report on what would earn them the most financial loyalty and security.

It would all be over before it started. The games. The mating arrangement. Any plans for a future monarchy that wasn't centered around tyrannical injustice.

All because she had just shifted to save a male who, according to the wrong potential bystander, would possibly seek to ruin her and, by extension, her father.

"Bronze. Please. You need to listen to me. I must rise and—"

With the precision of a matador but none of the showmanship and a fair bit more grunting, Bronze shook out her cloak from behind his back and let the heavy fabric settle over her body. Once she was fully covered, he lifted her hair through the collar, fanned it out over her shoulders, and replaced the relic around her neck.

But his touch didn't stop there. Even after she was fully concealed, his fingers lingered on the curve of her shoulder before brushing the tips of her hair and traveling farther down until he'd caressed every vertebrae along her spine.

The stroke was no more than fingertips on fabric, but she felt it everywhere. Her skin tightened in response to her hammering heart, and when she risked a glance at the spot on his chest where his own organ beat, the similar rise and fall of his body matched hers.

Both were breathing rapidly. Both were seemingly struggling for more.

"I have a rule," he said, breaking the spell and assisting her to her feet while she did the same for him.

"Inform me later. Right now, we're exposed and too close to my father's lands for anonymity. Besides, you're injured." Oh God, and was he ever. The most egregious of the wounds was the bite on his calf, where angry red flesh hung open, revealing mangled muscle that would need far more than simple stitching to heal. How he was even putting weight on the leg, let alone standing upright, was either a testament to his warrior's mettle or the sheer arrogance of his sex.

Likely both.

"My rule is never let them run."

"Why not?"

"Because running away is so much more enjoyable when you have someone to do it with, whether it's chasing or coercing. Why let the coyote have all the fun?"

Clara blinked away the absurdity of his words and shook her head in disbelief. "You're insane. Do you know that?" She gripped the edge of her cloak and was about to rip it off to cover his wound—or his mouth, she wasn't sure which one yet

—when his hands wrapped around hers, making her drop the hem.

"You'd be so much fun to run with, princess. Next time, let's plan it a little bit better, though. There are only so many more surprises like you a male like me can handle."

If she were any other female, she'd have known how to handle such a remark. She'd have the knowledge, experience, even the skilled repartee to fling back as a rejoinder. And if he were any other male, he'd be stoically kind to the point of animatronic and humor her for the sake of her bloodline.

But she was not any other female, and he was not any other male.

Yes, he certainly was in store for many more surprises. She just had to trust that he was strong enough to withstand them all before her luck ran out.

Because the truth of the matter was, despite what she'd planned for her original course of action, she was beginning to like the angel. Very much so.

And wasn't that the biggest and most perplexing surprise of all?

Oh, what a pair they made, truly.

Clara pulled her hands out of his and took a few steps back. "If surprises frustrate you, then you're really not going to like what I have to tell you."

"What's that, my lady?"

She gestured toward a copse of trees in the distance and gripped her cloak tighter, armoring herself as best she could. "We're here."

CHAPTER 12

Bronze had no idea what he expected to find when he reached the lycan lands, but the discombobulation of modern-day attire mismatched with far more leather and animal hides than this side of the century had any business seeing was too much of an assault on the senses. Perhaps it was the fading pain of the coyote bites adding to the delusion currently taking up residence in his brain matter, but he almost wished for another dose of fangs on flesh just to jar him out of the reality he'd walked into.

Holy fucking shit.

The community Clara escorted him through could only be described as an old village but in the strangest, most bastardized sense of the concept. There was an abundance of modest stone buildings and wooden cabins, some of which featured roofs with modern asphalt shingles while others were topped with— he narrowed his eyes—actual thatched roofs. As in, clumps of dried vegetation that had gone out of fashion somewhere around the dawn of indoor plumbing and the zygote phase of antiseptic use.

Of the few people—*lycans*, he corrected himself—milling

around, it was clear that the time, tone, and tenor of the mortal realm had fuck all to do with how they lived. One male, who couldn't have been older than twenty or so in mortal years, wore dark brown leather leggings similar to what he'd first discovered Clara wearing. The tunic he had on, however, was a thin beige linen that looked like it had been yoinked straight off a two-centuries-old laundry line and then belted at the waist with a strip of even more leather, which was likely cut from the same cow as what he covered his ass with. The male's hair, though closely cut at the sides, swooped up in a rusted red wave that didn't hold a candle to Bronze's auburn follicle situation but reminded him of the henna from North Africa used to dye hair thousands of years ago.

Another male, this one pulling a wooden cart behind him as if he himself were a beast of burden, looked like any movie set extra for a nineties motorcycle film. Black leather vest cut to allow for maximum arm movement and not much else. Green camouflage khakis that were only as baggy as his thick thighs would allow. Shitkickers with soles sporting more rubber than tractor tires. And a puss that could curdle milk before it had even left the teat.

In all of Bronze's immortal years, very few circumstances had made him, well, *reevaluate* his depth and just how strong of a swimmer he really was, and this one topped the list. As he trailed behind Clara through what he could only describe as an old-timey tourist trap with an identity crisis, the pain in his leg reminded him of another, far more acute crisis of his own.

At first, Bronze figured the sluggishness in his powers was due to his lack of sleep and the shortened time available to recharge his elemental energy. Thinking back on it, however, he'd been so concerned for Clara, he was lucky if he'd gotten at least four hours' worth of regenerative sleep at all. It wasn't like he hadn't pulled all-nighters before, and no, four hours was hardly enough for a sustained power diet, but it was usually sufficient to get the juices flowing the next day, provided he didn't do anything too taxing.

Like taking on three pissed-off coyotes on their own turf.

His metallic armor failing him in a fight wasn't the most comforting realization, but it wouldn't have been the first time, and he could logic out the whys of it.

What *didn't* make sense was why the fuck he was still limping along with a chewed-up leg or why his angel fire had zero interest in responding to his call. His powers were hardly sentient. Like his ability to heal, they were as much a part of him as his big mouth and megawatt smile. There was no contract. No days off. They always showed up for the job. So why the hell were his powers—and, by extension, *he*—moving at the speed of molasses?

And that, right there, was the other terrifying thought that kept his mind from staying on the task at hand and wandering to other circumstances he preferred to keep well and truly buried.

If he didn't even have the strength to stitch up his meat, let alone reliably call on his powers, how the hell was he supposed to make it through whatever trials the lycans had in store for him so he could nab the other relic and get gone?

Then yet another pang of worry knocked around his ribs on the heels of the others, making him fully aware of just how hollow his chest cavity had become over the eons.

Clara. Even as she walked ahead of him, with her bare feet poking out from the hem of her cloak and hinting at the rest of her bare state beneath, he couldn't shake the image of how he'd seen her after the coyote attack. Naked, newly turned, and flushed pink and pretty with the fresh heat of battle. Every flash of her instep as she led him further into her world was a reminder of what else he'd seen . . . and not seen.

She had been there, on the ground, her white hair engulfing both her and her sweet secrets, and all he could think was how badly he wanted to brush that gorgeous mane aside and lift her from the forest floor, only to lay her down properly upon it again in another fashion. Of all the creatures he'd encountered over his very long, *long* years in the mortal realm, none had ever stirred him up so thoroughly, to the point where he would have sliced off a sizable chunk of his wings just to transform into a beast alongside her and give himself over to whatever drug she emitted that called him there and kept him.

Bronze simmered over the circumstances, not liking that each step he took landed him in a deeper hole than before. His fondness for the little lycan was threatening to grow into something far greater than simple attraction. Yes, he'd given his word that he'd see their contract through, but he'd also taken great pains to remind himself of his impartiality on the matter. These were not *his* people, after all. He had no claim to them or even so much as a passing interest. Clara had even said that once he'd won her hand outright and they'd commenced with the formal necessities, he'd only be needed in brief official capacities. Fine by him. Perfect. Fucking wonderful.

What *did* interest him, however, was the unbridled access that came part and parcel to his winnings.

Access to the royal coffers and properties. An unquestioning allowance to search and scour the lycan stronghold as he saw fit. An opportunity to locate the other relic Rhode had advised him of and get the hell out of Dodge so he and his brothers could maybe finally return home.

Bronze shifted his pack to his good shoulder and tried not to think about the mounting distractions, be they female- or flesh-related. There was a prize on the horizon far too significant to demand anything less than his whole attention.

It wasn't just a homeland he'd lost when he was sealed out of the Empyrean. The sooner he could get Clara settled on the throne and that relic settled in his hand, the sooner he could focus on fulfilling another contract he'd made long ago.

CHAPTER 13

The sun was just cresting its arc in the sky when Clara and Bronze ascended the steps of the king's strong-hold. For some reason, the stones beneath her bare feet didn't feel quite as cold as they normally did after a shift, when she'd indulge her desire to forgo her boots. Perhaps it was the warmth of Bronze's sturdy frame at her back or the muscle of her courage giving off more heat due to her continued use of it, but she welcomed the sensation with a newfound appreciation for a strength she didn't know she possessed until recently.

Had she really frightened off those coyotes by herself, after shifting in front of a male no less? A *foreign* male? Her cheeks heated uncomfortably just thinking about it, but then her wolf's self-assurance rose up inside her with a warning growl of approval.

Both she and the creature had marveled in wonder when Bronze's skin shifted and liquid metal poured over and hardened around every chiseled slope of muscle, but it was her wolf that had whined in terror the instant his armor suddenly faded and that coyote's fangs punctured his flesh.

The rest was a blur of predatory determination and fierce

worry like she'd never experienced before. It was both acute and alien, and nearly stole the breath from her lungs.

She'd never been more grateful to see that charming mouth twisted into a wry grin when she'd first laid eyes on the angel after coming out of her shift. It was almost enough to make her forget that she wasn't actually mating him for any emotional attachment.

But goodness, the relief that struck her once she determined he wasn't fatally harmed had hit her just as strongly as she had the coyotes.

Preferring not to examine that too closely, she mentally chastised her wolf for bringing the memory up.

Once firmly inside the stronghold, Clara and Bronze made it as far as the foyer outside her father's receiving room before one of his elite guards standing at the entrance saw them and immediately ran toward her and Bronze.

Broderick, one of the more open-minded of the king's males, smiled at her with exuberant relief but didn't take his eyes off her battered companion. Or his hand from the hilt of his weapon strapped across his chest. "Lady, are you all right? Where have you been? The king has been asking after you all morning."

All morning. So her father hadn't noticed she'd left last night. Good.

"Thank you, Broderick. Yes, I'm quite well. I had some business with a few of the local farmers along the edge of the western territory. It's June, and the lupine flowers have just begun to bloom for the season. They don't grow this far into the mountains, and I promised my staff I'd press some of the blooms for them, but the farmers only permitted me to go out there before the start of business this morning. I didn't want to get in anyone's way, so I left early and quietly, hoping to be back by midday."

Whew. The lie flew from her tongue easier than she'd

expected, and judging by the curt nod of Broderick's dimpled chin, it had worked.

"And who is this male?"

Clara dared not risk turning back to look at Bronze, but she gathered, just from how thick the tension had grown in the small hallway, that there was much the angel wanted to say, no doubt with a fair amount of foul language thrown in. To her eternal gratitude, however, he remained quiet.

Thank the Moon Mother for small mercies.

"On my return, I ran into a bit of trouble with coyotes. This male, Bronze, came to my aid, as you can see. I wish to introduce him to the king so I might formally express my appreciation before seeing to his injuries."

Broderick narrowed his eyes in Bronze's direction and assessed him again, but before he could open his mouth to speak, another voice traveled through the open door.

"Then please, daughter, don't linger in the hall with him like some insipid traveler who doesn't know how to ask for what she needs. Let me see the male."

King Halpin's command carried through the ancient stones of the keep and straightened the spine of everyone it reached. Broderick, for all his brawn, still flinched slightly before clasping his heels together and returning to his post outside the door. Even Clara, who'd lived all ninety-four of her years under the scrutiny of that baritone, ducked her chin out of habit. Bronze, however, didn't even register the barest perception or interest. An awareness, yes, one that had been studiously employed since they first set foot onto the lycan lands, but there wasn't an ounce of deference in his demeanor for the male he was about to meet.

That will change, she thought, though she wasn't as strong in her conviction as she'd once been. Goodness, not even a day in the angel's presence and already his arrogance was rubbing off on her. If this kept up, what else might she adopt?

Clara didn't want to think about it as she led the way into her father's receiving room, ignoring the counselors and advisors huddled around the king, and halted at the edge of the burgundy French Aubusson rug. She was careful to keep her toes just shy of the shadow cast by the massive black walnut desk that nearly spanned from wall to wall. As a young lycan, she'd learned to stay out of her father's shadows. As a grown female, she'd learned to stay out of even those shadows that were extensions of him.

Instead of staying behind her as he had done in the foyer, Bronze stood next to her, with his hands braced behind his back and the toes of his boots hanging over the edge of the rug, disinterestedly bleeding all over the thing and firmly engulfed in the imposing shadows of her father's desk.

"Father, this is Bronze. He is—"

"Not a lycan."

Clara's stomach plummeted. The king's booming declaration was low in timbre but loud in proclamation. A tremulous silent warning echoed around the room. Then her father slowly rose from his seat, and Clara called on years of patience to resist rolling her eyes at the display of dominance. How many times had she witnessed his knuckles braced on the desk as he forced his muscles to fill with a strength that had begun to flee over the last century of disuse? There had been a time when the silver in his beard had been prized and distinguished, born of his gray wolf's coat and a mark of lycan supremacy. Now, the silver had overrun the rest of his beard, and its sleek precision had long been tarnished with the advancement of age and narrow-minded ableism.

"No, I am not," Bronze responded.

Clara couldn't comprehend what would have compelled Bronze to admit that so soon. Although, it wasn't as if they'd discussed it, and thanks to her ongoing foolishness and lack of foresight, they hadn't exactly determined a workaround.

Dammit. Why hadn't she thought of this? No humans were allowed in the lycan lands. They weren't allowed to know of her species' existence at all! But he couldn't exactly confess to being an angel, could he? One who possessed power her father couldn't conceive of? Oh, no, that wouldn't go over well. The blow to the king's ego alone wouldn't be one any of them would so easily come back from.

The king lifted a bushy brow, seemingly intrigued, or perhaps desirous of carrying out an execution so early in the afternoon. God, she hoped it wouldn't come to that. "You are not a human, either."

"No."

"Then what are you?"

"Father, he—"

"A demigod."

It was Clara's turn to lift a brow as she flicked her warning gaze in Bronze's direction. It was one thing to throw her father's arrogance back at him but to lie so boldly about something so significant?

The king folded his arms over his barrel chest. "Is that so?"

"Yes."

"Who is your sire, then?"

"An unknown mortal male. My mother is Saulé, celestial goddess of the sun."

Every lycan in the room held a collective breath. She had never heard of such a goddess, though she never had a cause to study cultures that did not have a connection to lycanthropy in some way. When she read the uncertainty on the others' faces, however, it was clear they hadn't an awareness of such a goddess either.

Which meant her father likely had no knowledge of the subject.

Oh, this would not go over well.

Clara waited in no way patiently to see how he would react.

"And you, it would seem, are also the great coyote killer of the Northeast. Judging by your injuries, it was not so easy a takedown, I gather." King Halpin's steely gray eyes roved over Bronze's form but held neither a note of approval at Bronze's supposed victory nor disgust that the male who allegedly saved his daughter was not of lycan blood. It was the usual mark of her father's indifference to her existence, perhaps worsened slightly due to Bronze's blood collecting on the king's rug.

"I overheard what my daughter declared. I take it you wish to see to your wounds and collect some form of reward for your efforts." The last words were spoken with such belabored annoyance that Clara could no longer contain her ire.

If her first small act of rebellion had been fleeing in the night to the human lands, then each act would only snowball from there, surely. Wasn't that how stubbornness worked?

She didn't know where it came from, but that gripping thought struck her hard and dug its heels in. *What would happen if I kicked that snowy clump down the mountain?* "Actually, Father, Bronze is here to compete for my hand."

The king's eyes shot to hers, and her muscles went rigid. A flush of anger rose up and colored the king's complexion a deep crimson. Whether it was for speaking out of turn or the actual words she'd said, she wasn't sure. Either way, she was over it. It wasn't like she'd been given many turns to speak her mind anyway.

If she had any hope of rebuilding what the avalanche of her actions sought to bury, she'd need her snowball to gain momentum.

There's no turning back now.

When her father didn't immediately respond, however, she took advantage of the silence to stake her claim. "I'm aware that you've made a betrothal arrangement on my behalf with Lord

Raff from the western territories, but I should like to propose another alternative."

"You should *like?*"

Three words. They were three simple words, but they were the most her father had said to her directly in over a month. She tried not to let the pain of it show and barreled through.

"I should more than like, actually." She lifted her chin and made damn sure to address everyone in the room *except* her father. "I deserve to have a say in my own future and, more importantly, the future of the northeastern lycans. Therefore, with your advisors and counselors as my witnesses, I am calling for the formal enactment of the Betrothal Games. This male, Bronze, has proven himself worthy to me and, as such, is who I choose to serve as my champion in the games. As king, you have the right to select the other two competitors as you see fit."

Clara didn't bow. She didn't drop to her knees or lower her eyes or make herself appear as if she didn't deserve to have just as much of a say in her future as the males around her.

But she *would* wait, and as the silence stretched on, the echo of her words seemed to grow louder with each heartbeat.

Odd. She expected shouting, fist banging, even a thrown object or, worse, a physical blow of misplaced anger aimed at an advisor or two. Perhaps a shift to wolf form in a display of dominance. The laugh that burst forth from her father, however, took her entirely off guard.

"Betrothal Games," the king bellowed once he'd managed to collect himself. "If it comforts you to think of such a thing as a game, then by all means, call it what you must. I prefer to think of it as strategy, mind you. Your mother, were she still alive, would agree with me. There is only so much one territory can do to thrive without the benefits of trade and expansion."

Seeming to remember himself and who he was in the presence of, her father carefully softened his features and came out from behind his desk. "Now," he said, laying his hands on her shoulders, "what's all this nonsense about games? You are nearly a century old, Clara. Far out of your youthful years. The time for fanciful daydreams should have been left in the past. Look, I can understand your nerves as much as anyone, especially after meeting this—Bronze, was it?"

The angel stood silent. Only Clara seemed to notice the tense tick of his jaw and the shards of citrine-colored ice that flashed between blinks.

"Um, Your Majesty, if I may." One of the king's high advisors —Pascal, if she recalled correctly—stepped forward. "The lady is not wrong."

"What?" the king gritted out.

Oh boy. Here we go.

"That is, there is a law, though it hasn't been enacted in several monarchies, wherein if the betrothed heir takes issue with the ruler's choice of mate, the heir may call for a formal request to enact the Betrothal Games. It is a competition of sorts where three champions compete for the hand of the heir. The winner is sworn in as the monarch's formal successor. It is an old law, sir, but a valid one. I believe its origins were based on ensuring the power of the monarchy's succession through literal feats of strength."

Clara stepped out of her father's hold, through the thickening silence, and went back to Bronze's side. Beneath the concealment of her cloak, a warm, sturdy hand pressed into the small of her back, calming her wolf instantly.

"Horse shit!" the king yelled. "Lord Raff is arriving tomorrow. The papers are already drafted, and I've signed my portion. The alliance is as good as done, and once he gets here, she's the price I have to pay to ensure our people have a bolstered army to defend against the encroaching humans." Again, he spoke as if she wasn't in the room. Then he surged toward her, surprising all the males with a swiftness not witnessed by their king in some time.

All the males except one.

Bronze threw himself in front of Clara and silently warned the king back with his eyes. Every soul in the room stiffened at the display of the king's aggression toward her, and Clara had to work quickly to conceal her own shock.

The lycans would not have been able to survive the centuries they had, hidden among the humans, if not for the strength of their monarchies or their laws. As such, it was forbidden under lycan law for any monarch to outwardly threaten physical harm against another member of the monarchy. Doing so could result in exile, being purged from the family bloodline, or even death.

Once Bronze had safely put her out of range of the king's temper, Pascal stepped forward. "Your Majesty, the lady has made the declaration in front of witnesses. It cannot be undone or ignored."

"Witnesses," her father ground out, though the word was hardly intelligible around the elongated fangs that thickened his speech. His gaze flashed to Bronze, who stood as immobile as a mountain, and threw his own silent challenge into the fight with the angel. The king bared his fangs and looked at Clara over Bronze's shoulder. "It seems I'm not the only one who knows something of strategy. The rest of you," he yelled, "leave. I shall discuss this with my daughter in private."

"Fat fucking chance," Bronze said through gritted teeth.

"It's fine. I'll be fine," she assured Bronze in hushed words she was careful to make sure didn't travel. Her shaking hands circled his biceps. "You can be right outside the door the entire time, but this has to happen this way. I knew I would have to face him."

Neither Bronze nor the king said anything. Only when her father turned his back first, seemingly unconcerned about

Bronze's threat, and went over to the serving bar on the far side of the room did the advisors begin to funnel out.

Clara had no idea what compelled her to do so, but before Bronze put his arm around her shoulders to direct her out of the room, she glanced at her bare feet.

They were still standing strong despite being fully engulfed in the shadow of her father's desk.

CHAPTER 14

Clara barely had time to return the relic to the royal coffers and change into a fresh set of leathers and linen before the sounds of her father's temper had begun to die off from within his receiving room. It was yet another indication of what awaited her on the other side of the door. While some predators grew louder and more vicious the higher their emotions flared, gray wolf lycans were different.

There was always so much more to fear from their silence.

Bronze marched them up to the door, and she had to grit her teeth at the arrogant display. If she was finally going to drum up the courage to cross that threshold and tell her father what she'd rehearsed for years in private, the last thing she needed was another male's arrogance distracting her from the task.

She needed to focus, concentrate, and *not* have Bronze reprogram her confidence with some chauvinist display of male aggression.

No matter how much it secretly made her smile.

Goodness, if she kept this up any longer, she'd just about lose her nerve altogether, which would utterly ruin any hope she and her people had for a better future.

"I told you to wait in the infirmary," she said to his back. "I can't imagine this will take long, and you bleeding all over the carpets isn't likely to endear you to the cause. Believe me, there isn't much the king can do. I made the declaration among witnesses. The *right* witnesses, mind you. His most trusted advisors and knowledgeable counselors. He may be a bit pissy and sore about it, sure, but all he can do now is play the cards he's been dealt."

Okay, maybe *a bit pissy* was an understatement, but she had to calm the fire somehow.

"Oh, there's plenty he can do," Bronze asserted darkly. "He's a male in power with an entourage of lackeys and more strength than—"

"Hey!" Clara whirled in front of him, forcing him to slow his advance, but he still wouldn't take his eyes off the oak door behind her. She had never seen that type of tenacity from him before, even when Bronze had soared ahead after the coyote. That had been instinctual, though. Biological, even. Two predators exerting claim to the same land. This, however, was something wholly different and unnecessary. Yes, she had employed her own sort of strategy, as her father had pointed out, but by the moon, it had worked, hadn't it? So why was Bronze unable to see her win for what it was? Her own form of quiet strength.

Clara let her voice fall into the conversational tone she'd grown accustomed to using around him during their time in the forest, hoping it would endear him to listen as he had when it was just the two of them. "You know, it doesn't sit well with me, how you are right now." She spoke softly, repeating his words from earlier back at him. And it seemed to work, as a glimmer of recognition sparked in his gaze. He trained his features back on her as she'd hoped, though the strain around his eyes and mouth hadn't eased.

Progress. She'd take it.

Clara slowly moved her palms over his chest in the lazy

petting motion she'd seen mothers do to their pups when they got too riled up. "Strength can be subjective. Neither of us would be here otherwise. I think you made me realize that."

Those hazel eyes dipped beneath the truth of her words, and the relief was so intense, it nearly caused her eyes to mist over. Wherever her angel originally hailed from, it was good to know that some emotions were universal. She read the shame on his face as clearly as the sun's arc in the sky.

He understands.

Bronze caged his hands around hers, securing them to his chest while stalling out the rubbing movements and increasing the warmth between them tenfold. "Do not, for one iota of a second, ever think I haven't seen just how strong you are. I've known full-blooded Empyrean seraphim warriors who wouldn't have had the courage to put themselves at the mercy of the unknown the way you did."

"I was desperate."

"You were fucking ferocious," he stressed. "Not fearless, perhaps, which is wise. We all need to fear something, but to get past it to do what needs doing is . . ." His throat swallowed around words he seemed to struggle with. The lack of composure and poise was a rare moment, even in the short time she'd known him, and she imagined it wasn't something the angel let others see often.

Clara tucked that thought away and gave him two swift soft pats of thanks against his chest. "Then, as you said, let me do what needs doing."

Bronze held her gaze until the door closed behind her, breaking the connection. Inside, the emerald and eggplant brocade tapestries featuring the family crest hung from the walls with the weight of the monarchy bearing down on the stones. Strange. She'd never noticed it before, but everything in her father's study took on such an air of heaviness she wondered how the foundation of the keep didn't collapse altogether. The black walnut desk cluttered high with documents. The mantle above the stone hearth supporting far more family history than the ancestral chalices and trinkets above it. Was it the burden of the monarchy that made even her shoulders sag slightly, or was it something more?

Fortunately for her, she never had to pay it further consideration as the weight of the past was soon lifted, or more accurately, diverted. Once she closed the door behind her, the king wasted no time expressing his thoughts on the significance of that past and how her act of defiance would go over in the future.

Her father hadn't even bothered to rise from his seat, so accustomed was he to having his words carry throughout the room regardless. "I could ask you why you made the choices you did, but I wouldn't be the ruler I am without the ability to glean information and form my own conclusions."

"And what would those conclusions be?"

A wry smirk twisted his mouth. "Well, given your unusual and quick attachment to the first male I've known you to ever show any interest in, my first guess would be that you let him fuck you and have all too late figured out what those consequences might look like."

"Father!"

He cut off her cry with a swipe of his hand. "But then I got to thinking, how would you even know of such an option as the Betrothal Games? As Pascal pointed out, it's not a more well-known part of our legacy. And then I realized you wouldn't know about it," he said flatly, any amusement he felt from drawing his own conclusions dissolving into the air. "Not unless you had spent considerable amounts of time researching the subject, preparing for exactly that event, and planning for the perfect circumstances to converge at just the right time. Which brings me back around to why."

Icy fingers of nerves sent stabbing prods throughout Clara's stomach, and her wolf growled against the pain of it. But so much had happened to her, *because* of her, in the last day or so that the chill of her father's attention no longer stung the way it once had. After all, if a river could not drown her and wild predators could not challenge her, then how terrifying could a simple conversation with this male truly be?

For it would only be a conversation. Despite her assurances to Bronze that she could handle her father, she dared not risk spreading the angel's trust too thinly. He was still injured, after all, and she would not put herself in a circumstance that would incite him to possibly act on her behalf, especially beyond what his body could safely perform.

But yes, she *had* prepared. She *had* planned. It was why, despite the terror threatening to grip her spine and shake her flesh free, she rode above the avalanche with skis firmly fastened to her feet. Clara held on to that kernel and the unique brand of strength it provided her.

By the Moon Mother, she would need it.

Clara lifted her chin higher and shot a warning look of challenge into her father's gray gaze. "I know our conversations have been few and far between over the years, so you may be unaccustomed to my preference for not repeating myself. I'll forgive you the discretion."

His hooded stare darkened.

"Yes, I have had little reason to say much in your presence, because you've always seemed pleased to hoard the wolf's share of the conversation, so this will be an adjustment for both of us."

The king's rising fury flared his nostrils so wide, it caused the overgrown graying hairs of his mustache to curl around his scowl, further accentuating the creases and craters that had been carved over centuries.

The male wasn't just old but ancient by lycan standards. The sum of that imagery and her awareness of it tipped over into a hopeful pounding in Clara's chest that had begun to chip away at the frozen shards he'd not only wrought over the long years but weaponized.

"The games will go on because there is no law that currently prevents them. Ignorance of your own people's laws is no excuse," she declared.

"Neither is treason, daughter. Do I smell an uprising? Is that it?" He spread his arms wide. "Is this all a simple bid for a throne you have no hope of inheriting anyway?" That statement caught her off guard but only momentarily.

No, she'd done everything by the book. By definition, there was nothing treasonous in following the law. She had been careful of it and had taken great risks to ensure she played by the rules. It had been the only way to make it all work. Her father had always been so focused on manipulation and gaining ground his way. Therefore, to get anything past him, Clara needed to do so by the book. Regulations created by others, especially those enacted long ago, were never areas of concern for him, now to his great detriment. He'd always preferred to make his own rules.

"I am not interested in what you smell, Father. It has no bearing on the laws that have governed us for centuries." Her voice was small, but her words were clear and succinct. They were sturdy, if slight. "As I said earlier, I have taken actions to enact the games. Those actions cannot be undone. I have chosen my champion, and as the monarch, you are entitled to choose the other two who may compete for my hand. I've already spoken to Pascal. He's taking care of the formalities as we speak and drafting the official notices. In three days, the games will commence."

The king pressed his knuckles into the desk and slowly rose, his eyes searching hers. She knew the look well and braced for the change of tactic he was preparing to engage.

"Where did this viper come from, I wonder? I can empathize with not wanting to marry a male you've never met before, but I am your father. You should trust that I would not match you with one who would not be suitable. Lord Raff is beyond wealthy, so he shall keep you in comfort. He is the warlord of the western and northwestern territories. It is a fine match."

"For you."

"For our *people*."

"You cannot ignore the humans. You cannot continue to govern with the mindset that one race must fall for the other to rise. We are all creatures living among the same land, vying for the same resources." Clara clenched her fists. "Yes, Father, even the vipers. For more clarification on that point, I would direct your attention to the face that stares back at you each morning. So no, I do not believe it is a fine match for me, because I no longer wish to be blindfolded, then pointed in a direction of another's choosing and told to march. And it may be that I end up in the same place as when all this started, holding the hand of a male you chose who only wants to drag me along for the sake of what resources are attached to me. It may be that your alliances stay intact, and I'll have to bear the consequences for finally speaking what my heart needed to say, but at least I'll have tried, and our people will have seen me do so."

She was trembling. A full-blown attack of the nerves. Never, in the history of ever, had she spoken to another living soul like that, let alone her king and monarch. The toll it was taking, not just on her body but on her soul and her she-wolf, was more than she ever anticipated. But oh, it was worth it. To see her father standing before her, face red and fangs bared, stirred up to the point of near violence knowing he couldn't touch her lest he lose any chance for the future holdings and expansion he'd worked so hard for, was enough to make her run away a thousand times. To take a thousand leaps into a frigid river.

To take a thousand chances in a foreign land hoping to find the one angel who could push her through those doors, despite hating that she had to do so.

Clara turned on her heel before her knees gave out. The king barked something at her back, but she was still shaking too hard to make sense of the words.

Just as well. She didn't think she should be called upon to decipher much at the moment, especially not the consequences of what she'd just done. Her mind was a jumble of sleep-deprived strength and dizzying amazement.

So it was an even bigger wonder when, as soon as she closed the door behind her, Bronze's powerful arms wrapped around her and buffeted her fleeting strength with that of his own.

CHAPTER 15

The way Bronze saw it, he had, at best, another sixty seconds of patience left on his lit wick before that oak door to the receiving room lived out the rest of its life as wood pulp for toilet paper. And none of that double-ply shit. He wanted splinters.

Phrases like "let him fuck you" and "viper" echoed overloud in his already cramped mind. Funny thing about rage. No one ever talked about how thick and heavy the stuff actually was and how, once someone yanked on its rip cord, it inflated to such unimaginable limits that it forced every sensible thought to get the fuck out or get crushed beneath it.

Every single one of the king's words that Bronze's celestial senses picked up stoked the fire that had been carefully banked within him ever since he'd arrived in the keep. But as soon as he heard the horseshit about this Lord Raff keeping Clara in comfort, his composure snapped. He had no problem standing outside the door, playing the part of silent sentinel and getting the side-eye from the lycan guards while daddy and daughter duked it out. Who didn't love a good stare-down? But for some reason, the idea of Clara not just engaging in contract negotiations but being an actual object of them made his sword hand twitchy.

A contract was an oath. He knew a bit more than most about that subject, but no fucking way would he stand by and listen to Clara being casually listed as a goddamn line item.

Bronze's fury launched him at the door before the guards got it in their pea brains to look up from their navels. But instead of worn wood scratching against the inside of his forearms as he ripped the oak off its hinges, it was Clara's soft form that brushed against his skin.

Soft and shaking.

"I . . . I think I need to sit down," she mumbled against the wall of his chest, her tiny fists balling up his shirt. "Quickly."

Well, fuck. No one had to tell him to do anything quickly. Ever. Especially not her, after hearing the battle of wills and tongues for which she'd just single-handedly led her own campaign.

Bronze tucked her into his side and hated how slight she felt, even if the warmth of her skin was still cool enough to knock his inferno of fury down by a couple of thousand degrees. Her shoulders were hunched so far forward, she was liable to topple over if he didn't hold her upright.

"Lady," one of the guards said, though the lycan kept one eye trained on the room still occupied by the king. A sharp crash resounded from behind the door, followed by the tinkling of glass on hardwood. Another impact, this one forceful and blunted. Furniture, Bronze suspected.

The guard's worried eyes shifted between his allegiances. "Lady, do you need—"

"She's good," Bronze cut the male off, picked a hallway, and propelled them away from whatever blast zone her father had left behind.

Because an asshole like that *always* left shit behind.

"Infirmary," Clara whispered as her grip tightened on him.

"Down the stairwell up ahead, then the last door on the right at the end of the hallway."

"On it."

Bronze ignored the heavy stares at his back as he guided them through the keep. He kept his eyes trained on the precision of his steps, not wanting to inadvertently trip her, but even traveling the short distance, his peripheral senses picked up on a whole lot of *one of these things is not like the other.*

As he made it to the bottom of the stairs and escorted them past the kitchen, he caught a glimpse of lycans in black slacks, some in matching black button-down chef's coats and some in cotton aprons, toiling over pans above a stone hearth. The smoke from the fires vented up through the chimney above the stove, but even with the rudimentary ventilation, an abundance of smoke still filled the space, as if someone had forgotten to switch on the cooking range hoods. Through the smoke, he could just make out the tips of their knives, or at least, he thought he could. Were those black blades? Certainly not stainless steel or even patinated carbon steel. Nor were they the bone-white hue of the weapon worn by the first guard they encountered when they arrived at the keep.

"Here," Clara said, pointing to the infirmary's entrance. "Take the first room. I just need a few minutes."

Bronze tucked them into a room that looked like a hospital's private suite of sorts. While he closed the door behind them, Clara hobbled over to the bed and collapsed. She had yet to fully open her eyes and instead let her head settle between her legs while she breathed in the faintly sweet air in the room.

He hovered over her, unsure what to do or what to offer, because the only thing he had a mind to focus on was the calibrated arc he'd swing his halberd at to sever the king's head at just the right spot so the male's beard didn't hang lower than the cumulative disappointments of his people.

"Matches are in the top drawer to your left," she breathed.

Bronze stalled out where he stood. "Matches?"

"For the lights."

Well, *that* certainly gave him pause. Though he gathered they were belowground, he couldn't fathom why the wall sconces adorning the infirmary suite would be anything more than decorative. Generally speaking, fire of any kind was a big no-no in medical settings, much to the plight of many a smoker.

Wait . . .

Bronze finally dropped his pack and walked over to the door he'd just shut, scanning the walls along its perimeter. No light switch. He checked the wall space above the porcelain sink and below the cabinets. Again, no light switch, nor were there any overhead lights or tableside lamps. Then he looked at the sconces once more, inspecting them further. Inside the simple glass cages sat honest-to-God candles.

Fucking *candles*. In a medical suite.

That out-of-his-element feeling he'd had earlier crept up his spine in slow warning prowls. Worried he was missing a very large piece of the damn puzzle, he found the matches and quickly lit the lamps.

What the flames illuminated was not the picture he wanted to see.

The cot was not so unusual for a hospital, except if it featured none of the electronic aids or metallic handrails he expected. It was little more than a mattress with a hard plastic frame, small resin wheels, and the obligatory set of overwashed mass-produced sheets. The bedside armchair wasn't anything altogether out of the ordinary either, with its uninspired wooden frame and ho-hum cushion in basic boring beige. There was no blood pressure monitor on the wall, however, nor any rolling IV pole. Without a window to let in any sunlight, flickering shadows danced fast and loose across a stone floor that looked about as hygienic as a borrowed bowling ball at a seven-year-old's birthday party. No amount of bleach could touch the bacterial critters that stone could store.

The king's physicians didn't use linoleum for a medical suite? And mages forbid there was a patient with compromised breathing; how the hell would they maneuver oxygen tanks or respirators next to ye olde flickering fire hazards dotting the walls?

Bronze slowly spun in place, making damn sure he didn't miss what his suspicion was telling him he'd never find. *Impossible.*

Even as he thought the word, the truth of his surroundings and what he'd seen ever since he got there solidified into sharp focus. There were no electrical outlets in the room, no hookups for respirators or oxygen, no monitors for vital signs. No ethernet cables or even so much as a damn night-light.

"You don't use electricity," he said softly, his words tinged with stunned disbelief.

But Clara must not have heard him, because when he turned to face her, she was just bringing her head up from between her knees and the flush in her cheeks was quickly fading to its more natural rose-kissed hue. "There, I think I'm better now. Oh, goodness, I still can't believe I did that."

Whatever realization his brain had landed on seconds ago, and whatever it was so eager to panic about, fled with the insignificance of a runaway thought.

Bronze was no stranger to hefty doses of hubris. Hell, there were times he gorged on the stuff like a recovering vegan attacking a cheese plate. But he'd never seen pride look so perfect as it had on Clara's features. Her shaking had long since subsided, and her shoulders no longer sagged under the weight of someone else's expectations. It was her eyes, however, that stunned him the most.

Clear, vibrant, and sparking with an excitement he'd yet to see from her before.

It was more than enough to make him forget about . . . whatever he'd been stressing over a moment ago.

"He's wrong, you know," Bronze said, closing the distance between them and taking a seat next to her on the bed, eager to finally rest his injured leg and see for himself that her father had truly done nothing more to Clara than talk to her.

No bruises or red marks on her skin. Good.

Clara gifted him a sad smile, no doubt realizing her feat of strength came at a high cost. "Wrong? About what?"

Her hand lay gripping the edge of the thin mattress, mere inches from his. Owing to no feeling other than instinct, he lifted her hand up and cradled it between his warm palms. The tips of her fingers were still cold, but despite her soft rush of breath, she didn't pull them away and instead curled them closer into the center of his hands.

The simple touch extended all the way to his core, until his angel fire throbbed with warming recognition.

"I heard what he said to you, and I want you to know that there are worse things to be labeled than a viper. In fact, vipers notoriously get a bad rap, usually by the uninspired or uneducated. They're low-hanging fruit for nasty metaphors, but in reality, they're some of the most amazing creatures this realm has ever seen."

She looked at him quizzically, and a corner of her lips lifted. "Vipers? Are we thinking of the same snakes?"

"Oh, most definitely. Let me tell you something about those beauties. Did you know that, for all the venom they carry, they still have the ability to *choose* whether to inject their victims?"

Her shoulders bobbed on a snort of disbelief.

"It's true. They don't always go for the kill, because they don't always need to. However, when they're cornered or feel threatened in any way, they administer an open-mouthed bite, and at the last second, they can make a conscious choice whether to rotate their fangs to avoid lasting damage to their prey. Their true power is being able to wound with a dry bite, but doing so without releasing a drop of venom."

Her eye roll came right on cue, but he was ready for it. What he *wasn't* ready for was her fingers loosening slightly within his grasp and then burrowing further in a way where they found snug homes between his. It wasn't a tight handhold. Just a tentative linking, but one that he wasn't so eager to break anytime soon.

"Not only do vipers choose whether to inject their venom, but they also decide how much to dispel."

"Wouldn't they always want to kill what threatens them?"

"The snake uses its cunning to take into account many different facets of the situation. Don't forget, their eyes see more than others do. Their vertical oval-shaped pupils can widen or narrow fully, enabling them to take in more light than their prey would. To see what other creatures can't. They can also give birth to live young, which, I imagine, affords them some additional perspective on the power they have and choose to wield."

"You almost make them sound pleasing."

Pleasing. Yes.

When had his heart ever beat a rhythm so light and happy against the cage of his ribs? Not since the heat of the Empyrean's sun cycles had warmed his battle skin and he'd shared a laugh or two with another sort of brother.

Under another sort of sky. Under another sort of circumstances.

The remorse came just as it always did whenever he thought of Malik and the promise Bronze had sworn to uphold as he held his dying friend, but this time, it left just as swiftly as it had arrived, chased away by the hope illuminating Clara's beauty.

And by the mages, she *was* beautiful. He could no longer pretend he wasn't affected by it. The truth of it sat warm and secure between his battle-roughened palms and filled other parts of him with an insistent ache.

"I've already told you what I find pleasing, princess."

There. Right there. *That* was the money shot. The way his heart bloomed when Clara's shy smile pinned him to the spot was enough to make him want to craft new compliments in new languages just to see that adorable flush creep up her smooth cheeks whenever he said them.

He shook his head, in awe of all he held for once, and whispered, "You have no idea how much strength you carry in your choices. I've seen you *choose* to let three coyotes live, despite the injuries they caused. I've heard the love you have for your people and have seen it shine through in soft words with the loudest message. I've seen you square off against your king, only to rotate your fangs at the last moment. Trust me, princess, I could not think of any qualities that I'd want more in a monarch." Then he lifted her clasped hand to his mouth and pressed his lips against her heated skin. "And I've never been prouder than to be chosen as your champion."

The bright mist in her eyes wavered with threads of uncertainty. "You don't owe me any of those words, you know. That wasn't part of our arrangement."

The barb surprised him, and that was perhaps why the sting threw him off course.

Ah. Their arrangement. Yes. She was right to remind him of it, but he was startled to find that he'd lost sight of his primary purpose so easily. The paving stones that guided their short journey had been cemented by his singular focus: get the other half of the relic and return home. Somewhere along the lines, however, the road had altered and swayed from its original course to one that favored frosted hair and shy smiles. Now, when he looked at the angle his boots were pointed toward, it was always decidedly in her direction.

And so far, territorial coyotes notwithstanding, he'd not

stumbled over a single step. No, his stride had been surer than ever, emboldened with a purpose that had begun to tip the scales in a direction he hadn't expected.

Perhaps there was a way to see Clara through this *and* bring the relic back to his brothers. Was the possibility of two homes so hard to imagine?

It is when there's someone waiting for you to return. When you made a promise that has yet to be fulfilled.

His jaw tensed, the reminder of his guilt quickly souring his mood. "I've got enough debts to last until the stones of this stronghold turn to sand and are swept away by the sea. Believe me, my lady, I've learned better than to add a single more debt to the pile. It ain't happening."

Without meaning to—or maybe a little bit meaning to—he turned closer toward her, resting more of his thigh on the mattress between them so he could see her more fully. Mages, she truly was stunning, especially how her breasts lifted higher over the collar of her laced-up shirt the longer he held her hand. If he looked close enough, he bet he could make out the flutter of her pulse every time her lips parted on a nervous sigh.

Damn, this was not good. As anyone knew, details fucking mattered, and he sure as shit shouldn't be homing in on the perfect parts of her that had absolutely zero bearing on whether he could find the—

"Oh my God, you're still bleeding! I completely forgot!"

Huh? Bleeding?

Clara ripped her hand from his and, faster than a seagull dive-bombing a french fry-holding beachgoer, had him flat on his back with his legs on the bed. Whatever air rushed out of him had somehow also managed to buffet Clara toward the cabinets on the far wall. When Bronze craned his neck to try and ascertain what she was searching for, he immediately wished he hadn't. Clara turned toward him sporting a king bed's worth of gauze, gauze rolls, and some half-filled bottles of dubiously colored liquid.

"Clara, I'm fine. Really. The bites have already started to heal." But his words were directed to the hollow of her neck and the female's distracting cleavage that landed him on his back in the first place as she leaned over, nearly smothering him.

Normally, it wouldn't be a bad way to end an afternoon.

Too bad nothing about their day had been normal.

She yanked his shirt to the side to expose his shoulder wound before shaking her head and letting the fabric fall back to his collar. "How could I have been so careless? Stupid *stupid*," she muttered to herself. She pinched at the hem of his shirt. "Off. Take this off."

Unfortunately, he fumbled too long with the edge that was half tucked in, and the delay cost him. In the absence of anything to care for, her idle eyes widened with shock, as if remembering a lit candle left too close to a curtain.

He knew that look. That was the look of a female realizing there was something far bigger and bloodier that demanded her attention. Something she *missed*. Something she was about to correct ASAP.

Shit.

"Oh, no you don't," he rushed out and stopped her from yanking his khakis down. One swift tug and she'd get an eyeful of far more than some leg lacerations.

Far, *far* more.

"Clara." A painful growl rumbled beneath her name. It was enough of a warning to give her pause.

Thank the mages she'd only managed to lift his shirt free of his waistband. At the rate she was going, if she hadn't paused with her hands where they were, he didn't put it past her to get him full-ass trauma naked in less time it would take to douse the candles in the room.

And speaking of which . . .

"As much as I can appreciate your enthusiasm, what's with all the— *Mmph!*"

She drew his shirt over his head, stealing his question as well as his few remaining protective barriers. "This is all my fault! I can't believe I didn't think of it sooner. I should have brought you here immediately and not have wasted time fighting with my father while you stood there, bleeding and brave as you were."

"Clara, for the last time, I'm fine. I'm immortal, remember?" He tried to grab up her arms, but she was already kneeling over his shoulder, pressing him back into the mattress, with some foul-smelling salve in one hand and a fist full of gauze in the other.

"Oh, this one's not too bad, actually. It looks like the skin's already begun stitching closed. Fascinating," she said, and he had to hold back a chuckle to keep from rocking his body any closer to her breasts, which swayed behind those laces that would take no more than a bite to sever. Maybe two.

Stay still, asshole. Stay absolutely perfectly sti—

"Who is Polina?" Clara's voice took on a quiet resonance. "And why is her name tattooed over your heart?"

CHAPTER 16

Clara didn't move. She wasn't sure whether her joints locking up was out of fear of what those six tiny shimmering letters on Bronze's skin represented or due to the plane of tense muscle supporting them. A damning heat prickled her skin, and she tried to avert her gaze. But where? She was practically lying on top of the male. Every corner her eye searched out only came away with more of that smooth, taut skin stretched over bounding muscles that jumped beneath her fingers every time she prodded a tender patch.

And tender it was. The slashes from the coyote bite that extended down his shoulder and over his collarbone weren't particularly deep—or, at least, they weren't any longer—but they left a precarious trail toward a tight disc of a nipple. One that seemed to tighten further beneath her labored breaths.

Somewhere between the travesty of the coyote's cruel marks and the tempting treasure that kept a taut rein on her awareness lay the scrawling script of another female's name.

Then the hot talons of mortification sank into her.

He had a sweetheart. Another female. True, they'd both made it clear that affection was not a factor in their agreement, but she'd never considered that the reason they hadn't discussed it was because he already *had* a female who satisfied his needs in that regard.

The realization flooded fresh heat to her cheeks. *Honestly, could you be more of a fool if you tried?*

"I'm sorry. It's none of my business." On weak arms, she pushed herself off the bed, already regretting that her shame shone clear as day on her face.

He grabbed her wrist and tugged gently. "No, it's all right."

Bronze sat up and shifted so he made space for her beside him. His tightly packed abdominals contracted beneath the weight of his hunched shoulders. Then he ran his fingers through his hair, and that strange flash of citrine sparked in his gaze. A gaze that was notably not directed at her.

"Polina was . . . a sister."

"A sister?" The confession surprised her, though it shouldn't have if she'd been better at following the threads of her most recent experiences more closely. After she awoke in the angels' infirmary room, Bronze had formally introduced himself and the others. How had he referred to them? His brothers and extended family. So it shouldn't be strange he also had a sister, right?

The realization should have been a comfort, but then why had her muscles ceased to relax?

"Before my brothers and I landed in the mortal realm, we resided in the Empyrean, Heaven's highest realm, as I've mentioned before. The angels you've met at our den are all sentinels like me, except for Rhode. He was the seraphim commander in charge of the most elite intelligence unit but is a brother just the same."

Clara nodded her understanding and was doing her best to stay focused. There were just so many words and phrases she'd never heard before. It was a hard-to-swallow pill of just how small her world had been her whole life and what she thought she could absurdly stumble into and maneuver unawares.

"I had a dear friend, Malik. He was a seraph in Rhode's intelligence unit, but the male made for a shit spy. He knew it, I knew it, and so did everyone else. However, he'd learned he had other skills that lent themselves very well to the spy game."

"Who were you spying on?"

"Cyro. The ruler of the demon charmers."

"Demons?"

"Yeah. Soul-suckers who eradicate mortals like pests and have a huge hangup over the Empyrean's Eternal Flame, which is the source of all light and life in the realms. Cyro can't tolerate the stuff. He and his cronies—who can eat, sleep, have sex, and generally commingle with the rest of the human race so they assimilate more easily—can only reside in darkness. Any light whatsoever, be it celestial or solar, torches them out of existence. That's why Cyro's been trying to snuff out the root of his grudge for eons, and we've been doing our best to prevent it."

"Demons," she whispered to herself, trying to shake off the shock of it all. Then another horrid thought occurred to her. "Was Polina one of these demons?"

"No," he quickly assured her. "No, Polina was . . ." His eyes got that faraway look to them again and seemed to dip lower under the weight of a past Clara was struggling to comprehend and dying to know more about. "She was Malik's younger sister. A real brat and a half during her early years, but a truly sweet and wonderful female once maturity set in."

"She sounds charming."

A haunted smile ghosted his lips. "She was."

Was.

By the blasted moon, had her brainless poking and prodding just drudged up the memory of a lost loved one? And there she'd gone and practically forced him to explain the woman's name on his skin as if Clara had any right to the truth of it?

Her hot shame got to work, as usual, painting her a greater shade of idiot, so she did her best to quickly rally and change the subject. "You mentioned your friend had other skills."

Thankfully, *blessedly*, Bronze took the bait, or perhaps he was just as eager to change the subject as she was. "Yes. The reason Malik didn't excel in that branch of intelligence was because of an old battle injury that compromised his short-term memory. But while that portion of his mind was damaged, another portion was altered in a different manner. Some of his other senses grew tenfold, to the point where he could sense shadows on the ground long after their owners had left the area. I never quite understood it. None of us did, really. Something to do with an increased sensitivity to thermal temperatures and the auras they left behind. I don't know. Whatever it was, though, it meant that Malik could detect when a charmer had been nearby."

"Quite useful for a spy legion to know, I imagine."

"Quite."

Clara waited for him to continue, but her focus dipped slightly when he swallowed and candlelight rode the wave of his neck, highlighting the dusting of rebellious auburn hairs he hadn't managed to shave as close as the others.

"After one particular mission, Malik detected a league of charmers who had inched too close to the Empyrean's gates. But the energy was a bit off, for some reason. Not quite as strong as if they were still in the vicinity but not so weak that they hadn't been there very recently. Malik had trouble placing the timing of things, so when he finally got around to reporting his observations to Rhode, his memory of what he sensed was no longer reliable. Furious with himself and determined to correct his mistake, he returned to the scene outside the gates. But by then, the charmers were waiting for him."

Bronze idly traced the swirl of his tattoo over his chest. "I found him shortly after. He was still alive but they'd, uh"—he cleared his throat—"they'd hacked off his wings so he couldn't return and report back. We'd learned that when Cyro found out about Malik's ability, the demon ruler had his mystics, the magic users, craft a way to mask their thermal presence. It worked."

"That's . . . that's awful. I'm so sorry." Clara grabbed his hand and held it to her chest, hoping to impart some sort of belated comfort for the memories she'd forced him to drag up.

Bronze followed the line of his arm, down his biceps, over the bend of his elbow, and up the ramp of his forearm where it ended in a warm bundle against her breasts. His stare was a heightened reminder of the male's uncut measure, thrilling Clara to the point of confusion.

He'd never looked at her like that, and it was doing all sorts of funny things to her insides.

"Before he died, he made me promise to take care of Polina. In the Empyrean, oaths are sealed onto our skin as tattoos."

"And what happened to her?"

He shook his head. "I don't know. In the days that followed Malik's death, me and my brothers were called upon to enact the Sealing and close the gates of the Empyrean against Cyro's advancing armies. The magic we used to complete the task cast us out of the realm. We've been here ever since."

"You've never been able to return home?"

The slow shake of his head might as well have been an anvil on her chest. Did he feel it, too, then? The weight of expectation that might as well govern every moment of her life? She couldn't take a step down a hallway or select an outfit without being reminded of the hands that scrubbed the stones beneath her feet or stitched up the seams of her blouse.

She had a responsibility to her people. In her father's eyes, it was to mate and to breed. When she caught her people's exhausted gazes, however, the responsibility felt like so much more and had nothing to do with who she invited into her bed.

Fleeing to the human lands and taking the steps to enact these silly games had been the only thing she could think of to live up to the weight of that responsibility.

But God, it had been so long, so *long* since she'd done anything for herself. Spontaneity had always been a flimsy fantasy, one reserved for those who had lighter hearts and less propensity for chaos staring down their future.

A future that threatened to be just as bleak as frigid river water should the games not go according to plan.

Without her realizing it, that familiar deep desperation had her clutching his hand tighter against her, and a sharp breath hissed into his lungs. But he didn't pull his hand away. He just kept it there, relaxed and warm against her breasts, and when she loosened her fingers slightly to free him, he still didn't remove his hand.

The sensation was altogether transfixing, as was the way his rigid pectorals rose and fell in a more labored fashion.

When on earth had the room gotten so small? Or his presence so big, so overwhelming?

So tempting.

Oh, yes. He was so very tempting. She could admit that now. Alone as they were, was it so bad that she wanted to be the object of his temptation as well?

By the Moon Mother, she was tired. So very tired of plotting and planning. And where had it gotten her? Dead nearly two times over, a father who was furious with her for poking holes in his reign, and an angel who—

She didn't remember doing it or how it happened, but somewhere between her last thought and her next breath, she'd moved Bronze's hand higher, until the tips of his fingers settled within the shadowy curve between the tops of her breasts.

This male made her want so much more than she'd ever

known she could have. Touches and tastes that, if nothing changed, she was liable to go an entire lifetime without ever experiencing fully.

Yes, she was foolish in many things, but she was also a female. A princess. A future monarch, Moon Mother willing.

And a viper.

She could choose when and how to strike. This male had taught her that when even her father thought to label her as nothing more than a common whore.

"Bronze," she breathed, her sharp breath stealing more than her fair share of oxygen from the small room.

One more soft inhale was all the fortification she needed to close the gap between them and capture her prey with a hungry kiss.

CHAPTER 17

There were good ideas, bad ideas, and *really* fucking bad ideas.

Clara's warm lips pressed against Bronze's fell somewhere in the realm of all three. Likewise, the kiss brushed over him in a measure that was just as tremulous. The good: a warm, answering tenderness that was sweeter than any confection. The bad: an urgency that lurked beneath her searching lips, reminding him of who she was, where they were, and exactly what was at stake. And then the very bad: his hand was trapped between her mounded breasts, and the threadbare hope he had of limping out of that room without disappointing either of them was quickly unraveling.

But by the mages, her mouth! Kisses weren't meant to be like this. They were meant to be raw, eager, demanding, a precursor to the baser instincts of what two bodies needed. Sure, there could be tenderness to start, but it was always—*should* always—be fleeting. An appetizer before the main course. Soup before salad. Drinks before dessert.

They weren't supposed to be fucking perfect.

The sweet pressure of their kiss shifted as Clara angled her head slightly before resuming her clinging rhythm, and boy, did that make him smile. She was a curious one, his little lycan. And judging by the rhythm she soon adopted, a damn quick study. With his free hand, he held her to him, fully aware he was indulging in more of her intoxicating pull as well as his own deception.

Outside of his brothers, no one still breathing knew of Malik, and even fewer knew of Bronze's pact regarding Polina. No matter how many years had gone by and no matter how many realms he'd traveled through, time did jack shit to ease the memories of his best friend's body draped across Bronze's lap as the light left the male's soul.

Malik. Fucking *Malik*, who'd been stacked like a mountain and weighed twice as much, had been felled to no heavier than the weight of Bronze's halberd once the charmers had shorn off his wings and stripped him of his battle skin, weapons, and anything that might be worth bringing back to Cyro.

It was by some miracle that the male had even had breath to speak the plea that Bronze had been powerless to ignore.

Bond with Polina. No matter what happens, she'll be safe with a sentinel. You must do this, brother. For me.

At the time, Bronze had been so wrought with agony that he'd have given his own wings, his powers, if Malik would have asked for them, if they would have stuffed the leaking light of Malik's soul back into his shredded body.

Interesting thing about death, though. It didn't matter what side of the coin you rubbed for luck. That midnight train ride came for you regardless, and it was *never* late.

So, the oath had left his lips in the same slow trickle that Malik's blood flowed out of him. A few searing pulses later, the tattoo had been branded onto his chest, sealing his fate. And then the Sealing had done the rest.

He'd done nothing but spin out of control ever since.

Until Clara, who he'd known for such a short time, had the

absolute gall to nearly get herself killed so he might have the privilege of rescuing her.

He tightened his arm around her and moaned into her sweet mouth when her exploring fingers skimmed over his goatee. The delicate scratches and smooth whorls of her fingertips along his jaw and beneath his chin were far more than the rhythmic delights of a curious lover.

Her touch was a balm to his ravaged soul, and if he had any honor left in him, he'd gently push her away and lay himself bare. Tell her everything. About the relic. Polina. How he absolutely fucking hated the idea of mating her in ceremony only, when his fire roared with an instinct to claim her as far more.

But any honor he'd once had was still sealed off somewhere in the Empyrean, waiting for him to return and fulfill the eternal oath he'd made to a fallen brother.

No. Whatever indulgences he'd grant himself a taste of would be just that, and only what she freely offered. If she needed a male, a mate in name and appearance only to see her through what lay ahead, he could be that for her but never more.

That was all he could ever permit this to be.

WHEN BRONZE'S hand caressed Clara's back and pulled her closer, a wave of relief rushed through her limbs, and she settled the rest of her weight against him.

God, she'd wanted to touch him. Even bloody and bandaged as he was, she didn't think any amount of gore could fully detract from all the glorious strength on display.

Strength he was now wrapping around her.

She sank further into the pull of his mouth, reveling in the salty seduction of him. By the Moon Mother, he smelled exquisite, and her wolf whined in rapt agreement, causing her heart to make requests of her body on her behalf. Curious, oh so tempted, and with a desire spurred on by her lycan nature, she darted her tongue out.

When he didn't pull away and answered with a muffled moan and a sweeping greedy kiss of his own, her body thrilled at the connection. Dark heat pooled between her legs and was only made worse by the constriction of her leather trousers.

If only all of her spontaneity in life had been rewarded in such manners, instead of spurned. Her path up until then had been as rigid as bone, with no way out, no hope for change or choice or chances.

Until Bronze had said yes. It was a vote that had never been cast in her favor on a ballot before and one she wasn't entirely sure how to secure. Were there limits to his role in this ruse? To his affection?

Oh, hell, did she really care if he kissed her like that and didn't laugh at her when she finally mustered the strength to try and stand on legs that had never been used before?

He was a mate in every sense of the word. A true leader who would inspire males to follow him and people to rise up for him.

And for the moment, he was hers.

The realization made her grip his hand tighter against her aching breasts, which had begun to strain against the laces of her blouse. What would be if she loosened them?

What would be if she asked *him* to do it instead?

As soon as the thought materialized in her mind, it skittered away on a sharp breath. Bronze moved his hand, the very hand she had been secretly willing to enlist into action. Simmering need shot through her, tightening every nerve ending that came into contact with his skin, and many that didn't but still sought him out like a flower to the sun.

Surely he would touch her now. Just give one light tug on

her laces and alleviate some of the pressure against her already full heart.

His hand retreated, and the disappointment was the kindest *no thank you* she'd ever experienced in her life. As clear a refusal as there'd ever been. A gentle reminder of their arrangement.

Then that strong hand returned and positioned so it could intertwine with hers perfectly.

"Clara," he murmured against her mouth, then dragged her name in a sweet trail until his kiss stowed it safely beneath her ear.

She'd never heard her name spoken in such a way. Like it was necessary and elementally vital. Like the way her wolf needed meat or her lungs needed air. The sensation was almost as dizzying as the tortured tingles left in the wake of Bronze's mouth.

"What do you need, my lady?"

What did *she* need? How the heck should she know? The past few days had been a giant exercise in step first, think later. But something *was* taunting her, dragging her attention toward sensations she had no frame of reference for . . .

"I . . . I don't . . ."

"You don't need or you don't know?"

Oh, holy hell. Who was she kidding? She needed, all right. Her whole body was a firework of demands that had exploded every which way. But how could she possibly pick a route? She was like a log adrift, bobbing toward a waterfall she couldn't see the bottom of.

"I don't know," she breathed.

Her doubt was lost on another scorching kiss as he wrenched her beneath him and stretched their clasped hands above her. Bronze was everywhere at once. His scent, his heat, his damnable mouth. He gave her no opportunity to think, which she supposed was part of the point.

Who the hell would want to waste an iota of time thinking

when there was so much to feel? And who knew how much longer he'd indulge her? Time was a fleeting factor for both of them.

Then her sharp resolve snapped into focus, chasing the chaos from her mind like an unruly pack of pups.

She knew exactly what she wanted.

Clara tugged on her hand, directing it southward until it reached the laces binding her breasts. His sentinel's eyes grew darker, giving a wicked contrast to the citrine sparks that hungrily flashed. Then she looped his index finger beneath a single lace.

And waited.

And waited.

Please.

The rip rang out overloud in the spacious medical suite, and the white linen flaps of her blouse parted, exposing her bare breasts. She only had a moment of cool air kissing her nipples before his mouth warmed one chilly peak while his strong warrior's palm possessively gripped the other.

"Perfect. So fucking perfect, princess."

Her hands were now free, but the blanket beneath her wasn't. With each swipe of his tongue and pump of his hand against her newly exposed flesh, she clenched that cotton as if it were a life preserver and she were an unmoored vessel in a storm-tossed ocean.

The relief was short-lived, however, and soon, she was gripping anything she could to make the aching parts of the rest of her ease. Shoulders, biceps, strong hips. She'd have torn out a chunk of the stone wall if he hadn't caught up her hands and settled them on the sides of his waist.

Did the male have a death wish? Surely, she would rip out whole parts of him if he kept this up. Weren't his kidneys not far from her fingers?

But she got the sense there was something more she should be seeking. Something else she should be asking for.

Instinctively, she curled her fingers into the waistband of his khakis and tugged.

The maneuver pulled his mouth and hand free of her breasts and miraculously, as if his head was tied to a string connected to her searching fingers, lured him lower down her stomach. What a thrill to have such power over a male! Even more thrilling, she learned, was the delectable breadcrumbs trail he left of soft, insistent kisses on top of her blouse covering her abdomen, as if he was worried about losing his way back to her breasts.

Impossible, but who was she to argue?

But oh God, the ache! She squirmed, near to thrashing. It was a panic of a different sort and not one she'd ever experienced. She'd had a lover or two before, though more to satisfy her curiosity than anything else. Her trysts had been short, sweaty, and over long before any sort of enjoyment had been achieved on her part.

None had been like this. Never like this.

"I know, princess," he said. Then, right when his lips were millimeters away from the laces of her trousers, he levered his head up and asked, "Permit me?"

"Permit you to do what?"

That self-satisfied smirk returned just for her. "To make you feel better."

Oh, hell. She was all in for it now, wasn't she? Her spontaneity had set up shop, and it had no intention of moving until it was satisfied.

Until *she* was satisfied.

"Yes," she gasped. "I permit you."

If she'd known how fast an injured angel could move, she'd have chosen her words more carefully. No sooner had the final word left her tongue than his hands had shoved her trousers down to her thighs. If her heart had thought itself a wild mare who had broken free before, it had nothing on what the sight of Bronze's mouth descending to her core would do to it.

Mumbles came next, or perhaps sighs. More gasping, for sure, though her brain hadn't the appropriate span of higher reasoning in that moment to discern between them. All she could focus on was the brush of Bronze's goatee against her inner thighs and the passionate placement of tender kisses in a place that she didn't even think could process tenderness.

She trembled further at his touch, both at the lapping of his lips and the passionate, masterful presses of his palm, which had found its way back to her breasts. And then the helplessness set in as a foreign wave of pleasure bumped further against her shores.

"Bronze," she whimpered. "What's happening? What are you doing to me?"

"Pleasing you," he said against her core as he gripped her on either side of her rib cage and slid her down farther to him, exposing more of her to his mouth.

Farther toward an exquisite feeling and what she irrevocably knew would be a total and complete loss of control.

Heat blazed like fire over her skin, claiming her body in a searing tsunami that assaulted every available sense. A cry erupted. Was that *her* voice? The trill shattered whatever logic she thought she possessed into fleeting specks of starlight across an eternal universe. Energy whipped her left and right, in sync with Bronze's slowing tongue and careful calmness. And just when she didn't think her body had any more aftershocks left in it, a final swipe and secret kiss pulled one last greedy jerk out of her.

She had no control over what happened next. No inkling of what it would mean for her skin to scatter from her flesh and reassemble in the warm embrace of a male who murmured light hushes up her thighs and still tracked reassuring tender kisses across her quivering abdomen. Her breaths barely had a chance to return to a steady rhythm before he placed a parting kiss over her navel and covered her with a blanket.

Then, strangely, he settled in beside her, tucking her against his warm chest but still cradling her face away from him slightly. "One day, princess, we're going to finally have a discussion about the lack of lights and electricity here because it's absolutely killing me that I can't see you the way I want to right now."

"Electricity?" Oh, that's right. Before he nearly sent her to the Moon Mother herself, he had mentioned something about that, hadn't he? "You're correct. There's no electricity here. Certain things don't—"

Heavy footsteps pounded through the hall outside their suite. "Lady? Are you down here?"

Shit! Clara turned, forced her hands over Bronze's mouth, and held him as still as she could.

"No sign of her," muttered a frustrated male, whose worried tenor tones alerted her as belonging to Pascal. "I'll search the gardens, then. Broderick, talk to the housekeeper and have the staff see to it that Lord Raff's rooms are ready."

"Sir? But he's not due until tomorrow."

Cold dread turned Clara's already misted skin clammier.

"The lord will be arriving earlier than expected, I'm afraid. A messenger just informed the king that he'll be here within the hour."

CHAPTER 18

Bronze had always been more of a stemless wineglass sort of fellow, and seeing the array of drinking vessels laid out before him, he was reminded of why.

Damn, did he need to break shit. Right the hell now. Unfortunately, it wouldn't do to go down the line of fine table settings snapping stemware like they were twigs. It wouldn't be nearly as satisfying anyway. Wineglasses weren't necks, unfortunately. One neck, in particular, was too thick to even detonate the satisfying *crack* Bronze had in mind for the pompously prestigious Lord Raff, leader and warlord of the western lycan territories.

Really, was the guy trying to impress anyone in particular, or was bending over on a regular basis to receive all the ass-kissing just part and parcel of political office out west?

Aside from the male's display of physical strength and prowess, there wasn't much to recommend. Hours after Clara had swept Bronze from the infirmary and set him up in a spare dormitory, she'd come to collect him for the evening meal. One, which she had been informed by her father's staff, would be a welcome banquet for Lord Raff and his entourage. The look on her face, however, when she'd relayed the news to Bronze was equal parts fractured composure and worry.

It was a far cry from the expression he'd prefer to see on her face and what he'd spent the last few hours reliving in his mind as he lay on the small cot, lit by more dim-as-fuck candlelight, and stared at a whole lot of nothing doing.

He should have been strategizing, should have been using the hours at his disposal to scout out the portions of the keep immediately accessible and then branch out beyond there. Clara had mentioned royal coffers. One didn't need a set of neon traffic wands, a bloodhound, and an overabundance of road flares to suggest that would be the best place to start his search for the other half of the relic.

Then again, it was kind of hard to find the motivation when Clara's slackened face flushed with pleasure brought on by his mouth played on repeat in his mental reels. Even with his eyes closed, he could still remember every inviting curve and crevice that bounced beneath the wall sconces' meager glow. He'd never given the possibility any thought before, but that female had somehow mapped out his personal path to the first inklings of ease his soul had known in some time. Lips, throat, collarbone, breasts, the dip of her navel, and lower was the exact circuit that had his mind running laps while it should have been focusing on what and who he was there for.

Goddammit. There was that word again. *Should.*

What he *should* have done was not puff up his still-slightly-oozing chest at the sight of her replete post-pleasure grin melting into the most enchanting smile he'd ever had the good fortune to witness. Was it astonishment she reflected back at him? Surprising curiosity? Likely both, if she was not accustomed to a male's touch, or at least that kind of touch. It was clear she'd never had an orgasm before, but she wasn't nearly as shy as he'd expect of a cloistered royal.

And like fucking clockwork, that thought alone had his

merry-go-round mind bringing it all back to the brutish lycan sitting at the king's elbow.

Bronze brought his wineglass to his mouth and drank from the thing just so his hand didn't smash it into shards, pick out the choicest of shivs from the bunch, and hurl the glass at Lord Raff's eye, which was only a hair shinier than the sweating pate of his bald head.

When the male and his traveling party arrived at the stronghold, the crowd had resembled a crew of bear-like boxers who were still waiting on their thirty-five-year-old callbacks for *American Gladiators* that hadn't come. Pity, that.

They certainly grew 'em brawny and bushy out west, however. Lord Raff was the only male without hair on his head, though the length of his black beard more than made up for the scarcity happening topside. Similar to the northeastern lycans, leather seemed to be the preferred fabric, but where Clara's people tended to swap in bits of more modern attire, such as khakis and button-down shirts, the western contingent apparently enjoyed a whole lot of camouflage. Every single one of the fifteen or so lycans sported thick olive tactical pants with beige boots, which were topped off with basic black thermals cinched tight beneath dark brown leather vests. Lord Raff's burgundy military-style tunic was the only standout and clearly signified him as the leader.

Or a seasonally inappropriate candy apple.

"As I was saying," King Halpin bellowed, more for effect than necessity, as the table they were all seated around was no larger than what the Hilton's staff would put together for a standard conference room luncheon of barely salaried middle managers.

Bronze took in the cacophony of bored, yet dutiful expressions and had to wonder whether mealtimes were always such a snoozefest. Honestly, did the king think his subjects bought any of this showmanship crap?

"We are honored to have the privilege of receiving Lord

Raff, ruler of the western territories. This visit has long been anticipated, and I look forward to the discussions of our future alliance. Together, by joining the northeastern and western contingents of lycans, the established power of our combined efforts will not go unheeded."

"*Presumptive* alliance," Clara spoke into her wineglass before taking a sip. Though not loud enough for the serving staff to hear, her declaration twitched the ears of every lycan at the table and drew the intense gazes of the two males at the center.

The king's cheeks deepened to an altogether alarming shade of crimson as he turned toward Clara. "Yes," he hissed through tight lips. "I have made Lord Raff aware of your . . . request."

"It is not a request, Father. It is law."

A sharp collective intake of breath flowed through the dining hall, yet unsurprisingly, everyone's eyes, save for those of the western lycans, immediately sought out something other than the king. The westerners, instead, shared a common glint in their gazes, as if excited for some form of entertainment after a long journey.

Bronze, meanwhile, stared daggers at Clara's paunch pissant of a father and made damn sure his sparkling smile reflected every ounce of sinister glee and pride he had for the male's daughter.

The king shifted his gaze back and forth between Bronze and Clara, but the scrape of adjacent chair legs on stone brought everyone's attention to the male at his side.

Lord Raff.

The lycan lifted to his feet in a slow, measured movement that forced everyone's eyes to track his great height. One hand was still holding a wineglass, which looked like it belonged to a child's kitchen set in the ruler's massive paw, while the other was folded behind his back in some bullshit display of diplomacy. An expectant and unsteady silence stilled everything around them.

The dude wasn't anything close to a bull in a china shop. No, he was more of a Kangal, the kind of ancient livestock guardian dog with a spiked collar and a quiet temperament that attacked without notice and wouldn't bat an eye if a few livestock occasionally got picked off in the process . . . after running through a meadow of demolished china.

Bronze's smile melted into a sneer, and he positioned as much of his elbow and upper body in front of Clara as he could without undermining the authority her shy voice had worked so hard to muster this night.

"Yes, lady. King Halpin has informed me of these Betrothal Games you have enacted and which, by agreement with your father, I am to compete in if our alliance is to come to fruition." The male took another sip and rounded the backs of the dinner guests' chairs but never took his black eyes from Clara. "Tell me, do you know why the inner circle that has journeyed with me consists of only fifteen lycans?"

"I do not, my lord." Her admission rocked unsteadily out of her throat, causing the king to smile in satisfaction.

"Piotr, the most lethally precise longbowman in my arsenal, was called away right before we were due to depart for your lands. His younger sister, Anya, was injured while attending classes at one of the human community colleges. She was studying finance and hoped to one day use her expertise to see whether human tactics could be applicable and helpful to lycan business structures. She wished to become a financial facilitator of sorts, aiding other lycans in their businesses to help them understand how to become more profitable, how to scale up their earnings, and learn when it was appropriate to hire more staff or to let employees go. These are skills that are much needed among my people if we want to survive into the future of the types of commerce the world seems to be heading toward."

The matter-of-fact tone sent off warning bells throughout

Bronze's skull. All too quickly, he remembered he'd left his weapons in his room at Clara's request, and the lycans were not ones to use utensils to eat, preferring instead to pick at their food with their fingers. There wasn't a knife in sight.

But he still had his angel fire. One flick of a thought and this asshole's scruff was going the way of a barbecued dodo.

Lord Raff ambled closer to them and put his empty wine-glass down on the table in front of one of his males, a large blond lycan with a military fade, bulbous chin, and icy eyes that seemed to miss nothing. Without preamble, Lord Raff purloined the male's wine and brought it to his lips. When he downed the drink in three large swallows, he set the glass back on the table and returned his focus to Clara.

"Do you know how she was injured?"

"You know she doesn't, asshole," Bronze interjected.

Those black orbs cut right to Bronze, and Lord Raff's smugness took on an edge of hostility. "Let me guess. The demigod."

"I'd bow, but I just ate." Bronze patted his stomach indolently. "Wouldn't want to get anything twisted in there and wind up with indigestion."

"Bronze, please," Clara whispered.

"No, lady. If this male is to be your supposed champion, perhaps some perspective is in order. I should have clarified. Forgive me. My best longbowman returned home not to be at his sister's side but to help bury her. You see, on Anya's way home that day, she shifted into her wolf and traveled through the forest at the northeastern edge of California, as was her usual habit. It is not a human public hunting ground, mind you. She and all of my people know better than to traipse through any of *those* woods, but it leaves precious little left for us to live and hunt in safely. But not so little, mind you, for the humans to hunt in kind. Apparently, their laws are nothing more than poorly governed suggestions. Despite their legislation regarding the ban on hunting wolves, it is still done. The canines, and us when in that form, are viewed as exotic prizes, revered for little more than our pelts and bragging rights from one human hunter to the next." Raff rounded the corner of the table and halted his advance a few feet in front of Clara, then clasped his hands behind his back. "Anya, unfortunately, was no exception."

Bronze had to give it to the asshole. He knew how to command a room and pause for effect. While Bronze had no wish to diminish the loss of another soul, whether lycan or mortal, and truly felt the death of the innocent female as keenly as anyone in the room, he also saw the warlord's play for what it was: more goddamn strategy.

"I am sorry to hear that, Lord Raff," Clara offered with deepest sincerity. "I meant no disrespect."

"Of course you didn't, and that, my dear, is the problem. We, as lycans, have spent far too much time in the human lands living as if our own people didn't matter, as if we are not also worthy of respect." He swept a brawny hand out to encompass all at the table. "How many here have suffered from human hunters and poachers over the years? From what your king tells me, your circumstances are not so different from ours. Relegated to living in the forest lest humans find you and learn that there are stronger, faster beings out there that could tear them apart if given the freedom to do so. Forced to trade and barter with those who would see us annihilated just for the opportunity to share one-tenth of the wealth they enjoy so freely. I'll admit, our territories do not boast the former glory they once did. Our numbers are dwindling to the point where it has become easier to remain small, remain hidden. Though it pains me to say it, the west has become a sparse and dangerous place for lycans and will worsen should we continue to take the easier, less abrasive paths available to us."

The hall fell silent in anticipation of Lord Raff's next words. When none came, a far more shocking thing happened: the warlord dropped to one knee before Clara. His large thigh was nearly as broad as the side of a barn and level with her bent waist as she sat in front of him. A meaty hand grabbed up hers and hovered it possessively in front of his bearded jaw. "I have learned, lady, over many centuries that the easy things are not worth having."

The kiss wasn't brief. It was slow, insistent. A fucking brand that marred her beautiful skin. Affection had no place in what Bronze was witnessing, and the dark shadows in Lord Raff's gaze promised the same.

This was another move. A power play. A message.

Heat punched up through Bronze's core. He was going to rip the asshole's arm out of its socket and make a tripod of the lycan leader—*after* his angel fire singed off all the important bits and fed the well-done meat to a few deserving coyotes.

His fire was there. It was *right there*, punching against his core, yet the power of it was no stronger than the lit end of a cigarette.

What the fuck?

Bronze tried again, calling on his angel fire, summoning it, roaring for it, but the flaming tendrils barely licked beneath his skin.

Not good. Not fucking good.

Sweat mottled the back of Bronze's neck. Amid his panic, Lord Raff dropped Clara's hand, who promptly swiped it back. Then he stood and walked over to stand behind the male whose cup he had drained of wine earlier.

"King Halpin has informed me of the Betrothal Games, and after consulting with his advisors, I have been made aware that I am to compete for your hand in mating. It is an honor I do not think you yet understand the magnitude of. With our union, princess, these great lycan territories will finally join as one and see the prosperity long denied them. No longer will we cower in our forests or wallow away under the ineffectual laws of an inferior species. We are lycan, blessed by the Moon Mother!

And thanks to you, princess, your people will have the opportunity to witness the true strength of what the next generation of *lycan* leadership shall look like and who will usher them into a new wave of security and affluence." Despite directing his words at Clara, Lord Raff kept his eyes on Bronze and punctuated the power of his stance. Most notably, his very *lycan* stance.

The king stood to join the warlord. "Thank you, Lord Raff, for your insightful words. We all pray to the Moon Mother for the soul of young Anya and that she be welcomed back to the sanctuary of the moon's embrace with all due expediency."

Lord Raff bowed his head in acknowledgment.

"Now, there is one small final matter of business before we can resign for the evening. My daughter has chosen her champion, the demigod Bronze. Lord Raff has delighted me in accepting the position as a second contender. Therefore, it is only fitting to reward our guests with another esteemed opportunity to demonstrate the true power of the lycans."

Bronze seethed against both the power that wasn't surfacing and the power that was playing out before him.

"The third selection, as is the will of the king, will be none other than Lord Raff's second-in-command, Byron, and the fiercest, most devoted ally among the western territory lycans." The king held his hand out, gesturing toward the brawny blond male seated in front of where Lord Raff stood.

A perfectly placed knight in a game of chess.

The king lifted his wineglass. "The games will commence in three days' time. Whosoever wins all three obstacles shall win the hand of my daughter, as well as the allegiance of my kingdom."

CHAPTER 19

Clara's foul mood swirled around her in a fog of frustration. Not only did the air in her chamber hang thick and bitter over the pointless adornments and fluffed-up furniture of her supposed station, but it also burned the back of her nose and throat with the stinging truth of what she faced.

What she *truly* faced.

The eager morning sun had taken its liking to her quiet room for some reason, shining through the window with a cheerfulness that belied the sad realization of her circumstances. Another day, another dawning enlightenment that though she'd grown up under her father's rule and spent her lifetime studying the manipulative maneuvers of his males, she simply couldn't hack it when push came to shove.

Her wolf prowled about in her mind, just as restless. After their evening meal, Clara had said her goodbyes and bolted for her room, where she promptly locked herself away to shed hot tears of feminine embarrassment. The session hadn't been an entire lost cause, however. Though low in number, there were a few moments of clarity where her wolf had calmed down to the point that Clara could sanely evaluate just where the encounter with Lord Raff had gone awry. Once she started there, she told herself that whatever brave new logic that had taken hold of her brain and had charted this course for her in the first place would surely come back around like a hired transport who'd left a passenger or two behind by mistake. Except it didn't.

Clara walked to the floor-length mirror, her steps slow and ghostlike, afraid to encounter what would stare back at her. Was there something about her innate appearance that instinctively identified her as a dupe? This morning, she'd gathered her hair into a high ponytail before brutally securing the thing into the tightest bun imaginable, lest it prove to be the reason the two males currently holding the power did not take her seriously. Not a stitch of makeup touched her features, which wasn't unusual, as she never cared much for the stuff. Surely, that would be less of a distraction, right? Less frivolity to lend to her form. Or would a sharp cat-eye slash of black eyeliner deliver a sharper statement to the males? If she recalled correctly, the ancient Egyptians were quite fond of kohl rimming their lids, as much to widen their eyes and command attention as it was to protect themselves from the sun.

Oh, nonsense. Clara could tattoo skulls and crossbones beneath her eyes and her father would likely not notice. Similarly, whether she wore skirts and sweaters or her preferred leather trousers and loosely tucked tops and tunics, she didn't think her wardrobe would paint her as anything more than the foolish fraud she'd been labeled as at that dining table last night.

"Oh, for goodness' sake," she huffed, swatting her reflection away and pulling a sleeveless emerald-green tunic over her long-sleeved white shirt. But as she pulled each wooden toggle through the small leather loops on her bodice, another tumultuous worry tugged back. Hard.

What if she couldn't maneuver the pieces on the board the way she'd planned? Lord Raff was a ruthless sort, that much was clear. And her father seemed more than happy to fall in line with whatever the brute had in store. It was obvious the westerner had strength and command on his side. All her father had to bring to the arrangement was a bit of money, some arms, and a kingdom full of people tired and jaded enough to follow the hand that fed them.

The king, her own father, had no qualms about playing her like the pawn he no doubt imagined she fancied herself to be.

A pawn. Not a queen. Never that.

Even Bronze had proven that point so eloquently and in front of a foreign audience. She'd started so strong too and was prepared to fire back at her father's decidedly intentional glossover of the games. And she'd done so. Boldly. Quickly. Gladly. But she hadn't been prepared for Lord Raff's tale or, perhaps, the warlord himself. No, his ruthlessness struck the heart of her emotions, for how could she abide suffering akin to what he'd described of the poor Anya? Clara would be no better than the hunters themselves if she didn't feel some small semblance of remorse.

In the end, it was Bronze who had to step in and fielded the floor on her behalf while her stunned silence dragged her back to the starting gate. For any other person, his interference would have been a blessing. For her, it was just another brutal reminder of why she'd sought him out in the first place. Her plan had always been one of manipulation, hadn't it? Bronze should have been nothing more than a game token to move around the board as she saw fit. A smiling shield and witty mouthpiece for her to govern her people through once they were mated.

But he had been there for her and had publicly raised his voice against those in power who sought to silence her. It was, in every sense of the word, heroic. Then why did she feel as if, in saving her, he'd only succeeded in humiliating her in other ways?

Do not think about his mouth on you or what his hands pulled from your body.

That, too, had been the other reason for her sleepless night. Somewhere between being ushered into that medical suite under his strong arm and brazenly baring herself to what his skill wrought, there had been a quiet sense of, yes, completion but also happiness. A light and airy joy she'd not known before, one that wouldn't see her miserable for the sake of the greater good. Instead, he'd only seen to her comfort, her requests, and that was only *after* she'd made the rash decision to finally chase what both she and her wolf wanted for once in their lives.

Ugh, did she want more of Bronze? Was that at the root of what had kept her up last night? It would be a massive problem if she did. An error of catastrophic proportions.

It didn't help that she excelled far more at making errors than fixing them.

Clara wrenched the door open and made her way toward breakfast, though she was loath to return to the scene of her mortification and wondered how she'd feel if her and her father's situations were reversed. Could she *truly* be the one to shame another so publicly if it meant her end goal would be achieved? Would that be who she needed to become? A ruthless, heartless, manipulating deviant with no moral compass except for what rang true in her mind, regardless of the consequences? Would she need to continue that ruse with Bronze and manipulate him into the player her people needed?

Boy, did she need a coffee and perhaps one of those extra-buttery croissants the cook prepared when her father wasn't keeping tabs on the butter stores. Anything to prevent her mind from trying to balance out the scales of the mess she'd gotten herself into.

The struggle continued to bumble around her brain while her stride—and stomach, thankfully—led her safely toward her destination. A few rooms down from the staff's quarters, a door swung open, and Bronze spilled out into the hallway, looking far more perturbed than she'd seen him the night before. Back then, his tight features had shown a cheerful restraint, as if what was happening in front of him didn't matter, because he was happily going about murdering someone in his mind. Now, however, his face was drawn, downcast, with deep furrows pulling at the corners of his brows.

"Good morning," she said.

He stalled out a bit, then turned around. "Oh, yeah. Good morning."

"Are you well?"

"Sure. Peachy keen."

"Your injuries have not healed fully, I take it?"

"Nah, they're good. Bit slower than usual, but I'm all patched up."

"That is good to hear."

They walked in silence for a few beats, and Clara nervously nibbled at a cuticle, stalling for however many steps she could scrounge up before she'd have to face her father and Lord Raff again.

"So, uh, about last night . . ." Bronze said.

There were certain words said in a certain order that were so triggering for a female, they might as well have an altogether different, truer meaning become the new definition. Like any male, Bronze's particular lilt to the expression was heavily seasoned with one underlying note: regret. It was unmistakable, even down to the tired way he dragged his body down the hall. Whatever strength she'd known him to possess had been replaced with the weight of poor decisions in the new dawn's light.

The sinking feeling that had started off her day continued to pull her down further, except this time, it had the foresight to rake claw marks across the burgeoning bloom of hope and fondness she'd begun to harbor for the angel. "What about last night?"

"I wanted to know what your plan was."

Her . . . what? "My plan . . ."

"Yeah, given the parameters of our arrangement and the bomb that exploded yesterday. I know you didn't expect any of it, and I want to make sure we're okay. I hadn't planned on stepping out of line, but I kind of couldn't help myself given the situation, you know?"

A bomb. Was that what he was calling what they'd shared? The single-most mind-altering encounter she'd ever experienced with a male was, in his eyes, little more than an explosion with a blast field that left a wave of collateral damage in its wake? Clara swallowed past the hurt tightening her vocal cords, surprised that he was beginning to mean enough to even warrant the biological reaction.

Was his part in her pleasure just a manipulation, too? A throwaway space on a game board he had to pass through anyway, so why not engage in the play?

The hair at her scalp seemed to pull inexplicably tighter, worsening the tension headache already beginning to form. By the Moon Mother, she wished she could just claw the bun out, shift, and run as far away as her wolf would carry her.

It would be so easy to run. But then the words from Lord Raff floated over Bronze's inquiry, until they flared hot in her mind. *Easy things are not worth having.*

And she *had* been easy, hadn't she? All it had taken were a few charming looks and a fair amount of skin on display on his part and she'd fallen prey to his tempting manipulations.

Clara halted mid-stride, leaving Bronze to continue several paces ahead of her. White-hot rage stung her eyes and wound tightly around the part of her that was coming to care for the male.

How utterly simple of you, Clara, to think you meant anything more to him than the honor-bound duty of his celestial station.

She tried to swallow past the tension stiffening every muscle in her body, until the whispers of his words from yesterday penetrated through the toughening fibers of her mind.

He'd called her the viper, hadn't he? Well, perhaps it was time to embrace that persona. As she pushed down the hurt and rejection, her remaining strength cleared some headroom for another emotion: determination. Yes, she could be the viper. She would choose when to strike, when to wound, and when to kill.

"Are you having second thoughts, warrior?" Her tone was colder than the polar ice of her wolf's ancestral homeland.

"What? What are you talking about?" The look of shock twisting his features was almost genuine. Almost.

Clara clenched her fists and buried them in the pockets of her tunic. "You claimed you were honorable."

"I *am* fucking honorable. I pulled you out of a river, didn't I? Where the hell is this coming from, Clara?"

"You tell me. Is the behavior you demonstrated last night indicative of the tenets of your species? You'll have to inform me because the only frame of reference I have includes a very small sample size."

Auburn waves danced around his chin in whips of disbelief as he shook his head. A play of emotions flickered across his heated gaze like the flames of a funeral pyre. "Something happened. This isn't like you. Did Raff say something after I left last night? His room's down the hall from yours, isn't it?" Then he stepped forward with a heat of his own and made to grab her shoulders, but she quickly stepped out of reach. "What did he do to you?" His eyes pleaded for a scrap of something with which to make sense of her reaction, but she was giving him none of it.

"Do you still agree to honor our arrangement?"

"You know I do," he said thinly.

"Good. Then we'll continue on as if last night never happened. I'm sure Polina, wherever she is, will be grateful for your continued devotion to your honor."

The feathered brush of her tunic's hem against his pant leg as she whirled from him might as well have been the roar of a human freight train. No longer hungry, she stormed away from the direction of the hall and ran out of the keep, toward the closeted patch of forest her wolf needed.

Only when she was fully engulfed by the safety of the familiar blue spruces and mighty oaks did she manage to rip her clothes off and let her wolf take over.

The soul-deep howl of agony that the creature bellowed into the open air was unexpected, yet unavoidable.

Her wolf, it seemed, wasn't the only part of her that had shifted.

CHAPTER 20

Bronze had a fucking Black Friday receipt's worth of items that had done nothing but follow his sluggish ass around for the two days and change that Clara wouldn't speak to him. On a good day, it would have been hard not to take the spurning personally, but now, on the day the first game was due to take place, it was proving impossible.

Turned out, he had been right. Like the viper he'd pegged her for, the female sure as shit knew just when and how to wound. When she fired her parting shot at him and flung Polina's name into the chaos of his confusion, it hadn't just ignited his mental kindling. No, it'd obliterated his thoughts on a cosmic level, sending them to the furthest reaches of his past and present so there was no hope of collecting his sanity again.

All she'd left him with was the dim outlook of a future he'd momentarily lost sight of. Well, fuck that and the horse it rode in on, which was ironically the very creature that was clopping along outside the arched window he stared out of. Somewhere between his phone and celestial powers having left their letters of resignation, he'd begun to get wise to the fact that something was very, *very* off about how the lycans lived.

The window to Bronze's dormitory faced south and overlooked a wide meadow flanked by densely packed forest. Not unusual. What *was* unusual was the well-trodden dirt paths that snaked from behind the keep and trailed in intersecting coils along the outskirts of the meadow into the tree line. He tracked a horse-drawn cart or two, which wouldn't have been entirely unusual for a culture that didn't use electricity, except for the cargo they carried: six thirty-two-gallon rubber garbage cans, a stack of mounted cardboard signs with arrowed phrases like *Restrooms* and *VIP Seating*, and a driver sporting a Boston Red Sox cap, stained utility pants, and a cigarette that needed to drop its ash two horse shits ago. The more Bronze spent time exploring the territory, the more he got the sense that the lycans lived in some bizarre twenty-four-seven Renaissance Faire, complete with ye olde functional privies and a whole lot of finger food.

Something was going on in that meadow, however, as more and more carts, supplies, and lycans were finding their way to its center. Bronze could only assume that was where the first game would take place.

Which would have been fucking great if Clara hadn't left him sitting outside her door for two days twiddling his dick and offering up apologies for sins he hadn't known he'd committed. Bronze let his eyelids fall closed and, for the millionth time, replayed their—was it even an argument?—so he could desperately search for some piece he'd missed. She'd meant to wound him. That much was clear. But why? Threatened animals always lashed out. Had he threatened her in some way?

When he'd woken that morning, his body had all the coordination of highway roadkill. It'd started when he got out of bed and promptly knocked the extinguished lantern off the small nightstand after he inadvertently flung his blanket too wide. Then there was the old-man bend-at-the-waist boot debacle that came with bodily groans no male who still had one foot out of the grave should ever make. The entire routine left him hobbling as if he'd just tried to power through one of Chrome's He-Man weightlifting sessions and his muscles had gone on strike for being overworked without the promise of rest-related overtime pay. For some reason, his powers hadn't regenerated overnight as they should have, which baffled him given the sheer amount of stone and cement walling off the place. There should have been more than enough metallic minerals and elements for his celestial power to draw from, for his metal to connect with, and yet his tank had been drained to E. The cold realization hadn't quite carried to the rest of his awareness until he could no longer ignore the magnitude of his energy drain.

The last time he'd felt anything remotely close to a decent charge on his power was following the few hours of sleep he'd managed to snag back at the den the night before he and Clara set off for the lycan lands.

So, yeah, he hadn't exactly been in the best of moods when Clara had come at him with that honor-bound warrior nonsense, especially after he'd lost a fair bit of sleep fuming over how Lord Raff and her father had pulled the wool over her eyes. It'd been clear from her quiet trembling during dinner that she hadn't expected the maneuver. The change of play was a dirty power move that greatly altered the trajectory of Clara's plan in the males' favor, and like hell would Bronze stay silent while they trod all over her. He certainly didn't have a reputation for keeping his mouth shut, so why start then?

But it was the morning after, when he'd seen Clara's tense expression, with her white hair pulled back into a no-nonsense bun and a look of dogged disappointment playing across her features, that he realized just exactly how much she appreciated his outburst.

That was to say, she didn't.

She needed him to come to her defense about as much as he

needed to own a seventh motorcycle, but hell if he'd been able to keep from throwing himself in front of any hurt aimed at her.

And then it had all backfired somehow, with her launching the honor-bound-warrior missile straight for the part of him that had forgotten why he was even there in the first place. The pain of the blow was nothing compared to the little redirection number it did on him. Though it hurt—physically fucking *hurt* —to see her storm off like he was the enemy she sought to liberate her people from, it was the reminder he needed to turn his attention to those he *could* help.

His brothers. Malik's memory. Polina.

Bronze turned his back on the scene outside the window and walked across the room to the notebook he had tucked away in his pack. The only good thing that had come from the past two days of Clara's cold shoulder was the surveillance he'd been able to do around the property. The king's keep wasn't overly large, owing to the fact that the northeastern population of lycans was probably no bigger than the population of Aurora. The stone structure and its surrounding property reminded him a lot of a regional high school campus, stretching up to three stories max. Long tight hallways with neatly ordered and predictable bedroom doors made up the bulk of the perimeter, while the center of the structure held more of its meat and pota-toes: annex, kitchen, receiving room, dining hall, armory, general common spaces . . . and two doors he'd never seen anyone go in or out of.

Winner winner chicken dinner.

He was willing to bet his brother Steel's brand-new espresso maker that one of those doors housed the royal coffers, where the relic was most likely located.

Bronze consulted his notes one more time before flipping the notepad closed. After whatever the hell games he needed to play this morning, he'd start his search there.

A low resonant horn blow carried among the stones of the

keep. A quick peek out the window revealed lycans herding toward the meadow in the manner of tailgaters filing into a stadium.

Shit. Guess it's time.

Bronze suited up as best as he figured and marched out into the hallway—directly into the path of Lord Raff. The male's meaty shoulder collided with Bronze's collarbone. The resulting spin made a carousel of the stones around Bronze before he managed to throw a hand out and catch his balance.

The western lycan hadn't stopped moving, hadn't even stopped to look at who he'd just nearly clotheslined, and Bronze saw why. Lord Raff walked with the stature of a lion and the breadth of a bear. His was a slow-footed stride that encompassed an innate challenge of its own. Unmovable. Unshakable. Uninterested.

Unmatched.

Bronze bared his teeth and grabbed whatever handle from his weapons vest was closest, ready to let a cacophony of curses and his dirk fly at the back of the asshole's head, when Clara's startled voice stilled his movements.

"Bronze! What do you think you're doing?"

Her loose waves and that half-corset/linen shirt number were back and barreling toward him at an alarming rate. Tawny eyes he hadn't seen for days were blown wide with worry.

Huh? Was that worry for him*? After verbally cutting his balls off and beating him with the set?*

"Firing off my shot, that's what. Lord Asshole needs a lesson in manners."

Then her eyes flew to the knife in his hand and carved out a connect-the-dots image that only stretched her features into a more alarming configuration. "Are those all your blades? *Metal* blades?"

He blinked. Then blinked again. "Um, yeah."

Okay, it was his turn to be confused. Right on cue, as if to highlight his bewilderment, another horn blast bellowed throughout the stronghold. The last of the lycan latecomers scurried from doors and hallways, eager to grab a seat for whatever the hell waited for him on that field.

Man, he really hoped it wasn't bears. His fondness for wildlife only went so far.

Then, like a magician frantically pulling scarves from a top hat, Clara began stripping Bronze of every weapon in sight and some not so in sight. When she came at his thigh holster with her fingers curled and her nails out front and center, he twisted away with a yelp and leaped back, making sure his junk was well out of clawing range.

"What the hell, Clara?"

"Off! Get it all off! Right now!"

"Okay, but tell me why first. Hey, easy."

"Hide them. Melt them. Do whatever you must do to make sure no one but me sees them. If you're caught with those weapons, they'll kill you on sight."

Once he'd finally managed to grab up her hands to prevent them from taking out more important bits, he urged as much calm as he could muster into his voice, even though a slight buzz of warning was beginning to work its way into his ears. "Let's talk about this. You've seen me with my weapons before and never said anything. It was *you*, Clara, who chose me as your champion to compete and then refused to speak to me for two days, which we *will* have a discussion about once today's competition is over. You're not getting out of that so easily. But we'll get to that. For now, why would someone try to kill me simply for being armed?"

"You don't understand," she said, shaking her head back and forth.

Damn right he didn't. "So make me. Talk. I don't think there's much time before I'm due out there."

Clara's eyes fell shut, and she sucked in a deep, labored

breath that did as much to calm her down as it did him. Which was not at all. When she opened her eyes, they were lit with a stern awareness that told him whatever came out of her mouth next was something he most definitely did not want to hear.

"You already observed that there is no electricity here. That is because, as I tried to explain to you once before, certain things in the human lands don't agree with our lycan makeup. Electricity is one of them. It affects our ability to shift and connect with our wolf, so we cannot live with it."

Bronze gripped her hands a bit tighter, suddenly finding a great desire for something to anchor himself against. Even as the weight of his daggers and firearms pulled down on his straining muscles, which still struggled to support what only a few days ago had been like a second skin, a part of him knew what Clara was about to reveal.

Knew it and was conversely strangled by the implications of it.

"What else doesn't agree with your kind?"

Clara's eyes bore the subtle sheen of a female who was equal parts frightened for her sake and someone else's. "Metal."

Excited cries and energized murmurs rose up throughout the makeshift dirt-caked arena, teasing the treetops with an anticipation the forest and its inhabitants seemed to have not known for some time. Wooden bench seats, erected in haste, lined up in bleacher-like fashion around a cordoned-off enclosure and groaned beneath the bouncing bodies of exuberant lycans. Those unlucky enough to grab a front-and-center seat were apparently unperturbed by that fact and still roared their enthusiasm from the ever-pressing crowd spreading out from the arena in a burgeoning bulge.

Bronze focused on none of it. It was all white noise eclipsed by the pounding truth bombs that Clara had dropped on him right before he'd entered the ring.

There was no metal anywhere in the lycan lands. And wouldn't you know, his little viper princess had been spot-on about one thing: she *had* tried to tell him earlier that certain things didn't agree with their lycan makeup. He had surmised as much about electricity, which seemed relatively harmless if not annoying, but fucking idiot that he was, he'd missed her use of the plural. *Things.* He'd never bothered to ask what other things.

It had something to do with their blood, she'd informed him hastily as she hid his weapons in his room and all but dragged him by his bicep toward the practice field. To his astonishment, lycan blood contained no metal, which was why consistent exposure to metal didn't agree with them. It didn't harm them, per se, but over time, the contact suppressed their lycan natures and prevented them from shifting into their wolf forms.

It all made fucking sense now as Bronze stood at one side of a dirt circle and peered at the crowd of mismatched lycans. There was no metal anywhere, not even on their clothing. No zippers or metal fasteners of any kind. It was why there was such an assortment of old-world linen tunics and leathers mixed with heavily modern drawstring khakis, vinyl, and whatever the latest polyester trends were. There were male lycans in baseball hats and T-shirts sitting next to long-skirted females in animal-hide cloaks. All at once, other pieces he'd filed away as odd began to surface. The strange black blades of the kitchen knives moving across cutting boards. The stone hearth of a stove combined with the notable absence of a proper aluminum ventilation hood.

The knives hadn't been made from some well-patinated carbon steel. They were ceramic, just like the wristwatches he saw peeking out beneath the chefs' coat sleeves. Likewise, the few weapons he had seen on the king's guards were either carved stone, whips, wood, or bone. He'd just never bothered to wonder why.

And then there was the giant blinking light of a newsflash that Bronze was still kicking himself over not realizing. The king's stronghold. The thing had the look of an impenetrable stone fortress, and Bronze took for granted that, as they all resided in the Fucking Granite State, the materials they'd used were surely granite as well, a stone rich in aluminum and alkali metals.

Wrong. So incredibly wrong.

Limestone. The whole place was built from limestone and cement mixed with the stuff. And limestone, *so* fucking unfortunately, was a non-metallic mineral.

In short, he was completely cut off from the earth's metallic elements, which meant he couldn't regenerate his celestial powers or call on them to manipulate metal in any way.

Which further meant that he was essentially no more powerful than a mortal.

A mortal who was still battered and bruised and now took up a very prestigious spot in a game where he had to best two warrior lycans without his metallic armor, angel fire, wings, or weapons.

Fuck.

King Halpin stood from a raised seat and held his arms up wide, silencing the crowd instantly. Clara sat by his side and kept volleying her gaze from one competitor to the next in worried assessment.

Bronze hadn't spilled the beans to her directly, because what kind of champion wanted to broadcast their weaknesses to the one they were about to fight for? But it was in her eyes, the way they swept across the playing field and never stayed too long in one place, as if searching for a way out . . .

Yeah. She knew something was up. He'd learned the hard way just how brutally sharp her perception was.

"We are here today to bear witness to the first of the Betrothal Games. This trial, like the others to come, shall be one that exemplifies the first credo of our monarchy." Beside the king, Pascal unfurled a burgundy banner decorated with moonstone embellishments. In the center of the tapestry flowed swirling opalescent text proclaiming, "With power, we run."

Running. Shit. His tired and barely healed calf tightened further in protest.

"I have devised a course that shall test the endurance and speed of each of these chosen competitors: Lord Raff, leader of the western lycans; his second, Sir Byron; and Bronze, the demigod." His name was underlined with a mouthful of scorn usually reserved for tax collectors and door-to-door pest control salesmen. "The objective is simple: retrieve the prized relic of our monarchy from the anointed table in under sixty seconds."

Wait . . . the relic was *here*?

It was a testament to just how fucked up his situation had become that Bronze had entirely missed the damn thing sitting right in front of him. Sure as shit, though, the very moonstone relic he'd last gotten a good look at in the den's clinic sat nestled within a perfect plum-colored velvet cushion on a small table directly in front of where the king and Clara sat.

Bronze and the two other competitors stood at the far sides of the arena. Lord Raff and all his two-hundred-and-seventy-five pounds of silent ego anchored the left position, eyeing both the relic and Clara. The male didn't pump his fists or work the crowd for applause. The rank boredom in his expression was tinged with far too much smugness for Bronze's liking, and *that* was saying something. To Bronze's right was Byron, who had already squatted down into a wrestler's stance, right leg behind him and arms out front, ready to tackle and torture whatever got in his way. And then there was Bronze, who was operating at an appallingly poor percentage even by mortal standards.

That relic was practically glowing at him, begging him to come snatch it up and take it far away from anyone and anything who didn't have a one-way trip to the Empyrean on their bucket list. All he had to do was run faster than two lycans —two *bulky* lycans who, on a good day, would only be slightly slower than Bronze.

Unfortunately, it was a far cry from being a good day.

Bronze surveyed the field. Were they just supposed to run across the dirt and grab the thing? Or was the objective to all arrive at once and wrestle it free? If that was the case, he'd fail before he'd even get his rear foot off the ground.

But why the hell would the king have them just doing relay races? Wasn't there more to a lycan's endurance than that? Or was it the speed that mattered, not the distance?

Dammit. He didn't have time to figure this shit out.

The king turned over an hourglass, and as soon as the pink sand began to funnel through the glass waist, a horn blared.

A blond blur overtook Bronze's periphery. Byron was jetting across the dirt, elbows bent at ninety degrees, palms flat, thumbs up, arms poised to pump and propel him toward the relic. Raff bolted as well but took a different route, one that carried him away from the soil spray of Byron's kickbacks.

Bronze should move. He needed to *move*, but none of this made any sense.

Think, asshole, and do it fast.

Byron was already halfway across the arena, his stride confident and his momentum gaining. Bronze jogged forward, hoping the action would at least shake loose the thing that was bothering him so much about the way the ground looked. Beneath his feet, the packed earth was solid and easy to get traction on, but up ahead, the soil seemed . . . different.

Bronze glanced at the hourglass. One-third of the sand had fallen already, soon to be half. He picked his heels up and pushed against the screaming in his leg from the gift the coyote left behind.

The explosion catapulted a plume of dirt high above him. Debris dimmed the sun's meager offerings through the partly cloudy sky.

Bronze skidded to a halt, nearly twisting his ankle. "What the fuck?"

Byron had been thrown back ass over tea kettle, his legs spiraling in a cartwheel midair worthy of a Cirque du Soleil acrobat. He landed a few feet behind Bronze with an unceremonious thud, while Bronze and Lord Raff had both taken a knee and covered their heads against the spray of soil and stones. Throat-choked grunts tore out of Bronze as more debris scraped trenches into his skin.

Hushed silence settled over the arena as the shock of their situation began to sink in.

Explosives. In the field. But how was that possible? Every bomb he knew of, and many he and his brothers had fucking made over the years, required metal detonators or, at the very least, metal casings.

Byron's low groans carried over the settled dust. Bronze risked a glance back and was surprised to see the male still had all his limbs attached. Oh, there was plenty of blood, and the lower half of his right leg was definitely facing the wrong way, but if the dude had stepped on something he shouldn't have, there wouldn't be a leg at all. Unless . . .

The sand had cleared the hourglass' halfway point now. Then Bronze locked gazes with Lord Raff, who not only observed the time as well but was also a good twenty feet from the relic compared to Bronze's fifty.

Both males pushed to their feet, but neither of them moved. The field was a hot mess of debris and churned earth. If there was something buried under there liable to blow, there was no way to tell based on how the ground had been impacted from the first explosion. But the relic was still there, sitting on its little velvet fainting couch like the world hadn't just blown up within the three-rail horse fence perimeter they were trapped in.

Bronze lifted one foot, more to test the vibrations in his leg than to see where he could safely put it down again, when a sharp glare nearly blinded him.

Huh?

Up ahead, Lord Raff was toe-stepping it from one foot to the next, making slow but sustained progress toward the relic.

Shit! Bronze was torn between forward momentum and the clarity that had eluded him since he'd first gotten there, the answers dancing just out of reach like a snowflake.

Snowflake . . .

Snow . . .

Freshly packed snow. A reflective surface . . .

The cogs clicked into place with a jarring *clank*. Bronze squatted down and Very. Fucking. Carefully. blew on the dirt that concealed what had been winking at him. The small circular glass object his puffs revealed caught the last trace of light through the clouds, blinding him with a whole lot of nostalgia he hadn't tapped into since after the mortals' World War II.

A glass landmine. A one hundred percent non-metallic explosive that hadn't seen its heyday since 1945, if he had to guess. Completely undetectable to metallic sensors and sensitive as fuck to any sort of friction.

Byron hadn't stepped on it full out or he'd be in pieces, but he must have disturbed it in some way. Perhaps some dirt he'd kicked up behind him had landed on it and had been just enough to detonate the thing.

Well, that was one sick way for the king to get around the lycan race's giant handicap. It also made Bronze realize just how high the stakes were and just how far Clara's father was willing to go to secure his interests.

Up ahead, Lord Raff had closed in on the table. Another leap or so would see the asshole holding Bronze's prize. If the lycan was bold enough to risk the jumps.

Bronze scanned the field, trying to hunt out any other signs of where the mines might be buried, when his mind snagged on what he'd mentally noted earlier.

Friction.

The mines needed friction to detonate. The fences surrounding the mines, however, were made of white PVC. Smooth. Friction*less*.

Only a third of the sand was left in the hourglass.

With his thighs burning, he squatted as deep as his hamstrings and glutes would take him and leaped several feet to his right, where the nearest fence panel was. Thank the mages for his well-callused hands, because those puppies snagged on the top rung. With a painful effort, he twisted himself up to his feet and balanced the tips of his toes on one of the five-inch square posts. Then, like a shot, he was sprinting. His long legs stretched in great smooth strides as he ran, unstoppable, from post to post, gaining momentum with each leap. The PVC was a flush touchpoint for his toes, propelling him and his freakishly long body high and far along the arena's perimeter until he was within arm's reach of the relic. With a final vault, he flew through the air and landed precariously on top of the small table.

Between his legs, the relic lay cuddled up in its velvet bassinet, none the wiser.

And Lord Raff was standing right in front of it.

Bronze squatted down and quickly gripped the curved moonstone, which had grown warm from the earlier sun, then batted the lycan's hand away right before the final grain of sand fell through the bevel.

In true mob fashion, the crowd threw up a roar.

Even though his chest burned from the exertion and his legs were keeping him upright by sheer force of will, Bronze couldn't resist holding the pose for just one more moment.

He jutted his hips forward and smiled. "You know, if you wanted to grab my dick and compare parts, you could have just asked. I'm always up for a modeling session. Intimidation and inspiration are two sides of the same coin. I won't be offended if you haven't figured that out yet."

It was telling to see exactly what kind of ruffled Lord Raff truly got. He wasn't the flushed-in-the-face type, nor did he go all swole-bro and punch stuff. The mask of cold calm that settled over his countenance spoke of promised retribution but clearly at a time of his choosing and under his preferred circumstances.

It was a warning Bronze knew well, one he had bestowed upon many demon charmers. Chilling to see it reflected back at him.

"You talk too much," Lord Raff said evenly. "I will endeavor to fix that."

"Take a goddamn number, but do it *after* you fix your boy up. Oh, wait, I forgot. You have no problem sacrificing your own people for the greater good. My bad."

"Bronze!" Clara's desperate wail pierced through the crowd and nearly punched a hole in his chest as well. She was running down the short staircase that led from her perch, her white hair and cloak billowing out behind her. Tears ran in chaotic tracks down her dust-smattered cheeks, but the smile that beamed his way was bright enough to patch up every aching part of him, starting with the bruised muscle right in the center of his chest beating faster with every step that took her nearer to him. "Bronze!"

Damn, he loved hearing his name on her lips. After two days of radio silence, he realized what her voice actually did to him and how darkly it dimmed his day when she withheld it.

He slipped the relic's leather strap over his neck and rose to his feet, intending to leap back onto the fence post so he could climb over and get to her.

Too many things happened at once. Her foot met the bottom step on a roll that stole his breath and that of every person in the stands. Her balance went next, pitching her, and then his heart, over the side of the low fence and into the landmine enclosure.

"Clara!" Bronze leaped from the table and dove for her, watching in panicked horror as the fence made contact with her midsection and her top half hinged forward over the rung. Her long legs tangled in the cloak and followed suit, dragging her whole body down until she would soon be flat on her back in the arena, giving the landmine topography more than its fair share of explodable living surface area.

Bronze's legs were the first parts of him to connect with the slim fence panel she rolled over, and by the mages, he hooked the backs of his knees around that fucker in the tightest triangle hold of his life and threw his arms out behind her back, catching her as she fell flatly into his grasp.

A deafening silence settled over the arena.

"Fuck. Clara. God*dammit*, Clara." He scooped her tightly to his chest, burying his head, his nose, everything he needed to fucking breathe, into her sweet, trembling body. "Don't do that to me again, princess. You hear me? Don't you do that to me again."

He didn't know whether the subtle nod he felt against his chest was her agreement or more of her uncontrollable quivering.

As he balanced his ass on one and a half inches of fence, with Clara in his arms and the relic around his neck, he knew he'd reached a tipping point of his own as well.

Because her sweet woodsy scent—a scent his body imagined was just for him—was tinged with something he'd never expected to smell on her. It was a scent that he'd first observed when he'd been shown inside the arena but had thought nothing of it then.

However, that was long before the last five seconds of her life that almost shaved the last years off his.

He knew what it was now, and that terrified him almost as much as being powerless.

It was the scent of true unbridled fear.

CHAPTER 22

It had been hours since the game had ended, and Clara still wasn't sure who had comforted who. After the final horn had blown, signaling the conclusion of the competition, healers had immediately seen to Sir Bryon and transported him to the infirmary. Lord Raff, not surprisingly, refused medical attention and instead walked off the field, sought the king out, and donned the same impassive expression that had been molded to his face since the first sands fell.

At least, that was what Bronze had told her, and she had to believe him, because she didn't know how long she kept her face buried against his chest or how long he held her to his. By the Moon Mother, she'd never known such terror. Her ankle rolling, the dusty ground coming up to meet her, the percussive explosion that quieted her heart, the spray of earth blanketing Bronze's back. All of it. Events and moments that spiraled out of control all because she'd pulled the pin from her grenade and started on this journey because she'd thought it would be easier to level the corrupted structure her father had built than rebuild on its shaky foundation.

And now *she* was the one who couldn't stop shaking.

At some point, their bodies had moved. He'd shifted off the fence rail. Her feet found the dirt. But up above? She was still a trembling mess and refused to let go of Bronze's neck until she could be absolutely one hundred percent certain all his vital pieces hadn't been blown from him. The two of them had eventually settled, though she couldn't say whether she settled him or he settled her. All that mattered was him lifting her higher into his arms, carrying her away, and gifting her with the warmest kiss of a new memory: her exhausted body being surrounded by familiar lavender-scented sheets and placed in her bed, lips rimmed with trimmed softness pressed against her forehead, and the sweet oblivion of finally crashing under the weight of adrenaline.

She'd awoken several hours later, alone and floating on a bizarre storm cloud of ease and discomfort. Food had been laid out for her on a glass tray by her bedside. It had taken several tries, but Clara had finally been able to grip the teacup without either scalding her lips or spilling the hot liquid all over herself. What little rest she'd managed to force upon her body had been fitful at best but ultimately beneficial. Her thumbs had been the first to stop shaking, but it took a while before the rest of her fingers had calmed enough to resume their normal functioning.

So close. She had been so close to losing him.

She brought the ceramic to her mouth, but even though its angled rim cut into her vision, it did nothing to block out the sight of Bronze taking the field as the extent of his powerlessness truly sank in. His face had fallen into a quiet panic that reminded her of, once again, being tossed out to sea. The way one's vital organs would shift to brace for an impact the body had no control over and was helpless to prevent.

It was a true paralysis in every sense of the word. What shocked her the most was just how acutely her body had mimicked what she imagined he was feeling in that moment. Her heart stalling out, breath slowing, eyes widening, lips summoning whispered prayers to the Moon Mother. All of it flashed in a blink, and then there was an explosion, followed by the inexplicable: an angel flying through the air. *Her* angel.

She'd been prepared for none of it. Not the cunning ingenuity of her champion, the brutality of the games, nor the ruthless indifference Lord Raff had shown after the bomb had gone off and his male was injured.

And then she understood why: because the ruler had not only expected to win, like all proud males would, but had appeared silently astonished when he didn't, as if a promise had been broken.

Clara's stomach roiled when she'd finally figured it out, watching where Lord Raff had placed his feet throughout the arena and how he somehow knew to stick to the perimeter, which enabled him to be far more sure-footed than the other two males.

Someone had informed him of the game's makeup, and since the law stated that the monarch was the only one who could devise how the games were constructed, it didn't take a genius to sort out the snake. Her father was giving his champion the upper hand as a way to even the already uneven score. Yet another thing Bronze had warned her about, but she hadn't considered, and damn her, she'd nearly lost Bronze because of it.

It was a situation she'd have to rectify immediately.

A soft knock at the door jarred her thoughts away from the nightmares plaguing her. Clara's bare feet brushed the smooth stones as she went to answer it.

Lada, one of her staff, had her hands full with items that needed stowing, chief among them the moonstone relic still tucked into its velvet cushion. In her other arm, piled high, was the stack of linens Clara had asked for when she'd woken a short time ago, thinking a bath might ease her mind.

"Lady," Lada said, offering up the folded bundle.

"Thank you." Clara took them and huddled the warm fabrics to her chest as the elderly woman dipped her head and proceeded down the hall. She'd only made it about a dozen or so steps when Clara's gaze shifted from the woman's rhythmic *step-shuffle* gait to Bronze, who had been leaning against the wall outside her door. With his arms folded across his chest and one enormous black boot supporting his weight against the stones, he looked like a male not to be messed with, and yet there he was, ripe and ready for the messing. How long had he been there? *He* was the one who'd urged *her* to rest, after all. Did he not trust she would do so?

Those questions floated away as quickly as they arrived, however, as she drank in the sight of him. By the Moon Mother, she'd not seen him in hours, yet it felt like lifetimes, the way her chest constricted and her heart threatened to leap from her chest. His gaze was searing and held a heaviness to it that felt like a caress. Or a claiming. Whatever it was, her mind and body accepted both possibilities with great inexplicable eagerness.

Bronze pushed off the wall and proceeded toward her, urging the very air around him to part in his wake. Her damn heart fluttered some more, then stilled slightly when he paused in the hallway to focus on what Lada held. He observed the old female a moment longer as she turned right at the end of the hall and took the stairway down to the royal coffers, where the relic was always stored. Clara smiled at that, warming to the blooming fondness for this male who clearly had concern for the elderly lycan's ability to descend stairs safely.

Clara was beginning to think she'd chosen poorly, for what male could be so kindhearted and selfless?

Hers, apparently, and she was losing reasons by the minute to regret her decision in choosing him.

Was it so terrible to want him, though? To admire him and all he'd done for her?

Oh, to hell with it all.

If this was her most egregious sin, then she'd go to her doom happily.

Her wolf sent tingling bays of confirmation and encouragement to her frozen limbs, urging warmth into her body that she no longer cared to ignore. If they were being forced to play by others' rules, then she was certainly within her rights to make up some of her own.

Clara turned into her room but left the door open, offering up the unspoken invitation she had no idea whether he'd accept. Would he understand what she was asking? Would he decline out of respect because he was too much of a gentleman to cross that particular boundary?

Only the Moon Mother knew, and Clara was driving herself crazy trying to figure out the mental faculties of another female —a deity, no less—when she hardly had a handle on her own.

Please. Just this once, let me have something for me alone.

Clara barely made it to her dresser across the room when she heard heavy footsteps follow close behind and the soft click of the door's closure.

He was there, in the room with her. She'd recognize the heavy presence at her back anywhere, even after only a few days. He'd made his mark, and there was no removing it. He'd survived and won the first game for her. Tomorrow would be the second trial, but for now, he was there, and the fact that she'd almost lost him made her desperate to ensure it didn't happen again.

CHAPTER 23

Clara lifted her eyes, met Bronze's gaze through the mirror, and saw a gathering storm reflected back at her. It was a punching answer to any doubt that had still swirled around them in the hall, and she'd be damned if she'd let her analytical mind cough up any more questions.

She needed to feel, not think. Lord knew she'd done enough thinking for a lifetime, and it had nearly gotten them both killed.

"Bronze—"

"Tell me you want this, princess." He prowled closer to her, never letting his eyes leave hers through the glass.

Before another question could rise up, she swatted the thing away like the pest it was and met his challenge with one of her own. "Tell me you don't want this, warrior. I think it is, perhaps, something we both need tonight."

"Not perhaps," he said sharply. "Absolutely fucking sure. I need certainty from you because I got out of the regret peddling business a long time ago. So I'll make this crystal clear. Tell me you want my hands on you."

"Yes," she breathed.

He stepped closer. "Everywhere."

"Yes."

"My mouth. Tell me you want my mouth on you."

It was no longer feet that separated them but the barest of inches. Then his chest bumped against her shoulder blades, and the heat from it nearly incinerated the fabric of her dressing gown.

"Yes."

"Every—"

"Yes, everywhere. I want all of you, but you must promise me one thing." She turned around to face him, and they both sucked in a sharp breath when the tips of her rigid nipples scraped across his chest through the fabric of her dressing gown. He didn't shy away from the contact, and neither did she. The challenges were simultaneously issued and accepted.

A single arched eyebrow was all the answer she would get, and Clara's wolf growled her lupine approval. This male, with his eyes flashing citrine and a body born of an immortal power so primal it predated predators, was hers to command, to invite inside of her.

"Promise me you won't stop."

The declaration hung heavy between them, like an irrevocable oath. For a moment, she feared he wouldn't accept her terms, that he was too honorable. Then he gifted her with that devastating half-smile that always managed to unravel her, and she knew she'd never be able to forget that grin for as long as she lived.

His fingers tightening on her hips was the only warning she got before his mouth was on hers. They met in a clash of kisses that was so violent, so needy, it could have brought down the stronghold with the force of it.

Her hips writhed in a seeking rhythm against his, searching for the only answer she and her wolf would accept. When the blunt barrel of his sex pushed her farther against the dresser through his trousers, she groaned into his mouth with eager frustration. Yes, *this*. This was what she wanted. Something larger and heavier than anything she'd ever been allowed to experience. The bruising nature of it didn't come close to matching any of the curse words she knew, but leave it to her champion to come up with some creative new combinations that had her flushing hot in places he hadn't yet touched.

"Mages above," he growled into her mouth as his hands skimmed over the peach-colored silk dressing robe. It seemed he tested every part of her, analyzed every curve, and then doubled back like some studious engineer. Not that she was complaining. Then his fingers curled into the open V neckline and paused, like a roller coaster cresting the top of its first rise before eventually plummeting to the ground.

"Yes. Do it." She licked a trail of heat down his throat, then slid her tongue into the divot at the base of his neck. His slight jolt made her gasp as well, and it was all she could do to keep her fingers coordinated enough to rip the shirt from him.

A moment. Bronze only granted her the briefest of moments to drink in the bare strength staring back at her from the lean slabs of muscle that caged her against the dresser. *Beautiful.* The observation, however, cost her greatly, though not particularly dearly. He captured her mouth again, and before she could chase his kiss any further, her dressing gown was pulled apart in one effortless tug. Silk separated from silk as the chilly air shocked her skin and his hands lifted her bare bottom to rest on top of the wood.

Her cry of surprise was savored by the drugging pulls of his mouth. Good. She didn't want him to interpret any howls of her body as anything other than complete and total exhilaration.

"Ease back, princess. I've got you." With one arm banding behind her waist, the other went to his pants. Working with more diligence than she thought possible, he freed himself and pressed the weight of his cock against her trembling inner thigh.

If she thought herself hot before, she had no idea how scorching the brand of his iron would feel against her sensitive skin. He held it so firmly to her she could feel the steady pulse of his life force beating into hers.

But her focus soon faded when his tongue, that infuriatingly masterful tongue, swept a trail down the column of her throat to her bare breasts. "Call me a bastard, but I haven't gotten these perfect tits out of my mind." He said it as if it was a sacred vow of some kind, where vulgarity was eschewed for the truth of his words. He dipped his head again and anointed each nipple with a reverent kiss one might bestow upon a king's ring.

Clara didn't know desperation could be painted so painfully on a male who was on the brink of pleasure, but it was there all the same. If he looked at her again, she was certain her heart would shatter into a thousand irreparable pieces for a male she couldn't ever truly hold, not with what lay in store for them both.

So, instead, she sought out his cock, which still lay hard and molten against her inner thigh, and gripped it firmly.

"Fuck, Clara."

Taking her cues from the way he leaned into her hold and how his forehead tightened into ripples of tension, she strengthened her grip and brought him to her slickened entrance. "You promised, Bronze."

"Oh, I know. I fucking know, princess. It's just . . ."

"Just what?"

He shook his head before settling his misted forehead against hers. "It's just a bit of paradise. I definitely don't deserve it, but I'll gladly take it."

Paradise. It was an elusive wonder she'd never allowed herself to contemplate.

"I should like to know it, too. Take me with you."

Bronze's chest grew impossibly bigger with each breath he took, as if some great part of the male had been stripped away and all that was left to sustain his breathing were giant industrious bellows.

"Always."

His surge forward brought something neither of them expected. His eyes sparked with flashes of citrine that battled for dominion with the dim candlelight's flames. The effect painted his bold features in an otherworldly tenderness. With the other few males she'd taken, she'd always been left as she was when she'd started the journey: unimpressed and unchanged.

With Bronze, however, Clara knew as surely as she knew her own name that none could ever come after him. None had ever made her feel altered at the cellular level and transported her over such exhilarating edges. She knew that every shudder racking her body was a sensation only granted to seldom few in the universe, and fortune had smiled upon them both.

Warm puffs of exertion tickled the side of her throat. She burrowed her hands beneath the back of his waistband, grasping the firm strength of his backside and urging him closer against her core.

Full. She was so incredibly full, and yet a part of her could never consume all of him. The rigidity of his spine, the stiffness of his shoulders, they all told a tale that this night would be one for quiet commiseration. A near loss for both parties. A close call that highlighted far more than either was willing to examine fully.

"Bronze. By the Moon Mother, you feel good. So full, but so good." She would have preferred her words come out strong and secure, like that of a future monarch's declaration. Instead, they came out raspy and desperate, fueled by far too much tenderness than she'd like, but hell if she could pull it all back now.

She cantered her hips forward, chasing his as he levered out of her in slow deliberate strokes. It took a moment, but soon they'd found their rhythm, and her forbearance on Bronze's sensuous pace soon lapsed into what she could only describe as a measured frenzy, if such a thing was possible.

He was holding himself in check, however. It was clear as day, painted all over the carved lines of his biceps and shoulders. This male, this warrior, had a preference for a punishing pace, but he kept it reserved, restrained, for her.

"Tell me," he rasped out and seemed to search her face for any sign that she was uncomfortable. "Are you okay? Does it feel—"

"I'd be better if you cared for me the way I need to be cared for." She gripped his shoulders and brought her body flush with his in entreaty, easing the swell of her breasts against his hard planes. "Like you did in the infirmary. No one's ever made me feel like that."

They locked eyes once more, her wolf's stare battling for understanding and encouragement with his sentinel's gaze. And then the world shifted. It was as if she released some sort of pressure valve, letting loose whatever bottled-up hesitancy still lay between them.

"Always."

Again, he said that word, but this time, she was not prepared for the shifting undulation of his muscles beneath her fingers.

He ran his cock wild then, spurring it on like a stallion. Great arcing thrusts drove her higher onto the dresser. Every bounce of her breasts was caught with an eager lapping tongue as he piled into her with more energy than she thought a male capable.

He was feverish in his pitch and called forth her wolf's rutting growls. Fingers curled into grappling claws, dragging him closer, deeper, higher, until a resounding cry stormed through her throat and erupted out of her.

Much like before, every part of her quivered as she was thrust toward a release she had only one frame of reference for. She quickly discovered that, while beyond good, that sample size was far too small for adequately assessing the explosion she flung her arms around him to restrain herself against.

"Bronze!"

He dipped his head into the crook of her neck and released a deafening roar in time with her wolf that pummeled her body with a force strong enough to bifurcate atoms. There were waves, and then there were tsunamis, and it was clear that, with his final eager onslaughts, they were both riding the latter.

When his soothing fingertips snaked around her back and pressed a trail of support along each ridge of her spine, she didn't know whether to slide off the dresser into his arms or let him move her however he liked.

Either option would have been fine.

But when his hand drifted to her arm, turned over her wrist, and held it up for his inspection, she thought she saw some of the light leave his eyes. A brief dimming of the eruption they'd just shared.

He swiped a thumb over the pale blue veins beneath her skin, and she tracked his pupils as they narrowed when his light pressure didn't reveal what he'd perhaps been searching for.

"What is it?" she asked. "Have I done something wrong? Because I have to be honest, I don't feel like I did something wrong."

"Perfect," he whispered, offering a gentle kiss to the inside of her wrist and wrapping his still-shuddering warrior's body around her. "You're perfect."

Content in his honesty and the song he plucked from her body, she smiled at the male, *her* male, and lamented the loss of all she held within when he carefully slid out from her. Before her bare feet had time to hit the stones, he'd shucked the rest of his clothing, scooped her into his arms, and settled them both beneath the warm blankets of her bed.

When she was fully wrapped, warm, and settled nice and snug against his bare chest, she wondered how long it would take before his pupils relaxed again and that light returned to his eyes.

Soon, she figured. If she had any say in things, it would be very soon.

CHAPTER 24

Perfect. The echo of that word boomeranged around Bronze's skull, touching points north and south with such force that it was liable to decimate any remaining foundation he'd fortified within. Clara was absolutely so fucking perfect that the truth of it was strong enough to make him forget the whys of what had gotten him there in the first place.

What would be if she was my why, though? Would that truly be so terrible?

He dragged his lips along the thin underside of her wrist again just to see the way her lips tried to resist curling into the smile he always knew he could coax out of her. He'd learned that neat little trick the first time he'd had her up against the dresser. After that, their coming together had been new and wild and savage. Her nails digging into his ass, the delicate bruises of his grip against her hips. The sex was needed for the both of them, more to affirm just how fucking short life could be. His own had flashed before his eyes when the fall of Clara's frosted hair had flipped over that fence rail, and even though he was technically immortal, that didn't mean he couldn't be killed, rather that his life was just long-lived.

It all would have ended in a heartbeat, however, if Clara had fallen on the minefield.

After that, no amount of holding her would ever have been enough to erase the could-have-beens from his mind, so he made to consume her instead.

Dresser, floor, dresser once more, up against the wall, then her gripping the door of the armoire as he blanketed her from behind and swore out oaths of a different kind against the back of her neck. For untold hours, they had been locked together in a storm with no ending, only moving in the rhythms of frantic need. And every opportunity he had, he would offer up a kiss to that smooth patch of flawless skin at her wrist, unmarred by any sort of soul bond symbol that would have sealed his fate and would perhaps stand to make sense of what was happening to him. Why he couldn't access his power . . . or, take it one mindfuck further, imagine a future that somehow, someway still saw her by his side as anything other than an aloof monarch.

But when they joined, the symbol hadn't appeared as it would have had they been soul bonds. *His* symbol. The mark of his celestial name written in the ancient language of the Empyrean. A distinction that only manifested when two souls contained matching sparks of the Eternal Flame and joined together to create the soul bond.

Yeah, none of that had happened for them. And honestly, it was fine. Good. Great. Better than great, even, because who the hell needed to lug around any more disappointment? And with these checked bag fees? No thank you. Bronze was so sick of the stuff, he'd rather lick Lord Raff's boots than haul around another ounce of regret.

As Bronze lay on his back, with Clara's naked form tucked to his side and her delicate fingers running idle swirls across his chest, he was relieved. Honestly and truly relieved. If Clara had been his soul bond, once she fell asleep, he wouldn't have been able to consciously leave her bed to follow the path of that serving female who had been holding the relic. He would have been glued to all of her sensuous sides and said to hell with the Empyrean.

As that wasn't the case, however, he was fully obligated to get swept up by the shock of seeing the relic bob down the hallway like a bag of laundry. The sight had hit him almost as strongly as the sight of Clara, clean and healthy and breathing, staring back at him with those molten maple eyes and a gasp on her lips as he moved within her, moved together.

As complicated as it was, he'd decided to stay with her then. And soon, he'd make another decision, then another, and another. That was all life was anyway, right? A series of choices that moved unattached nomads around the playing field while they hoped like hell they still got to pass Go and snag that eternal two hundred dollars every now and then.

Because she wasn't his. Fate had made that perfectly clear, and he had no right to make choices that included her beyond what they'd agreed.

"Lord Raff knew about the mines," Clara said softly into the cushion of her puddled hair against his chest. "I wasn't entirely sure what I was seeing at first, but after the explosion, the way he maneuvered around the field was so intentional that there was almost a pattern to it. Always on the tips of his toes, always two steps forward in quick succession, then a step to the left, followed by two more quick steps forward, all near the perimeter of the arena. Why would someone step in such a pattern if the mines were truly random and if he had not known they were there to begin with?"

Bronze snorted. "Sounds like the king's been sharing some secrets."

"Unfortunately. It also means we must assume that for the

two games to come, the king has favored his champion unfairly." She lifted her head, and the worried wings of her brows nearly unstitched him. It was the look of a daughter's lost respect for the male who had raised her. "I knew he was capable of this sort of treachery, but I just didn't think he would stoop so low as to use it in such a public setting."

"A threatened male can get pretty damn desperate."

"So can a gray wolf lycan and, apparently, a Canadian timber wolf lycan as well. Ridiculous, really, given their lineage."

Bronze tucked his chin to examine her more closely. "Lineage?"

"My father is a gray wolf lycan, descended from the gray wolves of North America. Fierce, powerful, incredibly dominant and stubborn. Lord Raff, on the other hand, is a Canadian timber wolf lycan, descended from the wolves of western North America and what the humans call Alaska. The timber wolf lycans are one of the largest wolf species in existence, well acclimated to the harshest climates, and are viciously protective of what they deem as theirs."

"Makes sense. I'm ashamed to admit it, but I had no idea your culture was so rich and varied." Bronze dragged his fingers through her silken strands, playing with the frosted tips. "And you, princess? Where does the other half of your kind hail from?"

"The Arctic."

"I knew you were coldhearted, but I never knew you were an original ice queen. Ow!"

Clara pinched his side but quickly soothed the small hurt with a gentle hand over his skin. "Everything is a joke to you, isn't it?" Her faux ire was masked by a genuine chuckle, however.

"The world would be an infinitely harder place without levity. It's been scientifically proven. Laughter creates dopamine, or what mortals call the 'happy hormone.' Dopamine serves as a sort of buffer between cortisol and adrenaline. It's what helps push us through to the finish line and why people who laugh often are more likely to accomplish hard things."

"What a wondrous world your mind is, truly."

"Honey, you have no idea. It's like Disney World up there." He winked, and she hid her smile against his chest, but his muscles still twitched when they picked up on her concealed joy.

"I am an arctic wolf lycan, descended from polar wolves that roam among the frozen tundra and forests of the great north. I believe the nation of Canada calls that area Queen Elizabeth Islands. My mother was also an arctic lycan, and I inherited most of her genetics, but she was mated to my father out of obligation. Her ancestral homeland is small, and there is only so much to offer in trade. Agreeing to mate him was a way out for her, as well as an opportunity to learn more of the world, despite the reputation my father had long fostered." Her stiff swallow paved a hard track against Bronze's ribs. He knew what was coming at him real fast and wished like hell he could stop the pain that was about to rise up anew for her. "She died in childbirth with me."

"I'm sorry, princess." He gripped her tighter, offering his support in the form of his strength.

"It was a long time ago. But now that you know what sort of lycan Lord Raff is, you must take extra care with him. His wolf is the most efficient of hunters, with unmatched speed and endurance, let alone the sheer size and weight of him. If he should let his lycan free, there won't be anything you could do to—"

Bronze froze as her words slapped something free in his mind that, up until then, he'd been fair-to-middling at not hyper-focusing on. But then she whipped the sheet off his vulnerability and started poking at the tender flesh he hadn't had time to care for yet. Bronze hinged up off the bed and shifted her off him. "Are you saying you don't think I can beat him?"

"You don't have your powers, Bronze. There's no metal allowed here, and metal is what you need to regenerate. You told me so yourself!"

As if he needed a fucking reminder. Had he not proven that he was more than capable of adapting? That he knew the stakes well enough to fight the battle before him, regardless of how much it differed from the one he'd prepared for?

"That doesn't mean I'm powerless. I thought I proved that to you, but I clearly didn't do a good enough job for you to actually believe me." Bronze threw his feet over the bed and punched his legs into his pants, then searched around for his shirt.

"Bronze, come back here." Clara wrapped herself in the bedsheet before trailing him to the door. "Let's talk about this. What did I say? I thought I was speaking a truth."

"Oh, you spoke a truth all right. Your truth, not mine. I gotta go. Better rest up before tomorrow's big day. Wouldn't want to embarrass you with a poor performance."

"Bronze!"

He slammed the door with a resounding *thud* and thanked the prime mages for solid oak construction. Despite what he said in there, he was *so* not strong enough to hear another plea fall from her perfect lips or see the respect she once held for him dim her eyes further.

There was more to a competition than the players, especially when there was an alternate game to be won. Bronze held on to that thought and armored himself with it as he made his way down the stairs where the serving lycan had gone earlier.

THE OLD STONES encasing the lower level of King Halpin's keep groaned with a pregnant energy that was almost predatory.

Every step Bronze took was heavy beneath the weight of unseen forces watching him. There was history here, encapsulated in the ancient limestone, and if Bronze was in any less of a hurry, he might have stopped to admire the scenery. Or at the very least put a palm up to the stuff and see whether the answers to his wishes would be whispered back to him. Yet left alone in the silence as he was, he didn't have the luxury of such fanciful exploits. Any thoughts about his powers that he needed to sort out would be best left for when he was in his dormitory and the back of his head was flat against the threadbare pillow on his cot.

Long-stowed images of Malik, and a few of Polina, surged through the mire of his mind as he examined the great oak door in front of him. Of the two doors he'd yet to see anyone enter or exit from, this one was the only entrance accessible by the stair-well the old serving lycan had walked down.

He didn't need Malik's shadow sensory ability to know this was where the moonstone relic had been stored.

It would be so easy to bust in, nab it, and make like he'd never been there in the first place. Clara and her father would have far too much going on to search him out, especially among the supposed human lands, where, deep down, the lycan leaders seemed to fear what they did not understand. Even if Lord Barf led the charge, he was not from this part of the country. Without the use of technology and relying on scent and inner fury alone, Raff would have very few resources available to go after Bronze.

And by the time Raff did pick up on his trail, Bronze could have that relic nestled safely in the sentinels' den, where Chrome and Rhode could put their massive craniums to good use and figure out how the hell to get them all home so he wouldn't have to wonder about Clara anymore—

"There are so many questions I *could* ask, but a wise lycan never offers up questions to which he does not know the answers to already, so it would be a waste of time for both of us." Lord Raff's quiet warning bounced off the stones, making the small hallway even more claustrophobic.

Bronze squeezed his eyes shut and cursed inwardly, not wanting to admit how his lack of celestial powers had allowed that asshole to follow him or just how right Clara's statement about him being powerless actually was.

Irony could fuck all the way off.

What Bronze wouldn't do for his sickle sword and a fully loaded Smith & Wesson M&P 9mm with the threaded barrel, no safety, and half a dozen magazines. Instead, he'd have to settle for his bare knuckles, fancy footwork, and big-ass mouth that had gotten him both in and out of more fights than the sky had stars.

Handy, that last asset. Truly.

Bronze turned his back on his literal door prize and pushed his punishing verbal weight into the lycan who had offered up his dance card. "If I didn't know any better, I'd say you had a crush on me. You know, if you wanted to cuddle, you could have just asked." Bronze spread his arms wide. "Plenty of me to go around."

Lord Raff stood at the base of the stairwell, unamused and uninterested. The stony lock of his forearms across his barrel chest was a challenge welcoming anyone to lock horns with him. And if Bronze wasn't in such a pissy mood, he might have taken the male up on his offer just so Bronze's body could stay nice and loose.

"Dances bore me, so I'll not engage in them." A stone-cold gaze to match the walls around them hardened on Bronze. "You are no demigod."

Shit. The assertion momentarily took Bronze by surprise, but eons of quick reflexes had taught him to suppress any sort of outward sign in the midst of the enemy. Instead, he stood silent, frozen, waiting for Raff to reveal more so Bronze could evaluate his next move.

Raff stepped away from the stairwell and, with his arms still crossed, began to walk in a slow semicircle around Bronze. "I have known a fair bit of power in my day, and you, my male, have none. Besides, I can think of no reason for a demigod to be seen skulking around the king's keep, patting down the door to the royal coffers the night before the second trial he is to compete in, or storming out of the princess's bedchamber moments before his little unescorted excursion down here. Unless, of course, his plan was to never compete at all but nab what valuables he could and flee in the night before the sun rose and no one was the wiser."

"Do you really like the sound of your own voice that much? Honestly, I know you guys aren't the techie sort, but you'd save your poor vocal cords so much effort if you could just record your boring-ass monologues and play them back at your leisure."

"Humor is the weakest of defense mechanisms. Jokes are often made to smooth over the most uncomfortable situations, such as imminent death or the catastrophic heartbreak of broken trust."

"Nah. You're just an asshole who hasn't had a reason to giggle since your second inadvertently tickled your balls. How is Lord Byron, by the way? Still . . . *kicking*?"

Despite Bronze's totally obvious and definitely intentional low blow, the icy facade he was hoping to score some cracks in held firm.

"Oh, he is healed. Timber wolf lycan blood is strong. We mend quite quickly, unlike humans and other *species*."

Bronze's veins filled with blood so heated, he was liable to explode and paint the asshole in Bronze's favorite shade of gore.

Raff raised a palm to Bronze, as if somehow sensing his opponent was on the verge of going nuclear. "Tell me, does the princess know you're down here, attempting to service her father's cache so soon after servicing *her?*"

"Shut your fucking mouth or I'll do it for you."

"No need. I've got all the confirmation I require, and soon, so will the king and his daughter. There is no reason to bother His Majesty with this bit of nonsense right now. The king and I are like-minded, after all, when it comes to goals and priorities." Raff prowled closer until flecks of russet twinkled in the torchlight within the thicket of his dark beard. "You see, *I* have never portrayed myself to be anything other than what I present. Strength, power, the need for an ally to unite the great lycan territories, and a willingness to rut with any royal female who comes with her fair share of land and—"

The punch split the skin on Bronze's fist, but the pain was well worth the satisfying crack of Raff's jaw as it swung in suspended animation from one side to the other, separating from that vital hinge structure that allowed the male to run his damn mouth.

Bronze braced his forearm against the male's thick neck like the iron bar he willed it to be and snarled at the lycan. "You so much as dream of her and I'll fucking neuter you with the blunt edge of those ceramic blades your kind is so fond of using . . . *after* I pummel your stones into flapjacks beneath my boots, you miserable piece of lycan filth."

"I wonder," the lycan mused calmly in between subtle coughs, "does the princess know how money-motivated you truly are? What would be if her beloved champion was not entirely the male she thought him to be?"

The knee that found its mark between Bronze's legs was Lord Raff's answer and warning to Bronze's ill-conceived threat.

Shouldn't have given him the fucking idea to go for the jewels.

As Bronze grunted through his foolishness and fell to his knees, with one hand protecting his groin while the other was fisted and poised to fly at the nearest chin, Lord Raff moved with eerie grace from the wall he'd been held against and marched toward the stairwell. "I'd wish you good luck, but I've never much favored the folly of it. I make my own luck. So, I'll just say this: may the best male win."

"Fuck . . . you," Bronze ground out, but his threat was gobbled up by the shadows left in the wake of Lord Raff's exit, as if even Bronze's words were too powerless to fight back.

CHAPTER 25

The morning sun chased away the lingering fog that had settled thickly over the practice arena. Damp dirt quickly had its moisture baked off, leaving a cool yet lightly packed surface on which the second Betrothal Game would commence. Tension heaped its burden onto Clara's shoulders, and the oppressive weight was beginning to become more than her wolf could handle.

Guilt made for an abhorrent support system. It truly did.

It had taken several precious seconds to realize the fault in her behavior from the night before. Unfortunately, time could never be called back once lost, nor could her words or the penetrating shock they'd struck Bronze with. And like any warrior, he took the hits well, barely letting on how deep the wound had really been.

But oh, she knew. She saw it in the puckered stillness of the lines at the corners of his eyes and how swiftly he armored himself with wit and fled the thing that wounded him.

She was that thing, that awful thoughtless thing, and now she was about to watch him walk into that arena for what may well be the last time, with the knowledge that her actions had already incapacitated him.

The entire situation eluded and confounded her, for her experience in groveling was limited to the profuse apologies she'd offer up to her father when he was displeased with her, regardless of whether or not she was at direct fault. But to grovel to a male who she not only respected but had begun to feel closer to than her own wolf at times?

In all their talk of being powerless, Clara had never thought the term would apply to herself, yet there she sat, primped and poised before an empty arena next to a king who'd rather barter his daughter off than love her. A princess in name only. A symbol.

A fool.

But not for long.

Clara squared her shoulders against the hushed murmurs of the gathered crowd and silently watched as the competitors marched bare-chested into the arena.

The shock of auburn hair pulled tight into a small bun at the back of Bronze's head gave her the confidence to proceed with what she had planned. And even though she willed those hazel eyes to find hers so she might implore a different, far more earnest truth into them than the one she'd spewed before out of panicked foolishness, she didn't let her disappointment show when they skimmed past her. Though it still stung, it was the least she deserved. She just hoped her cunning was enough to convey the full measure of her heart instead of the errors of her words.

The king stood next to Clara and, once again, raised his hands to silence the crowd's excitement. "We thank all who have gathered to observe the second Betrothal Game. Today's trial shall test one of the greatest attributes of our *lycan* heritage," he said, letting the emphasis on their species distinction linger in

Bronze's direction. "I look forward to shaking the hands of whichever champion can truly exemplify this credo."

Pascal stepped forward then and unfurled the royal burgundy banner with the words "With strength, we capture" held high for all to see.

Clara's stomach somersaulted over the knot of worry that had lodged itself there.

A strength challenge. When Lord Raff is almost twice the size of Bronze.

No, she chided herself. She would *not* discount the angel. If she did, then she was no better than the doubting female who'd broken the spirit of her male mere moments after he'd made hers soar to heights she'd never known before.

Taking the cue from her emotions, her wolf pounced on the kernel of doubt until it was nothing more than the whisper of a bad memory. And then, true to the lupine female's urges, she replaced her worry with new, far more accurate depictions of just how strong Bronze truly was.

Memories of his chest glowing and cushioned with more than enough strength to hold her trembling naked body above his as he eased and supported her over his thick arousal. Or positioning her with such care as he entered her from behind, much to her she-wolf's delight, and spearing her slowly, hunting out her release while holding back his own.

Oh, yes, her male had strength in spades, and didn't deserve an ounce of her pity or doubt.

Please let this work.

"Now, as you may have noticed, one of our champions is no longer able to compete. Sir Byron, Lord Raff's second, while mostly healed of the injuries incurred during the first Betrothal Game, still remains at a physical disadvantage and has, therefore, withdrawn." The king extended his hand toward the seat below him, where Sir Byon sat looking altogether indifferent, as if it didn't matter whether he was eliminated from a schoolyard game or the running for a job promotion. "We wish you all the best in your recovery, Sir Byron."

"I serve at the will of Lord Raff," the blond behemoth said with a monotone drawl and a dismissive shake of his fingers.

Meanwhile, Clara was seeing ten thousand shades of red at her father's use of the word *disadvantage*.

We'll see about that.

King Halpin clapped his hands together. "Lord Raff and Bronze the demigod are each wearing two leather armbands secured around their biceps. The goal of the game is simple: the first champion to capture both of the other opponent's armbands through a feat of strength alone shall be declared the winner."

But as the king sat back into his overstuffed cushion, Clara shot to her feet. "Before the champions can compete, however, each must be outfitted with a uniform of equal make."

She finally connected with Bronze's gaze then, along with Lord Raff's, her father's, and every other lycan gathered in the field.

"What are you talking about, Clara?" her father hissed.

Instead of matching his whispered words, she projected her voice even further, ensuring all in attendance could hear her. "I would like to echo the king's sentiments regarding how important it is that no champion is left to a disadvantage. While both males are to compete bare-chested, as is common among grappling, the looseness of their individual trousers may provide opportunities for injury. But not to worry, I have provided a remedy to the situation." Clara waved her hands toward two male attendants, who had been standing off to the side, each with a small stack of clothing in their hands. "With your esteemed permission, Your Majesty, the start of the game shall be delayed by five minutes to allow the competitors to change into the uniform fight shorts I have provided. And we must all thank the king wholeheartedly for his endearing determination to ensure that no individual, not even our chosen champions, should be at a *disadvantage* when competing for something so important as the future of this lycan monarchy."

With that, she clapped and clapped and clapped some more until every pair of hands had no choice but to follow her lead and weigh down the objection that was firmly poised on the tip of her father's tongue.

She had him. Oh, by the Moon Mother, she had him. Refusing her would not only go against his earlier words proclaiming fairness but would also undermine the integrity of the games and the cause they fought for.

"Very well," he muttered, then volleyed a heated gaze between Clara and Lord Raff, who communicated his form of displeasure while swiping the shorts from the attendant.

Clara sank back into her chair and felt the fire of her father's anger hot against the side of her face, but she didn't care.

Her part was done. She had succeeded in leveling the playing field, though she was still a bit put off by how stupid her father thought she was. Did he think she wouldn't notice the way one side of Lord Raff's trousers draped differently over one leg than the other? Of course the lycan was hiding something within them, and now both the king and Lord Raff knew she knew, too.

She could only hope Bronze would dispatch the lycan quickly so she could go to her angel. If she had to endure one more hour with him hating her, she was liable to leap into that damn arena herself just to win his favor back.

THERE WAS ONLY SO much denial Bronze could twirl around his noodle before he inevitably settled on two facts: one, his little lycan princess had just outmaneuvered his opponent in far fewer moves than he ever could; and two, they were both playing a very deadly game, one where lies were the currency and advancements were made based on the price of the bargain.

When Bronze had been instructed to remove his shirt and don the leather armbands, his a light brown while Lord Raff's were black, he wondered where the wild card was going to be hidden, because after realizing he and Clara had both picked up on the same cheater-cheater-pumpkin-eater vibe, it wasn't a matter of if but when.

The uniform swap was pure brilliance on her part and, judging by Raff's sour punim, dead on, as was what Clara's very public gesture meant.

A level playing field. Not an acknowledgment of one opponent's power over the other, but instead establishing that the true power was in the hands of the game and letting the fates decide who deserved to partake of it.

It hurt, the admission of losing his power, but not as much as how good it felt to unburden himself by lamenting his loss with someone else, even if it did mean the road ahead was steeper, harder, and, apparently, as he turned to face Lord Raff, paved with fucking ogres who had a preponderance of hair in the wrong damn places.

The familiar horn blared, signaling the start of the game, and Bronze lunged forward.

And feinted.

Lunged and feinted again.

Honestly, when the two of them came together, it was like an awkward middle school dance where everyone was holding onto shoulders and waists armlengths apart. Raff was physically larger. Nothing Bronze could do about that, and if he wasn't careful, that big-ass body would plow him into the dirt if the lycan even got so much as a whiff of the upper hand.

But Bronze had a longer reach. Best he could do was get in, jab fast, and tire the fucker out. Where Raff had strength, Bronze had stamina.

Two armbands were held in place by a bit of loose twine. That was it. All he had to do was outlast the snorting bull hurling toward him and swipe off two strips of leather. Easy peasy.

Bronze ducked and dove for Raff's bicep, snagging the edge of one armband with his middle fingernail but not getting enough of a grip to wrest it free. He jumped back quickly but was a hair too slow and couldn't avoid a swift blow to the side of his ribs.

"Fucking cheap shot, asshole," Bronze grunted, holding his side.

Raff smiled, all fang. "Quite."

After another few seconds or so of light-stepping it, Bronze crouched low, lunged again, then retreated. It took *for-fucking-ever*, but eventually, Raff started to show signs of wear. The widening nostrils with each breath, the extra second of recovery the male took before throwing a punch or two, with every third one regrettably landing where he aimed it. Despite the hits, however, it was working. Raff was slowly beginning to conform to Bronze's wrestling style.

Bronze had, at best, another dozen breaths or so before Raff would get wise to that fact, so he had to act. Now.

Hinged at the waist, Raff charged forward and snagged Bronze by the neck. Bronze dropped his arms and let his left one loosely settle on the outside of Raff's elbow, while he grabbed the male's wrist with the other.

Let him come to you. Make him think you're out of juice.

Letting his body fall lax, Bronze dropped his shoulders low but surged forward with minimal strength, just enough to make Raff think he was fighting back. It worked, and Raff stormed forward to counterattack.

Except Bronze had no interest in fighting back. Instead, he dropped his grip on Raff's right arm, put his hand to the ground to hold himself steady, and shrugged his shoulder away. The lycan lost his balance and his handhold on Bronze and pitched forward . . .

Just enough for Bronze to yank free one of the male's armbands before kicking out, rotating over, and pinning the lycan beneath him.

The crowd erupted in a cheer loud enough to be felt through the soles of Bronze's boots. But the loudest cheer of all came from Clara. He shouldn't have risked a glance, but he'd been about as helpless in that regard as any number of his overused muscles.

Goddamn, she was lovely, with a smile as bright as the moon and far too much pride beaming through her joyful expression for him to ever think for one second that she thought him to be truly powerless.

He was, though. Totally and completely. He knew that now and wasn't at all surprised she had him pegged long before he'd figured it out, though perhaps not in the way she'd originally meant it. When it came to her, he was truly and utterly power-less, and it was becoming enough of a damn problem that he wasn't entirely sure it was even a problem anymore.

She'd manufactured this whole event *knowing* her father and Raff would be playing by house rules, and she risked mages only knew what to ensure their treachery didn't grow roots.

She'd done it for him, not to highlight his deficiencies but to cut the tyrants off at the knees, and do so in a way that didn't incite a revolt or get someone killed.

Clara had figured out how to play the game so her opponents would have to fall back several spaces, all the while Bronze kept marching on at his assumed pace.

And he'd stormed out on her last night, with the taste of her still on his lips no less, like a tantruming teenager who was butthurt because he'd just been told he had to do his homework before he could play his four hours of video games on a weeknight.

Had there ever been a bigger asshole? He'd have to double-check with Chrome to be certain, but in that moment, he didn't think it was possible. Gold fucking star for him.

It was Clara who made Bronze realize what was about to hit him. Her eyes growing wide with shock. Her lower lip falling open. The screams.

Then Raff's growl came as he roared up beneath Bronze, reached over, grabbed him by the arm, and flipped him onto his back in a slam so hard it loosened Bronze's back teeth. Before he could move, Raff crawled up his body and knelt on Bronze's thighs, pinning him to the spot.

One tug down an arm, then another. Bronze's screams erupted as sharp claws raked through the soft skin on the undersides of his forearms, leaving bloody calling cards in their wake.

A rounded shadow formed in front of Bronze's vision as Raff leaned over him, blocking out the sun and bits of Bronze's sanity. "There is only ever one end. Remember that."

Two scraps of brown leather were tossed in the dirt at the side of Bronze's head, all while his brain had begun to clamor in time to the crowd's chants.

He had lost, and now he and Raff were even.

Which meant he was only one game away from breaking his promise again and losing Clara forever.

CHAPTER 26

The young female healer stood before Bronze, wringing her hands and begging him to hand off the job of wrapping his wounds to her care. "Are you sure I can't help you in this regard? I've already cleaned the gouges thoroughly. I recognize your preference to forgo any stitching of the flesh, and that is certainly your prerogative as the princess's chosen champion, but at least let me secure the binding. You are to give it the best chance at healing before the third game tomorrow, and I should not like the dressing to come loose while you sleep."

"Thank you, but there is no need. I can take care of my own wounds."

"Yes, sir." The head bow of disappointment was so heavy, it was almost—*almost*—enough to make Bronze feel guilty over turning away the kind healer. It was clear she cared deeply about her profession. After all, it wasn't her fault she got stuck with an ornery angel who'd just had his ass handed to him in the most public of settings.

The lycan closed the door behind her, leaving Bronze to admire the scene of his stupidity. The infirmary room they'd brought him to was much, *much* smaller than the one he'd spent time in with Clara when they'd first arrived. This one, with its butcher-paper-clad utilitarian cot and very little else, was likely for those who couldn't afford a side of office furniture with their injuries.

It was a perfect place to lick his wounds. Quite fucking literally.

The gouges Raff had scored into his flesh weren't the only parting gifts the male had left him with. There were just some things that stuck with a being, no matter how much time had passed. For Bronze, the sound of those two scraps of brown leather *thwacking* the dirt next to his ear would be the eternal metronome in his mind ticking back and forth between two of his most solid truths: *loss* and *mate*.

He sure as shit had enough in the first column to fill a black hole. The second column, however? That pain was about as fresh and murky as his newly appointed gashes before the healer had cleaned out all the gunk that clung to him from the arena. Over the eons, from time to time, he'd summon the idea of a mate to his mind and more so ever since Titan had been the first of his brothers to find his soul bond in his lovely female, Rose.

It had always been Bronze's duty, however, that would engage first, calling to mind images of Polina, but the thing was . . . the representation was always invariably a bit off. Long blonde tresses haloed over the slight stature of the woman he thought he recalled, but when he tried to narrow his focus, the best his brain could come up with was Malik's ugly mug stretched to fill out the face holding up all that hair. And Bronze had to believe there was more to Polina than the sum of her brother's features, but for the life of him, whenever his mind conjured up the word *mate*, it was his oath regarding Polina, not the female herself, that always floated to the surface.

Until recently, when a frost-haired lycan princess began

slipping into his dreams. With Clara, they'd tossed the mate moniker around freely, as if it was a frisbee to be played with. Whoever caught the thing in that moment was the proverbial keeper of the secret and actor extraordinaire, until they flung it back and could breathe a sigh of relief that the ruse was no longer theirs to uphold for a time.

Except, somewhere along the line, the ruse had stopped feeling so . . . ruse-y. It was in the feel of her hair, the taste of her skin, the strength in her back when she stood up against her father's oppression. In those moments, his heart had begun to clench more tightly, anxious and terrified for the time when he'd have to catch that frisbee again and pretend he didn't want to try the truth of the part on for size.

Maybe Raff had knocked loose more than just Bronze's back teeth.

"Bronze!"

For anyone else, a frantic lycan flinging a patient room door wide would have been enough to call not only security but the nearest Comic-Con convention to see whether they were missing some of their talent. For him, however, it was just enough to scatter the rest of the staff and afford him a measure of privacy with the female he needed to apologize to in a big fucking way.

"Hey, princess." Then he cleared his throat, trying to chase away some of the gravel. "Clara, look, I'm so sorry for how I—"

"I'm so sorry for the words I—"

The verbal collision caught them both off guard, casting an expectant pause around the small room.

Clara quirked her head to the side, and Bronze had to bite his lip to keep from smiling. It was easy to forget sometimes that his female was descended from canines and occasionally exhibited very canine-like mannerisms. Now was not the time to point it out to her, however. The prime mages had gifted him with a nominal amount of intelligence most days, but even he was smart enough to know to gird his loins if he let that observation about her fly.

"Why on earth would you be apologizing to *me?*" Clara rushed forward and started inspecting his bandaged arms. "I'm the one who said the most awful things to you. And you must know they were outright lies."

He opened his mouth to speak, but her raised palm silenced him.

"I know what you're going to say. That they were born from my emotions, and emotions don't lie, and yes, that may be true, but my sentiments were built on misconceptions and inaccuracies. They were words I believed at the time because I didn't know I could believe in anything else. Every male who's been in a position of power in my life has always proven that point ruthlessly. And it's all garbage. Believing something for the sake of believing doesn't make it true." She dropped her hands and clasped them in front of her. "True power does not pick and choose its recipients. It is not defined by role or lineage or—"

"Gender."

The look on her face would have been so beautiful if it didn't also crush him. *She still doesn't believe what she's capable of.*

Bronze cradled her face in his palms. "Listen to me, princess. It is indeed a rare thing to go up against one's father, let alone one's king, and publicly castrate him so effectively, all without a single lycan knowing. You want to talk about ruthlessness? About power? Oh, Clara, I wasn't angry at you, not truly. I was angry at myself for thinking I had made it this long in this realm on my powers alone. There was no way I was ever going to win that match, regardless of how you ensured a fair outcome. From the moment I stepped foot onto that dirt, my brain was already starting from a place of affirmed lack."

"It was?"

He nodded. "It's the first rule of any competition. If you start out thinking you're going to lose, then what's stopping you? All

I was focused on was the power I *didn't* have, the strength I *couldn't* summon. No shit I didn't win. All my attention was going toward what I was missing, so of course that's where my energy went, too. The whole thing was over before it started, and for that, I could never apologize enough. I cost you a match and may have jeopardized what you've worked so hard for."

Clara peeled away one of his hands and placed a tender kiss on his palm. "It's not over yet. There is still one more game. And you're wrong. We've *both* worked so hard for this. Whatever happens, it's something we'll face together."

Damn, he didn't deserve this. Not this soft and warm female who had just flung her arms around him, not the way his body curled around hers protectively as if trying on the part of mate for size.

None of it was his. None of it was real. But like he fucking cared at that point? If life had taught him anything, it was that second chances were not guaranteed. Sometimes the mages robbed you of the life you knew in order for many others to live theirs. Sometimes fate would strip your powers in order for you to prove your strength.

And sometimes a celestial goddess would break all the rules, claiming aces wild, and send exactly what you needed upriver.

"This feels right to me," he whispered against her hair.

"It does. It really does."

The rumble of his stomach was a fucking bullhorn of a moment killer. "Shit, sorry."

"None of that. I'd like to be finished with the apologies for at least five minutes. Let me go bring you some food."

For once in Bronze's life, he didn't argue and was more than content to let Clara walk away knowing she was just as eager to get right back in his arms.

CLARA WAS DEBATING between the apricot and the raspberry jam for Bronze's hunk of bread. The kitchens had cleared out from the breakfast rush, and the staff was enjoying the brief lull before the lunch prep, so she blessedly had the place to herself.

And also, quite fortunately, leftovers. She heaped the platter high with half a loaf of grainy bread, a wedge of hard cheese, two apples, and—oh, what the hell—two ramekins of *both* jams, grabbed the small coffee urn, and floated toward the door.

"Late breakfast, I see."

"Father!" Clara skidded to a halt and raised the platter high overhead, floating it above like a peacock feather on her fingertip. Once the items had stilled and the platter no longer swayed from side to side with the waves of the coffee, she brought it back to waist height and placed it on the counter.

The king jutted his chin toward the tray. "Is that for him?"

"For my champion, yes. He was injured, as I'm sure you recall. Lord Raff dealt him a difficult blow. I am helping him to heal and ensuring he is nourished in the interim."

"Does that require riding his cock as well?"

All the available air rushed from her lungs. "What?"

Her father moved into the kitchen, taking in the space as one would assess a recently inherited estate they had no interest in or use for. "Naivete does not become you, daughter. For once in your life, do act like you are a part of this family. You are many things, but ignorant is not one of them. Now tell me, has he gotten you with pup yet? Or is it too early to tell?"

The raging heat coursing through her veins aggravated her wolf to the point of nearly shifting. "How can you say such things?"

"Because I am the king," he snarled at her, bracing his hands on the counter. "A king who has made an arrangement with a foreign leader for your hand in marriage and, thus, an alliance to unite our kingdoms in a mutually beneficial arrangement. Raff brings the muscle and might, I bring the currency and your warm cunt. Did you really think you'd be able to outwit me with your little games and the demigod or whatever the fuck he is that you found like some lost plaything in the human lands?"

"Do *not* speak of him that way. He is more powerful than you can imagine."

"Powerful enough to dispatch the dozen guards I've ordered to stand sentinel outside his patient room after you left? He can't even manage to get rid of one lycan. How the fuck do you figure he can manage twelve and while injured no less?"

The dark stone of the kitchen walls began to creep toward her in painfully heavy increments. Even her wolf was pacing and circling through her mind at the claustrophobia of it all, her tail lowered and her whimpers pummeling Clara's nerves with a new sort of fear.

No, this can't be happening.

"I'll make this quick, as I haven't got all day. Unfortunately, due to your little show of *independence*," he sneered, "our subjects are expecting the Betrothal Games to finish in their entirety. However, if you wish for your champion to live to see the sunrise, you will agree to mate with Lord Raff, and the final game shall commence in such a way that the outcome will be secured in our favor. Oh, yes, daughter, I'm well aware you've caught on to my arrangements. But you are my blood, after all. So, rather than dispelling my tactics entirely, I rather thought this would present a good opportunity to bring you into the fold, so to speak. Give you a look at the family business, internal operations and all that."

It was all happening too fast. One moment, she was debating which jam she'd secretly been most eager to taste on her champion's lips, and the next, she was bartering for his life. Though, it wasn't really a barter, was it? No. This was pure unadulterated blackmail at its finest, from the male who should have been protecting her from the very beasts he was now subjecting her to.

But Bronze. Oh, Bronze! He'd never asked for any of this. All he'd done was save the life of a female who had begged him to do the impossible, and he'd followed her willingly for no other reason than altruism, a bit of responsibility maybe, and perhaps a small growing fondness between them.

Though it wasn't small on her part. That had never been truer than when she'd seen him fly through the air, bobbing on fence posts, to claim a relic in her name.

And now he would be killed for it.

"What is your answer, Clara? I have other business to attend to, and my guards are waiting. They have instructions that if they do not receive word from me by half past the hour, they are to breach his patient door and destroy him on sight."

Half past the . . . what?

Clara ripped up her sleeve and took in the time on her wristwatch. The bone-colored hand had just ticked past the twenty-eight-minute mark and was quickly closing in on the dreaded half hour.

"There's no time! How can you not give me any time to consider this?"

"Because there's nothing to consider. I will have my way regardless. I was merely giving you an opportunity to have a hand in your male's future before I secure yours. Now, what will it be? Will you play your part, or will I end his?"

Her heart forced the answer from her closing throat before the avenue for speech was lost to her entirely, before her head had time to analyze any possible alternatives, any way out of the hell she'd been dragged into.

The truth, when she was finally able to see it clearly, was mirrored back at her through the ashen reflection of her circumstances as they had always been. A broodmare to be won. A bloodline to be purchased.

Love had never played a part, and she was foolish to believe it would do so now.

"Yes." She sighed. "I'll do as you ask of me. Just, please, spare him. As you have remarked, he is not one of us. He is innocent."

The king assessed her with a smirk of satisfaction, yet no small measure of remorse. "*That* is yet to be decided. If he dies tomorrow, it will not be by my guards' hands. That is, so long as you cooperate."

She nodded, no longer trusting her voice to say anything that wouldn't end in Bronze's execution. As she walked out of the kitchen, trailing her father in stature and shadow, she never looked back at the food she'd intended to feed Bronze.

She couldn't bear to witness the flies that had no doubt begun to descend.

CHAPTER 27

As Bronze stepped out of the stronghold and into the drizzle-rain-drizzle combo that had made everything just wet enough to be miserable, he had the oddest thought about the arena. He had no idea why the concept hadn't come to him sooner, but now that it had, it made so much sense.

The place looked like the inside of a public toilet.

The circular pen had been thoroughly doused with far too much saturation for the ground to handle, which created a landscape of lovely brown smears. Small muddy ponds had cropped up throughout the practice ring, producing cylindrical shapes that seemed to bob among the matted-down earth beside it.

So, yeah, definitely a toilet. Only good news was that Bronze was about to step into the thing for the last time.

Except maybe he wasn't?

The warm rain mingled with the morning mist, which had no intention of getting gone any time soon. The lingering clouds hovered low above the arena and grassy meadow surrounding it, seeping through the outskirts of the forest like a mortal plague of gray shadows.

It was in front of that copse of trees that the crowd gathered —and everyone was silent. Like, pin-drop silent.

Bronze checked to make sure his bandages were nice and taut and strode to the forest's edge, wishing like hell he'd been able to see Clara at least once before the attendant had come to fetch him this morning. He'd not seen her since yesterday when a healer came to his patient room and informed him she'd been urgently called away. After she'd shared her apology with him and he'd shared half of his fucking soul with her.

The words they'd spoken had been buzzing around his mind ever since, until he finally allowed them to land.

When they did, they chose to nestle in tight and good to that spot behind his sternum that had been not only walled off but condemned to a duty that had become impossible to fulfill. He realized that now.

This feels right to me.

It does. It really does.

Shit, he needed to see Clara. To hold her again, tell her what the gooey center of him had known since she'd first whipped the thing up.

He loved her. Holy hell, did he love her. And he would tell her free and clear of any oath, of any relic, of any obligation to his family or his mages or a dead brother who, if he were still alive, wouldn't keep holding Bronze to a panicked and dying compulsion.

And perhaps the biggest noodle scrambler of them all: Bronze would do it all over again. He'd give up every power, every flight, every bit of his angel fire, if it meant he'd wind up back here, fighting for this female.

Bronze reached the center of the crowd where Raff stood and slowed to a halt in front of the king, who was alone except for his advisor, Pascal, to his right and Broderick, his guard, to his left. Where was Clara?

"Today is the final trial of the Betrothal Games. Lord Raff!"

The king extended his arm toward the lycan, but the crowd stayed silent. "And Bronze the demigod." Another arm gesture. More silence.

A trickle of warning pricked at the base of his spine. *What the hell is going on?*

Bronze scanned the gathered lycans, searching for the hood of Clara's favorite cloak or, at the very least, her white hair standing out among the throng. Nothing. Just a lot of somber faces beneath soaking-wet clothes and ominous umbrellas. Fucking hell, they looked like they were at a burial, not a tournament.

That unease from earlier ramped straight up to full-blown panic as he eyed Raff, who stood shoulders straight and arms clasped behind his back, donning his usual stony expression.

The king cleared his throat, pulling Bronze's attention back to the pompous prick. "As both remaining champions have each garnered a victory, the winner of this, the third and final trial, shall be declared the winner of the entirety of the Betrothal Games. By right of writ, the male shall receive my daughter Clara's hand in mating, a pledge of alliance and allegiance with this kingdom, and he shall be placed in the direct line of succession to the throne."

Why the fuck was he saying all this shit? They knew the stakes. Did the male think because he was surrounded by so many oxygen-replenishing trees that he had the right to use up more than his fair share of it?

It was all a fucking performance. A grand covert declaration of hostility that could only be made by one who had more expertise in stagecraft than sovereignty.

Bronze was *so* over it

Then Pascal stepped forward and unveiled the burgundy banner revealing the third credo of the monarchy. The swirling opalescent script blurred together amid the fog and rain, but it was legible nonetheless: "With the moon's senses, we protect and safeguard."

"Broderick, if you please," the king said.

Halpin's lycan stepped forward and gestured to another guard, and both males walked behind Bronze and Raff. There was a rustle of fabric, and then a heavy swathe of dark linen was draped over Bronze's eyes and fastened snugly behind his head.

Shit. It was a senses challenge. And he was competing against a lycan.

"For this trial, both competitors shall be blindfolded, and as our credo expects, now that you have been robbed of your sight, you must use your other senses to locate an object hidden in the woods behind me." Another pause, then Broderick was tugging at the back of his head again. Was he fastening something?

"Lest you think of removing your blindfold once you are beyond the initial perimeter of the forest, I have instructed that a small length of special thread be secured at the juncture of the fabric. Should you try to lift the blindfolds over your heads or remove them in any way, the thread will snap, and you forfeit the game. Each competitor must hunt for the object blind-folded, retrieve it blindfolded, and return from the woods blindfolded. Only then can he be declared the victor."

Of all the on-the-fly scenario calculations Bronze was doing, far too many of them resulted in a snowball's chance in hell of him out-hunting a biological predator like Raff. Not without his celestial senses and sure as shit not when it came to scent or hearing. Eyesight maybe, if he was quick enough, but scent?

A small square of fabric was placed in his hand. Soft leather coated one side, while the other was thickly napped with smooth wool. On instinct, he brought the thing to his nose, and every muscle in his body swelled beneath the pelting rain.

He knew this fabric. Knew its earthy scent and the bristly feel of it when it was soaking wet from the river. Knew how the cloth was a deep evergreen while the leather lining beneath it was the same tawny brown as the eyes of the female who'd worn it.

It was from Clara's mantle. The one she'd been draped in when he discovered her in the river.

His heart squeezed out hurried peals of panic. But just as he was preparing to run, to leap over the king himself and bolt into those woods to find her, something else gave him pause.

Something rich and earthy rose up from the fabric, more pungent than sweat but without the normal metallic indicators of bodily fluids.

Then he sniffed again, and as a stark realization closed around his neck, he nearly destroyed the fabric within his fist.

Normal metallic indicators for mortals. Not for lycans.

It was blood. Clara's blood.

CHAPTER 28

The horn's baritone bellow rattled the trees, and Bronze heard Raff take off with a burst of speed he'd had not thought the lycan capable of.

And it fucking terrified him.

Bronze sprinted toward the forest, keeping his head down and ears open to whatever he could detect. He had no time to cower under the eerie sensation that came with his loss of vision, nor did he sink into his survival instincts that all but demanded he slow down, stop, and step lightly lest he plow into a tree. That was what his hands were for, and he kept those suckers out and around him like iron clotheslines. He'd never kneecapped a three-hundred-year-old heart pine before, but he'd go at it with gusto if it got him to Clara before Raff found her.

Clara. Oh God, Clara! All at once, images slammed into his head, morbid scenarios that were a thousand times worse than the night he'd first found her. Deep gashes, blood soaking the forest floor, severed limbs, the final puffs of air being pushed out of lungs quickly filling with viscous liquid. You name it, and Bronze imagined it, no matter how haunting.

"Shit!"

He couldn't think like that. All he could do was keep moving forward. Keep scenting, keep listening, keep—

The side of his heel came down on a tree root. His ankle rolled, and then the rest of his body rolled some more, tumbling to the forest floor in an uncoordinated tangle of limbs. The impact evicted the air from his lungs, but his muscles were on autopilot. Rising. Slowly rising.

Get up. Get the fuck up.

He spared only half a second to test for injuries. Bruised, not broken. Then he pressed on. Faster, harder, until his breathing became the only sound he could hear and all he could smell was the salt from his sweat as it soaked into the blindfold. Goddammit, he was powerless like this! Every muscle strained to shift into his bronze armor. His wings begged to be set free, even though his fire and the celestial powers that fueled his transformation were little more than dying embers in his core. There but withered and starved. Useless.

Nothing responded. Fucking nothing. Not even a ripple of *yeah, we hear you, bro, but we're a bit tied up at the moment.* His formerly powerful body was nothing but a shell for empty echoes.

And then he heard it. It wasn't loud, not in the least, but it also wasn't the leaves under his feet, nor the sounds of his ragged breaths. It was *something*, though. There! He heard it again. Bronze did the hardest thing he'd ever done and stopped moving. A faint wince, like that of a creature in pain, then a wheezy inhale. Muffled moans but higher pitched, not the kind an injured animal would make.

Clara.

Bronze fled toward the sounds, homing his mind's eye to each cadence and pitch as if they were his heartbeat. With his arms still out in front of him, he moved as fast as he dared, until he broke through a thick cluster of trees and heard the noise as loud as a fucking bullhorn.

It was his name. Garbled, yes, with all the consonants blurred together, but he'd know his name on Clara's lips anywhere, and that shit was coming through clear as a cathedral bell.

"Clara!"

Screams of panic behind what must have been a gag rose up to answer his cry. By the mages, he hoped it was just a gag and not something worse. But she was there, close by. No more than twenty paces or so, judging by how the sound carried. *So close.* He stepped toward the echo of her voice—

The crack against his skull rang his bell so damn hard, he wondered whether it was just blood that slowly seeped out of his nose. He hit the ground with a roar of pain, but it was nothing compared to Clara's muffled cry that his senses still prioritized. He had to hand it to the king, though. Whatever the blindfold was made of, it was fucking solid. That shit didn't budge.

"Do you have any idea how positively fucking *annoying* you can be? She isn't even of your race, *demigod*. None of these creatures are. You are not lycan. You are not one of us. Did you really think you could outmatch me in *scent*?" The rage in Raff's declaration loomed larger, louder, until his fucking puss was inches in front of Bronze's, judging by the hot dog breath that caused his nose to twitch.

"You know"—Bronze winced around a pain in his ribs— "that's the highest number of words I think I've heard you string together at one time. Bravo. I'd clap, but I think I've got a couple dozen splinters in my hands. *Aagh!*"

Raff's heels crunched against Bronze's wrists, forcing them into the damp earth. Bones and tendons shifted beneath the rubber soles as Raff pressed down harder.

Bronze gritted his teeth and swallowed around a choking

cry of pain. "Please tell me you've taken off your blindfold. Give me permission to rip this thing from my eyes so I can wrap it around your throat, you self-important prick."

"I do not need my eyes to kill you, nor do I need anything beyond what the Moon Mother has bestowed upon me at birth." A sharp claw pierced the skin at the center of Bronze's chest and dragged lower, lower, until the curved edge glazed over his sex and curled beneath other far more tender parts of him. Bronze's breath caught in his throat, but he choked it back down, forcing his mind to work out a solution as quickly as possible.

"You've been a thorn in my ass from the moment you fired off your mouth at the dinner banquet. I should have dispatched you then if I'd known you'd be so much trouble, but hindsight and all of that. Now, however, it's done. *You're* done. The princess is *mine*. Her womb, her lands, her father's money, all of it is *mine!* I will *not* be a slave to the humans any longer! They may have their guns and their land, but I have centuries on my side and nothing but patience." Then he dipped his head closer, his foul breath causing Bronze's eyes to water beneath the blindfold. "I'm done playing games, and so are you."

Bronze tried to buck against the weight above him, but a subtle warmth landed on top of his right arm. It surprised him at first, enough to make him grow lax beneath Raff's hold as the lycan tensed above him to deliver the final blow.

Head. Radiance. Comfort. Then, surprisingly, the rain halted. If he'd had his vision, he would have imagined a subtle sun poking through the dense fog of clouds. A beam of gold striking the forest floor to chase away the drizzle. And then the strange warmth moved down his arm, over his strained bicep, and along his forearm, until each finger wiggled with a rebirth of energy and blood flow.

So many questions assaulted him at once, but none so expedient as to what his newly charged fingers had just brushed up against. Had that been there before? Rough wood. *Thick* wood.

A weapon.

There were times for questions and times for action. This was most certainly a time for the latter. With a soft grunt, Bronze gripped what his fingers sought—a heavy tree branch. Then a great primal roar erupted out of him, loud enough to shake the trees and stir the birds to fly. Loud enough to create a new oath and have it reach the Empyrean to proclaim for all who would listen that Clara was his, and he would not leave her helpless to her fate.

Bronze's cries stunned Raff, who lost his balance and was unseated just enough for Bronze to break free and swing his arm wide.

The impact wasn't loud or jarring. Rather, it was wet and dull and followed the body it had struck to the ground with due devotion.

With the weight lifted off Bronze's chest, he scrambled back and, giving zero fucks about the king's rules, ripped the blindfold from his eyes.

Well, shit. If Bronze had known he was capable of such good accuracy with a long wooden stick, then why the hell had he been losing at pool to Chrome on the regular?

Raff lay motionless on the forest floor, still blindfolded, with a long thinly angled branch protruding from his ear. Like, dead center. The twig—though the thing deserved a posthumous promotion after its bold act of service—was only six inches long, but it was a proud offshoot of the thick bough Bronze had grabbed and hurled at the male.

He didn't bother to check for proof of life. There was only one life he was concerned about.

"Clara!" With his sight available to him once more, Bronze whirled in the direction where he last heard her voice . . . and stopped in his tracks. "Oh, Clara."

His beautiful lycan princess was bound to a tree so tightly the rope dug beneath her ribs, leaving a concave depression on her torso. The moonstone relic of her proud heritage hung limply around her neck like some sick shrine of perceived activism. She had been gagged, as he'd suspected, but there was no discernable blood to speak of. Just a nick, then, most likely. A trick of the mind to get him so worked up, he'd fumble before he left the gate.

It had nearly worked.

But the thing that broke his heart the most wasn't the torrent of tears that ran down her dirt-smudged cheeks and over the stained rag covering her mouth, nor the way she sank against her bindings as if she had no strength left in her.

No. It was what they'd done to her hair that made him see red.

Bronze approached her not with the speed his heart commanded him to but with the gentle tenderness of freeing a wounded animal from a hunter's trap. "Oh, sweet Clara. What did they do to you?"

On the right side of her head, her beautiful white hair hung wet and limp over her shoulder. The left side, however, had been shorn close to her scalp, revealing patchy silver peach fuzz that, despite its lack of concealment, the rain didn't touch. It was as if her own body, mutilated as it was, refused to bow even for the storm's sake.

Bronze's soul shattered, jettisoning into a million fucking pieces for what she'd lost and what he'd failed to prevent.

He removed her gag first, then her bonds, and welcomed the weight of her slim frame as she fell into his arms. After entire centuries passed just holding her, convincing himself that she was well and alive and, mages willing, capable of healing just like he was, he finally heard the whispers spoken against the column of his neck.

"I agreed to it."

He tensed. "What?"

"The shearing. I agreed to it. My father was going to kill you if I didn't consent to marry Lord Raff and take part in the final game and whatever else my father wished me to do. Him cutting my hair . . . it was my penance for the trouble I caused him. The price I had to pay for publicly refuting his selection of my would-be mate and forcing him to enact the games. For a lycan female, their hair is very important, symbolic even. A sign of our lineage and bloodline. Our power. He knew that, knew what it would mean for me to willingly have him cut it, and so did I." Then she pulled back to look at him, a sad strength shining in her eyes. "And I'd do it all over again if it would save your life."

"Don't say that, princess. Don't ever say that to me again. I'm doing all I can not to storm back there, rip out the entrails of the male you call a father, and use them to string him and this asshole up by their boots so the coyotes could have a decent meal." He clenched her tighter to him with desperate relief. "Do you understand, Clara? I can't ever see this happen to you again. It wouldn't just kill me. It would break me. Mortals have no sense of how truly mad a male could go if his female was taken away from him. Death is not a kindness often granted to beings such as me."

The corners of her mouth lifted slightly. "Am I that female to you? With all the ones available in this realm and the others?"

Bronze didn't hesitate. "They're not you. Never could be. Never will be." He didn't want thoughts of Polina entering this private, panicked space with his princess, but when they did, for the first time, they didn't linger, nor did they track tendrils of guilt over his soul like muddy footprints.

Damn, it felt good. And freeing. Finally.

Clara bent down and picked up the discarded blindfold, inspecting the severed fastening thread at the back of it. "My father will use this as justification for not declaring you the winner, despite Lord Raff's death. The king is a vicious man with no end to his machinations and manipulations." She placed the fabric in Bronze's hand.

He couldn't explain why he did it, but something about that earlier warmth on his arm, which had led his fingers to locate the perfect-for-bludgeoning branch next to him, urged his thumb to swipe across the torn thread.

The brief pause in the rain Bronze had noticed earlier had rolled into a full-blown precipitation lockdown, taking with it the slight sprinkles of heavy mist. And when something drew Bronze's attention northward, the barest patch of blue sky appeared through the thick canopy of elm trees. The sun—bright, golden, and damn insistent—shone through the opening and focused its honeyed rays on the back of Bronze's hand right where it covered the thread.

I know that heat.

It had fled as fast as it arrived, however, pulling the dreary cloud cover back into place like a blanket over one's head. But when he moved his thumb away from the severed fabric fastener, a bundle of intact golden threads took its place, just poised for the tying.

Clara gasped, but Bronze could only smile.

Saulé.

"Someone up there likes me. Here, put this over my eyes and secure it. I'm ready to win you good and proper."

When Clara was finished, Bronze swept her into his arms and walked—way fucking slower, thank you very much—out of the forest, holding the most precious prize of all.

He didn't put her down until well after they cleared the tree line and the crowd's cheerful shouts had toned down to a joyous murmur. Behind his blindness, he waited . . . and waited . . . and yup, there it was.

"No! Impossible! This cannot be! Broderick, inspect the

blindfold. He could not have bested a lycan at scent without removing it from his eyes. Where the hell is Lord Raff?"

Broderick's thick fingers examined the fastener and then went stock still. Yeah, the dude totally knew that someone else's grease had been under the hood of his handiwork. The question was, how would he play it? "All is secure, Your Majesty. Bronze has successfully retrieved what has been hidden in the forest under the rules of the match."

Bronze whipped off the blindfold and appreciated the guard's subtle nod of approval.

Yeah, he's a good egg. I hope Clara keeps him around.

"Oh, and to answer your question," Bronze said, "Lord Barf is dead. He kind of met with the pointy end of a tree branch. You might want to go get him before the animals do. That's a whole lot of grade-A muscle meat to go around."

Pascal stepped in front of the king, a note of restrained exuberance tugging at his features, as if he was finally allowed to say the words of his heart. "I hereby proclaim Bronze the demigod as the official winner of the Betrothal Games! I will, henceforth, update the records and document his place in the official line of succession."

God bless that little lycan. There weren't enough ill-mannered jokes in the world to get King Halpin as swollen in the chest as Pascal's proclamation had just done. *Maybe* there were a few *yo' mama's so* thigh-slappers Bronze could have resur-rected, but none of them would have gotten the color of the king's beet-red fury just right. Ah, well. He couldn't win them all.

But he *could* make it very fucking clear what he and Clara thought of his ability to rule and how badly his daughter wanted him out of the picture.

And also how efficient Bronze could be at dropping bodies and making them disappear.

Bronze lifted Clara to his chest once more, to the delight of every swoony female in attendance and several of the muttering males, and addressed the king. "Go to the woods and clean up your mess. By morning, ensure the rest of the western lycans have departed the keep and then the three of us are going to have a nice little sit-down so we can all come to terms with your kingdom's new reality. And whatever else you need to say to me right now can be addressed to the back of my head because there isn't anything else I intend to hear for the rest of the day other than the words of my betrothed."

The crowd parted for him as he carried his prize back like a greedy pirate who'd just found a long-lost treasure after a decade of false alarms and wrong turns.

Clara drew his ear to her mouth and said with a laugh, "You're too much sometimes."

"Nope. Not hearing that."

Because none of it was enough. *He* wasn't enough, and whatever time he had left with her in this realm would *never* be enough, but he'd sure as hell soak up every second with her until destiny came to its senses and gave him his next marching orders.

CHAPTER 29

There was something to be said for giving oneself over to whatever primal urges decided to lay claim to your higher reasoning. For Clara, that had always been relegated to her wolf. She'd give the beast her head and let her run as widely and freely as the property would allow. It was the only sort of freedom Clara had been permitted to enjoy, provided she remained within their borders, and that wasn't an acquiescence on her father's part so much as a biological imperative.

But held high to Bronze's chest as she was, their breaths mingled with an urgency that was almost painful in their insistence. Her heart wasn't just clamoring against her chest with frantic eagerness but with almost the rabid panic of a berserker. A desperation that her wolf had known and understood long before Clara had gotten wise to the significance of what her body was feeling.

Bronze booted the door to her bedroom closed behind them, threw the latch, and never broke stride as he carried her . . . in the complete opposite direction of the bed.

"Where are we going?"

"Blood. Bath."

"A blood bath?" she teased, kissing his stony chin. "That hardly sounds appetizing."

"Don't distract me. I've finally got my eyes back, and I'm going to use them, dammit."

"Who am I to argue then?"

By the Moon Mother, she loved him like this. All growly and grunty and singly focused on what exactly she knew not, but she *did* know that he intended to involve her in it. And that was just *so* where she wanted to be. Her wolf growled in kind with approval and perhaps a bit of agitation that it had taken Clara so long to come to terms with this.

But they were here now. Her father would be dealt with. Her people would begin to heal just as soon as she and Bronze could establish hope in a better monarchy and ideally push her father out of the throne sooner rather than later.

Clara's feet finally touched the floor as Bronze squatted down and settled her on the edge of the tile shower bench, but his hands never left her body. They merely relocated to smooth over her arms, down her neck, across her brow, and anywhere else his worried gaze had touched first.

A smoky hazel gaze that battled between a far-too-familiar delicious intent and one that ached with the restraint of a boiling pot too long covered.

Oh, this will not do at all.

She grabbed up his hands and brought each of them to her lips. After she kissed both pulse points once, twice, and then a third time, she smiled as his breathing finally evened out. Once she was certain he wouldn't combust around her, she forced her brave warrior to still himself. With a few quick rolls of her left sleeve, Clara revealed a shy pink gash on the underside of her forearm that had already begun to stitch itself closed.

But the relief hadn't softened Bronze's features the way she had hoped.

"I did this myself," she assured him in what was hopefully a well-meaning tone. "My father didn't touch me. The blood required for the scent hunt was minimal, and it was easier all around if I cooperated. I am healed, though." Then she affirmed her declaration with a kiss to his deeply grooved brow.

Bronze jerked his head from side to side and squeezed his eyes closed as if blocking out the world. "Don't . . . Can't . . ."

"Bronze," Clara urged. "I am whole. I am well. All because of you."

Goodness, was he always to be this difficult? This was a happy occasion, was it not? They'd just won! Her father would soon no longer have the influence he did over her people, at least not solely and without her and Bronze's input. She'd gotten everything she'd sought to achieve, including a most magnificent male who always believed in her, despite the hardships thrown in front of him.

Still, he wouldn't open his eyes to look at her. Another moment of this and she would start taking it personally.

"Bronze," she said more firmly, tugging at his shirt sleeves. "We have not lost! Why won't you look at me?"

His chest heaved in great breaths but then settled slowly as each ragged bit of air escaped over a shuddering lower lip. She'd never seen him like this, so emotionally indisposed, so raw and fragile. Like a loyal pet who'd retrieved every ball you asked it to, yet still looked at you with sadness as if it wasn't enough.

The whole scene broke her heart, which had the nerve to grow far too full to accompany the care she held for this male.

Foolish, Clara. Once again, you are so—

Bronze's lids flew open, and he cradled her head with such speed, she nearly fell off the bench. Then his lips were brushing over the shorn side of her scalp, pressing, stroking, kissing every exposed part of her so that she couldn't help but lean into his strength any way he would offer it, even if it meant acknowledging the most vulnerable part of her.

"Lost?" He ground out the word against the side of her temple. "You want to talk about lost? I almost lost *everything* today when I realized you were taken. So, forgive me, princess, if my eyes need a moment to catch up to what my heart is still coming to terms with. That you're here, in my arms, and not bleeding out in a fucking forest where I couldn't find you."

A rush of memories flooded back to Clara and mixed with the images of what Bronze must have seen and endured before he'd found her in the woods.

Malik. A lost brother. A male who had bled out in Bronze's arms. A soul he'd been too late to save.

"Oh, Bronze."

He nodded stiffly but said nothing, because they'd both understood how today could have ended. What-ifs billowed around the spacious bathroom like unspoken secrets, making the air grow thicker and hotter with the impetus of what they'd dodged and what she could no longer live without.

Clara flung her arms around Bronze and smoothed the rigidity of his stern mouth away with the insistence of her own. Her kiss was open and eager, having no preference for anything other than the taste of Bronze consuming her from the inside out. And thank the Moon Mother, their passion was a language her warrior had no trouble speaking. If words eluded him, then she would declare her heart with the movements of her body.

"Off," he growled into her mouth, then grabbed her blouse at the shoulder and ripped it down, baring her breast. "I want it all off. I need to see you, to know you're all right."

He'd barely finished getting the words out before both their damp clothes had been stripped away in greedy tugs. Then he leaned over her shoulder and flipped on the shower. Steam soon swallowed them in a cocoon of passion, protecting them from anything that wasn't welcome in their small heated frenzy.

Which was, coincidentally, everything.

"Wait! The relic." She'd not undone the leather fastening yet, and she wouldn't risk—

"Leave it on. You've earned it. It's yours."

The words weren't just an insistent request but a reverent plea, even as he lowered his head to worship her breasts. But his devotion was somehow different this time, with the pulse of his cock beating against her inner thigh. Bronze was everywhere, and so was the connection to her people. Two halves of a whole that stitched together perfectly to complement the lycan monarch she always hoped to be one day.

The monarch she now knew had always been within her.

Because of him.

The impulse to see far more of him, to take in all she could of the male, was like a strike beneath her ribs, but she could no sooner lie there than ensure every part of him was cared for. Appreciated. Honored.

Loved.

The last thought tickled the back of Clara's mind as she pulled away from him, turned her back against the shower's spray, settled him onto the bench—while absolutely adoring the wrinkle of confusion between his brows—and dropped to her knees.

CHAPTER 30

Bronze was an immortal fallen angel. A feared sentinel warrior. A being created by the prime mages and lauded for his cunning and cruelty in combating the demon charmers.

And he'd just been plopped on his ass by the woman of his dreams and ordered to sit as if he was—and the irony was not lost on him here—a dog.

"Clara," he begged. *Again—dog.* "What are you doing?"

He was waiting for words. Waiting for an audible explanation as to why his princess had gotten to her knees before him and inched her mouth closer to his jutting erection that was so hard it was about to cut a hole in the tile beneath him. Because in what fucking world did he deserve this?

It was a dream. A miracle montage where *she* was the angel and everything around him was a temptation literal actual Heaven couldn't touch.

And then her mouth was around him.

"Fuck."

He lifted his head and tried to focus on the shower spray anointing the curve of her lower back and waterfalling over an ass he'd yet to stop dreaming about. Shit, no. Too much. Already, the suction and swirl of her tongue over his head was pulling him faster toward a curtain call. He shot his gaze to the ceiling, then back at her, then up again, throwing his hands out, bracing his palms against the cool slick tile and then swiping them away because he did *not* need another reminder of just how slick his current environment was.

"Clara . . . princess . . ." he breathed over a few too many strenuous swallows.

That was when the teasing *really* started. Slow, yet relentless. Curious, yet miraculously skilled. But it was when she dragged her tongue down the thick vein bulging along the underside of his shaft, then expertly cupped his balls, and *squeezed . . .*

Bronze lifted Clara off him and, palming the ass he loved so much, dragged her up his body until she was seated right where he needed her, with those powerful thighs hugging his hips and his cock sliding closer to her welcoming entrance.

"Baby," he whispered into her mouth as they exchanged desperate breaths in quick pulses, "I'm going to finally—*finally* —kiss my mate as I've longed to. Rightfully. Wholly."

Were there words after that? Maybe. In his mind, *definitely*, though they were mostly limited to the onomatopoeia variety, and all were lost to the welcoming shift of her hips that saw her hot core sheath him with such swift efficiency. Mouths came next, moving in a hurried rhythm that chased away any worries that had hunted him the past few weeks. Hell, his whole goddamn life. There was only the feel of Clara, in his arms, around his cock, expanding throughout his mind like a majestic starburst, searching out nooks and crannies that had only known darkness and illuminating the fuck out of them until they had no choice but to open themselves up to her beautiful brilliance.

The water had washed away all the debris and blood of the day—the nick from Raff's claw scraping his chest, the bits of shorn hair that had managed to cling to Clara's skin. But it couldn't chase away the heat. Never that. Instead, as her hips and breasts swung toward him in a syncopated rhythm that would play on repeat in his mind for as long as he'd remember, a burning ball of embers deep within his core churned as well. Hotter than the relic's smooth moonstone, which seemed to warm between them. Hotter than the approaching orgasm, which curled his hips tighter and made his muscles tense beneath the now-tepid shower spray.

Hotter than Clara's faith in him, which had never once wavered.

Bronze broke from her mouth as a wave of heat punched through him, lighting his limbs on fire and pulling a cry from his soul that made the very water around them quiver. His release was painful in its pleasure, erupting in wave after glorious wave that only strengthened the heat around him.

Heat that spread and spread and spread some more, until it wrapped around Clara and cradled her as it guided her through her own pleasure.

Bronze . . . Bronze, hear me . . .

Beneath the heat and flame and fucking perfection of it all, an ethereal feminine voice urged his eyes open. His lids were only peeled wide for a second, but it was enough for the whole of his existence to bloom with eternal clarity.

The relic, nestled safely between Clara's breasts, glowing with pristine opulence. Blue flame cocooning their bare bodies. Cleansing water dancing around them, misting into steam upon contact with the fire.

His angel fire.

The voice spoke again in his mind, through the shock, through the stinging tears that threatened to draw him away from the female in his arms. Bronze held Clara tightly to his body, tucking her head against his chest as they both rode out the spark that joined them in ways nothing else could. All the while, he kept his mind open, receptive to what the voice told him. All it revealed. All it granted.

All it pardoned.

And then it was gone, along with his fire, leaving behind nothing save for the soul-absolving clarity that Clara was unapologetically, undoubtedly meant to be his.

Bronze breathed through the shock of what he'd just learned and reached for the knob to turn off the shower. He grinned into Clara's hair at the serendipity of it all. "Are you all right? Are you harmed? Burned?"

"Burned?" She pulled back, though her thighs still rested comfortably on top of his and her stomach draped across his own. "In a shower?"

"Let me dry and dress you. There's something I need to talk to you about."

A stark calm froze her features, and a look of concern flashed behind eyes far too knowing, but eventually, she smiled softly, nodded, and, thank fuck, let him tend to her.

Once they were dry and he saw her nestled comfortably within his arms under a mountain of bed covers, he let himself inch toward the one thing he couldn't believe was waiting for him.

"What's this all about?" Clara asked, proffering a sweet kiss to the center of his chest, right over the scratch where Raff's claw had found its mark. "You seem troubled."

Before he could lose his nerve, Bronze grabbed up her right hand and turned it over . . .

And breathed through the gut punch of his life.

"By the mages, it's true."

"What's true?" Then she saw what he saw, and her eyes widened to match the perfect O of her lips.

The tattoo of his Empyrean name on her wrist wasn't gold, like the ones he'd seen on his brothers' mates, but was purely opalescent, like it had been ground from the most precious of seashells before being etched into her skin. Yet when he moved her wrist to catch the light, the same iridescent effect was achieved. Gone this way, and visible the other way.

A nod to her lycan heritage, one that was averse to metal but one that was still made perfectly for him.

"That is my name, princess, written in the old language of the Empyrean. *Sendran.* It is a mark that can only be bestowed upon the joining of true soul bonds."

A shining awareness lit her features. "Soul bonds? As in . . ."

He smiled and kissed her fully. "Mates."

"But how?" Clara tried to rub at the thing, but it stayed pressed into her skin regardless. And after a time, the worried rubs turned into sincere swipes and then, finally, soft caresses. "I don't understand."

Bronze fell back into the pillows and cradled Clara higher against his chest. "Many months ago, a goddess prophesied that I would meet a woman who would challenge me. A woman of lycan heritage who was, and I quote, 'so very fond of their games.'"

She laughed softly, though her reaction was tempered with notes of disbelief. "How remarkable."

"Quite. Her name was Saulé, and she was a celestial goddess who had done quite the number on my brother Brass and his now-mate, Molly. But anyway, it was Saulé's words that convinced me I was on the right path when I learned of your heritage. And even more so when the true origin of your moon-stone relic was revealed as well." He lifted the fang-like horn from between her breasts and examined it with no small amount of wonder. "This isn't just a relic of your people, Clara. It's a piece of the Empyrean."

"The Empyrean? How is that possible? How would you know that?"

"Because Saulé showed me in my mind when you and I joined together and enacted the soul bond. What you and your people view as a crescent relic of your Moon Mother is actually a piece of the Empyrean's gates, which had been severed from the structure at the time my brothers and I enacted the Sealing. Whatever dormant celestial magic was still contained in here was the very thing powerful enough to break the magical suppression of my soul's spark among your lycan land so it could finally spring free and seek out the matching spark in your soul." His throat tensed with the enormity of all the goddess had shown him, all he was now being forced to reveal to Clara. "This," he said, swiping a thumb over her wrist with as much tenderness as a warrior like him was capable of, "is the mark of the soul bond, of eternal mates. And now that this is truly free, so is my angel fire and all my celestial powers."

Of all the things Clara managed to snag onto, *that* got her attention. She bolted upright, nearly headbutting his chin in the process. "You have your powers back? Are you certain?"

"You didn't feel that heat or see the blue flames surrounding you as my power recognized you as its own to protect and serve? Are you telling me you really didn't notice *catching on fire?*"

She shook her head in disbelief, though her eyes hadn't left the relic she now cradled.

And then, because he was a bastard and couldn't resist, a teasing smile slowly split his face. "Did I just blow your mind to the point of actual memory loss?"

It wasn't a headbutt, granted, but the slap to his chin still stung regardless.

"So, we are mates, then?" she asked. "True soul-bound mates?"

"Yup," he said, sawing his jaw back and forth but smiling through it.

"But this relic is not of my people."

"It is. Saulé assured me as much. Once it split from the Empyrean, it belonged to whoever claimed it. If it was your

Moon Mother who blessed it thereafter and birthed the lycans, there is no taking away from that. It is yours, though whatever celestial magic that was in it has been spent in freeing the block on my power."

That was another thing he'd have to dissect when his mind caught up to the events of the last few minutes. The relic was just that now. A true relic. An ancient artifact with no more power in it than whatever the lycans believed it to hold.

There was no going back to the Empyrean, not with that, at least. The stark reality of it all was almost laughable in its irony. He'd gotten the very thing he was meant to find, and yet he found no remorse in the change of course.

Fuck. His brothers, however, would not take well to the news. In that moment, though, with Clara curled safely against his chest and her body melting into the promise of his protection, there wasn't a single regret to be mustered.

"I know," Clara murmured, her voice growing heavy with the events of the day and all they'd learned. And then her slim hand came to settle on his chest, inches below his right collarbone. "I kind of figured something significant happened when Polina's name disappeared before my eyes when we were in the shower."

Saulé came to his mind again, pressing out the ripples of his anxiety even as Clara offered a revenant kiss to the spot on his pectoral once owned by another.

Your oath is fulfilled, warrior. Guard your lycan well. You have earned it.

As sleep cast a heavy pall over them both, he held his treasure close to his heart. He'd never earned anything in his life, and yet somehow, in the span of a week, he'd managed to win the world.

It was a lot to process and something he wondered whether he'd ever truly believe. But he was not one to dismiss fate, nor turn his nose up at what it offered.

So tomorrow, he'd tell his female exactly what was in his heart and dive headfirst into whatever awaited them.

Bronze yawned, clutched the covers up over the bare side of Clara's head so she wouldn't catch a chill, and cocooned her against his chest.

Yes, tomorrow.

CHAPTER 31

Clara swatted away Bronze's hand for the third time since they'd left her bedchamber. "Stop that. If you keep rubbing at it, who's to say it won't up and disappear?"

"It doesn't work like that, princess." He'd managed to snatch her wrist back up and, with the stealthy skills of a ninja, press a tender kiss to the softly glowing mark there before she yanked it back again. It wasn't a hard yank, mind you. She didn't have that in her. But it was just enough to keep their private game alive.

The one where she pretended his devotion didn't melt the tender bits inside of her and make her wolf want to pounce.

Soul bonds. *True* mates. It was all too much to wrap one's head around, and the irony of the outcome had done far more than simply settling around her like the realization of their future.

It wasn't just a future of a co-managed monarchy, as they had originally planned, but a future together. Really *together*.

And perhaps the most wonderful comprehension of all was that it had largely happened without her meddling. The thing she'd been most worried about, the thing that had driven her to sheer madness and kept her up at night, was just how deviant she'd have to become to give her people the chance at happiness they so deserved.

But Bronze had changed all that, and the relief was still so immense, she hadn't yet managed to find the right words to describe it or thank him.

Or, perhaps even more significantly, share with him the other thoughts that lurked in her mind as she and her wolf reveled in his admiration.

Clara adjusted the wide headband that concealed the majority of her bare scalp and snuggled in closer to his side as they walked toward her father's receiving room. "I hope it doesn't disappear," she whispered against his chest, adding her hope to his earlier assertion and already feeling the warmth that grew on her wrist every time she touched the soul bond mark.

They still had so much to discuss, so much to make sense of. And while her heart desperately wanted to leap to the finish line and her wolf was eager to commence with the more carnal cele-bratory activities, her head knew better.

Leave it to Clara to possess the only brain in existence that successfully managed to blend foolishness and sensibility.

She stifled a soft chuckle as her wolf wondered, strangely, what such a combination would smell like. Perhaps selling scented candles called *foolish sensibility* was in her future.

"First things first," she announced to Bronze, who'd already stiffened his posture and shunned the carefree smile from his features.

He wore his weapons, as he was used to doing before coming to the lycan lands, though still well concealed at her request. The only difference was that he didn't need them now.

His angel fire and all his celestial powers had been returned to him, and what a wonderful night of discovery that had been.

"Father," Clara said in a chilly greeting as she and Bronze entered the receiving room.

True to fashion, the king stood in front of his desk, fists down, and a sour expression twisting the cruel lines of his face into something she had not seen before, but it still didn't look entirely out of place. He had been reading something—a note—and whatever it said not only commanded his attention but his body language as well. Pascal and Broderick lingered silently in the corners of the room, but otherwise, the king's usual entourage was absent.

"Thank you for meeting with us. I trust the western lycans have left."

"They have." The tone was harsher than she'd ever heard him use. For a moment, she was inclined to retreat into her familiar posturing, but then her wolf growled a low reminder in her mind and she paused.

No. You've earned the right to speak your piece. So has Bronze.

Clara stepped out of Bronze's hold and strode forward. Right into the desk's great shadow. "This does not have to be harder than it is. We only wish to speak civilly and establish a new chain of communication for the present monarchy. The union between Bronze and me is one our people will greatly benefit from, and it is my hope you will see that our people's needs should be placed above the monarchy's own. We have a responsibility to serve, and you have an opportunity to ensure your place in our new future. Bronze is next in the line of succession, per our current laws, and I will serve alongside him, but you are still the king and will be for as long—"

"Damn right I'm the fucking king!" her father snarled at her. The outburst had her retreating a stunned step. "And if you think for one goddamn second, I'll—" He froze. All the anger and volatility he was prepared to fling at Clara dissolved into a look of blank confusion.

Bronze threw Clara behind his back, and she could tell, from the warmth radiating off him, that he was banking his fire, calling it to be at the ready.

Oh, this was bad. This was *not* how she hoped this would play out. She made to step out from behind Bronze, who was so big and damned immovable, but the fangs poking free of her father's upper lip stilled her steps.

The king sniffed the air, then dragged his nose between her and Bronze. He sniffed again. Slower. Deeper. As if drawing the entirety of the room's air into his lungs.

Clara knew the moment her father scented the soul bond, and her heart plummeted into her stomach. It was in the twitch of his ear. Subtle but noticeable to those trained to look for it.

Oh no.

"You *mated* with him? It was bad enough you let a male of another species fuck you, but now you've actually *bonded?*"

This time, she managed to shoulder *her* way in front of Bronze, who still hovered close by but said nothing. "Who I spend my time with and who I choose to mate is none of your business anymore. Or have you forgotten the events of the last several days? I have won the right to live my life as I see fit. Bronze has fought to ensure that right remains so."

The king spit in Bronze's direction. Broderick flinched, his hand going to his weapon, but a warning flash in Pascal's eyes told him to stand down.

Surprisingly, Bronze did nothing, which only angered the king even more.

"You stupid fucking girl! All you've won yourself is a tainted womb and people who would rather claw out their own eyes than serve whatever spawn you promise them. You've corrupted the bloodline of this great monarchy and everything I've worked for." His eyes grew wild, crazed. His hands clenched into fists, then opened and clenched again, as if he had no control over the movements of his body.

She gasped in a ragged breath but couldn't bring herself to

retreat, frozen as she was to the French Aubusson rug. She'd never seen him like this. Angry, yes. Frustrated, of course. But this surpassed all of that, tumbling into a fit of pure rage she had no true experience with and no recourse to fight.

Her father had just . . . said those things to her. Had actually said, with words from his own heart, things no parent should ever say to their offspring. And he'd done so in front of an audience, including her new mate, even after she'd acquiesced to his public shaming in the final Betrothal Game.

She cast a helpless look to Broderick, one of the males who knew her father best, as if to ask whether any of it was true. Would he also view her differently? Had she misjudged what her ambition and hope would mean for the people she loved?

Have I gotten this all wrong?

Broderick merely took an uneasy step forward, closer to her father, though she didn't know whether it was to defend him or restrain him.

"Clara," Bronze warned. "Get behind me."

"Yes," she mumbled to herself, sensing the gravity of a mistake she'd not foreseen.

But she was far too slow.

The chair behind her father hit the floor before Clara had even lifted her foot out of the great desk's shadow.

Then that very shadow transformed into one of fangs and claws.

When Clara looked up, her father's gray wolf stood atop the desk. By the Moon Mother, he was huge. She'd forgotten how large and powerful he was. The howling snap of his jaw was a stark reminder, and the saliva that fell from his elongated fangs gave his message the ferocity he so clearly wished it to have.

Clara screamed as the wolf took flight. It leaped at her and scattered everything on the desk into a whirlwind of confusion. Teeth shot at her like a missile. She fell back against the rug and flung her arms over her face, bracing for her father's bite—

The roar that erupted above her was none like she'd ever heard before. A masculine cry of rage drowning out a predator's growl. There was a yelp, a grunt, followed by a *whoosh* she couldn't place, and then finally . . . heat.

"Up, lady. Up now!" Broderick's hands were beneath her arms as he helped her to her feet.

Good thing, too, because she had no idea what she was witnessing and her limbs had frozen in shock.

No, that wasn't true. She had words for all the components of the picture. The circle of blue flames. The snapping gray wolf in the center of them. The Aubusson rug reduced to embers where the flames touched it, though the fire, strangely, wasn't spreading beyond the concentric circle.

Yes, she had words to describe all those things. Just none of the sense as to the why of it all.

And then Bronze stepped out of her peripheral vision.

Goodness, he was glorious . . . and terrifying. A hard mask of brutality stretched across the angles of his face like stones coming to rest into long-familiar settings. Every muscle on his body was strung taut and locked up tight, as if relishing finally being called into service. The blue flames of his angel fire, however, were the most brutal of all. Targeted, menacing, and under the complete control of her soul bond. It was the power that had been freed by their celestial connection coming into being and was a force that was immense in its fury.

"You got a dungeon or something? Cells? Some form of detainment?"

Broderick placed himself in front of Clara, ensuring she was out of the way of the flames. "Yes."

"Throw him in there and keep this in the cell with him." Bronze extinguished the flames encompassing his right fist, reached into his back pocket, and tossed a closed metal switchblade at the guard. "Make sure he can't reach it, but keep it close to him. It'll ensure he can't shift."

Broderick caught the blade and held it away from his body. Clara took a few steps back from it as well, despite being used to the close proximity of Bronze's weapons. When she stepped back farther, however, her heel bumped against the edge of the desk, and she had to throw her hand out to right herself. Her pinky brushed the lip of a raised wax stamp, and the large wolf emblem upon it caught her eye.

It was a message bearing Lord Raff's official seal.

More guards entered the room, with Bronze shouting commands while Broderick echoed the orders to his lycans. But it all faded into the blur of the background as Clara brought the note up to her nose to focus on the words that, though in a legible order, didn't seem to make sense.

"Don't feed him," Bronze barked as he lowered the flames so Broderick and the guards could detain the king. "Unless Lady Clara allows it."

Vaguely, she heard her name. That was her name, right? Possibly. Though with how badly her hands were shaking, she didn't think she could put much stock in anything she'd previously taken as a certainty.

The words before her were succinct. No flowery language or unnecessary adjectives. Just pure brutal facts from a purely brutal warlord.

Clara's hand flew to her stomach, and she waited for the truth to hit her, for the sky to open up and declare that what she held in her hands was a fallacy crafted by the king to ensure further dominion. Another manipulation. *Something.*

But the seal was real, and the note was dated the morning of the final trial. It had been written by Lord Raff before he died.

"This can't be. No. No no no . . ."

The commotion in the room began to die down as the guards took her father away. Pascal had gone to accompany them at some point or see to whatever matters the old male needed to see to. Moon Mother knew he'd have much on his plate to clean up.

"Clara?" The worry had never left Bronze's voice since they'd first entered the receiving room, but it *had* shifted into something tinged with unease. When he said her name again, she recognized why the word sounded so off, so wrong.

There was no confidence in it.

That was when the first tear threatened to fall because she knew the words in her hands were true.

So she called on the Moon Mother for strength as she took in the sight of her soul-bonded mate and asked, "After you left my room the night we first made love, did you go to the royal coffers to try and steal from my father?"

CHAPTER 32

Bronze's head was hammering against his skull as if his brain matter was a kidney stone being worked over with the most efficient ultrasonic propulsion. And if that wasn't enough, he still wasn't entirely certain he had it in him to stand still while Broderick and his boys dragged a muzzled-and-leashed wolf out of the room by his tail like some animal control trophy capture.

Except it wasn't a trophy. It—because Bronze was *so* not ready to believe there was anything worth dignifying as a male in that piece of shit—was a king. Clara's king. Her father.

And, as far as Bronze was concerned, on borrowed fucking time in terms of breaths left.

When Halpin shifted and lunged for Clara, Bronze's soul had punched into action before his muscles had a chance to regroup, so deep was the shock of seeing a male of her own blood coming at her with a ferocity strictly reserved for enemies. But after so long without Bronze's power, he couldn't yet trust in its accuracy or strength. One millimeter off and Bronze could fry Clara instead of the king. Instead, he'd turned to what he knew would see him through and what had been tested time and again over the past several days: his strength.

It was just enough of a successful trust exercise to convince Bronze that, yes, he *was* fully capable of sinking into his power, calling forth his full angel fire and wielding it with ease.

Of course the first time he'd become whole in soul and strength would also be the first time his full power was called into service for Clara's protection.

So that was why, after the king had been dragged away, Bronze's brain was spinning out, his powers cowering on the fritz, and his heart slowing to a worrisome degree when Clara looked up at him from the note she'd been holding.

She spoke the words again, with clear diction and enunciation, to ensure there was no possible confusion as to what she was asking.

Which made total fucking sense. Because when you were accusing your soul bond of ulterior motives, you needed to make damn sure he had all the rope he needed to hang himself.

For the first time in all his years, Bronze didn't know how to respond. Oh, the rest of his body sure as shit knew to freak out and panic, but the part of his brain responsible for the sweet care and protection of his female had nothing, and maybe that was a relief, because lies never stuck around to see the fruits of their labor.

No, they were always the first to get good and gone, leaving the hard truth to clean up the mess they'd made.

"May I see what you're reading?" he asked over a hard swallow.

"No. You may answer my question first."

He knew better than to take a step forward, even though he was a blink away from rushing to her just so his body could impress the truth of his being into hers and chase the doubt of his lying words away.

There was no question in his mind. She knew. He didn't

know how, but she knew, and if he wanted any hope of keeping her in his life, he had to give her what she was asking for.

"It was my original plan to retrieve an item, yes, but it had nothing to do with making love to you."

A gripping chill crept over the stone walls, blanketing the room in a cold that seemed to freeze everything in place. Clara, likewise, stood frozen, her face a mask of smooth indifference and quiet calm.

When she spoke, only her lips moved. "Your . . . relations with me were secondary to your true goal? A goal that would have you stealing from my people?"

"No! No. Fuck, Clara, you weren't secondary to anything. Please, what are you holding?"

"Are you asking me so you can ensure your story is in line with what I have discovered?"

Cold. Her words were so cold, they cut through him like jagged icicles.

"I don't understand," he admitted honestly, and even that small acquiescence to the truth seemed to help thaw the tight band around his heart, just enough so the withered muscle could start to bleed out.

Clara held the paper out to him between the tips of two fingers, offering up only what contact was required. "This is an official missive from Lord Raff to my father, dated the morning before he died. I have verified the seal and handwriting as his own."

Bronze stepped forward lightly and took the note she offered, but he didn't linger at her side, instead shrinking back to the place he'd previously occupied across the rug. Like a fucking coward.

After a few hard blinks, he managed to make the words coalesce into something that resembled paragraphs, though none were what he wanted to read.

Your Majesty,

I wish to recount my observations of the previous night. Upon witnessing the supposed demigod, Bronze, donning his shirt in the hallway after leaving the lady's bedchamber, I followed him to the royal coffers you had pointed out to me during the tour the day of my arrival. There, he was intently inspecting the coffers' door, and I confronted him on his intentions. He evaded my questions, naturally, but it was clear he never intended to be caught. I also suspect that he had no true intention of remaining as the lady's champion and competing any further for her hand and, by extension, your kingdom's best interests. In my experience, once a thief acquires what they have been searching for, they tend to flee.

Use this information as you wish. As a testament to the strength of our future alliance, I share this freely so you and your daughter may go into the days ahead with open eyes and clear consciences.

-Lord Raff

Bronze let the note fall to the floor. It was either that or incinerate the thing and piss on the ashes. "Clara—"

"I shall have the truth now or nothing at all. I recall that night you were angry with me, as you should have been based on how I treated you, but I cannot understand . . ." Clara's eyes dipped lower a fraction, her only deference to a debate. But all too soon that arctic gaze returned to him, and the mask was set into place once more. "I never showed you where the coffers were. I only told you that they existed. The serving female who brought me linens that night, she was also carrying the moonstone relic to return it to the coffers."

Bronze saw the moment those cogs fit into each other like shark's teeth, and a true soul-crushing fear gripped him.

"You followed her," she whispered, understanding brightening her gaze but dragging down her features with even more disappointment. "Followed where she took the relic so you'd know where the coffers were located. In truth, I observed you noticing her, but I foolishly thought you were worried she might stumble. She was carrying quite a load down the stairs, and she is getting on in years."

Fuck. This was spiraling too fast. Every time his mind latched on to one thread to try and tame it, another would spring loose and unravel at twice the speed. All the while, Clara was shrinking further and further away from him, until he barely recognized the look she gave him, so foreign it was to see it splayed across her features.

It was one of disgust, repulsion.

"It was the relic," he admitted, his hands outstretched before him, desperately reaching for her even as she pulled away.

"What?"

And then his arms fell. Just plunked to the sides of his frame as if he had nothing left to offer save for whatever truth he could submit that he hoped would at least fill in the gaps left by his lies.

"When I pulled you out of the river and brought you to my brothers, Rhode noticed the relic around your neck as something other than what you know it as. It was a mirror image of what he'd seen in Cyro's possession, something with enough power to possibly open the gates of the Empyrean again."

"I thought you said your goddess revealed it as a celestial mechanism by which our souls could at last discover each other. *That* was what the magic was for, to finally free your powers."

"*After.* All of that happened *after* I'd already joined with you, and I had no idea the thing was capable of any of that."

She seemed to latch on to that piece of information, and he held the kernel of hope in his chest that he could somehow still get through to her.

Until she held her claw above the one thread he'd hoped she wouldn't snag and shredded it.

"So your goal the entire time was to obtain the relic so you might use its magic—the magic you suspected it of having—to return home. You never intended to remain here with me, in this kingdom, even as a visiting monarch as per our original agreement."

There was no going back from what she'd ripped open. He knew that now and knew that, as she stood there with those expectant eyes begging him to tell her anything other than the truth, he'd ruined the one thing in his life that gave him hope for happiness.

Bronze dipped his head, shame weighing the thing down, and spoke the truth. The entirety of it. "The tattoo you saw on my chest, the one with Polina's name, was born from a celestial oath I made with her brother, that's true, but there was more to it. I swore to look after her, not in the manner of her brother's best friend but as a mate."

An icy chill thickened the air further. "A mate?"

"Yes. My station as a sentinel would have afforded her more security. I had the skills and means to defend her should things with Cyro's armies get worse. But it was a promise made to a dying friend on the battlefield, Clara, not one thought out and the repercussions examined for eons to come. I made it out of love for Malik, not because I loved Polina as anything more than a fond acquaintance. Fuck, I haven't even seen her since I fell, and I don't even know whether she knows about the oath."

"But you've thought of nothing else since then, clearly. And you used me and my circumstances to try and find a means to your own end so you might discover a way back to her."

"At first, yes, but listen to me." He rushed toward her, but the warning in her stare drew him back.

"Why did you insist I wear the relic last night when we—" She cleared a sob from her throat, stomping out the emotion. "When we had sex?"

Had sex. Not made love.

He shook his head. "I don't know. I just did."

"Was it just for your own vanity's sake? Or were you so impressed at how beautifully you'd orchestrated this whole production that you wanted to marvel at your exploits while conquering another?" She leaned forward on her hips and flared her eyes. "Tell me, were you disappointed when you couldn't cut it from my throat? After all the times you had to bleed on my behalf in the games that I *begged* you to compete in?"

"No! Never!" His heart. Oh, mages, his heart. The thing hemorrhaged freely, each pump expelling more of the vital fluid that had kept his hollow shell of a body moving throughout the ages.

And he had been doing just that, he'd realized. Moving. Fighting. Fucking. Whatever his body demanded of him so long as he kept his eyes on the prize. Destroy charmers. Save souls. Kill Cyro. Get home. There had never been room for anything else. Perhaps that was why he always found a joke or two handy to offer up. Laughs were simple and fleeting. A quick dopamine hit that was gone as soon as it arrived but had the strength to change the vibe of a room and, more importantly, divert attention from what people would otherwise prefer to keep secret.

What they'd prefer not to dwell on.

Clara didn't move, didn't shake, didn't even look at him. There was no light in her eyes. Just a rigidity to her stature that he'd seen warriors adopt time and time again when they had no true fight left in them but were still resigned to their fate.

"Clara, please . . ."

The shift happened so fast, he nearly fell back on his ass. Clara roared a great painful howl to the ceiling, one that was a haunting mix of mortal and wolf. Then sleek muscle coated in thick white fur sprouted through her garments, and a muzzle holding far too many teeth was pointed right at him. Those tawny-brown eyes that had always reminded him of cinnamon and maple were now trained on him in the style of a predator. One large paw moved forward, then the other. Saliva dripped from her sharp fangs, landing in neat little drops before her, anointing the path she would take to annihilate her prey.

When she was a few feet from him, she snapped her jaws wide and swiped her claws at his chest. He jumped back at the warning shot and knew damn well she wouldn't give another.

After all, judges didn't bring the gavel down twice.

With all his options exhausted, Bronze turned from the room, shaking, and shut the door behind him.

Unlike the last time he'd shut a lycan in there, eerie silence met his back. There was no hurled furniture. No breaking glass. Nothing.

Just the absolute stillness of a broken heart.

CHAPTER 33

Clara knew the moment Bronze left the property, not because of any inkling or hunch, but because it was the moment she vomited up her entire breakfast and had resigned herself to lay on the cold tile of the bathroom floor for however long she wanted.

The rest of her life seemed like a reasonable length of time.

Eventually, however, her joints demanded her attention, threatening to never again move from the shape she'd twisted them into if she didn't get her butt up.

She'd settled on the chair in front of her mirror as a consolation to her body's needs, while still lending itself rather well to the suffering her soul wasn't ready to give up quite yet, even after the hours she'd spent locked away in her room.

Like hell she'd go near the bed, and as soon as Broderick was available, she'd ask him to torch the thing.

Clara leaned back and allowed the rigidity of the wood and the ornate carvings upon it to dig into her spine as hard as they insisted. Despite her wolf's whining protest, she'd sit there for as many more hours as she needed.

After all, when one was a newly appointed monarch, even by consolation, didn't they get to do whatever they wanted?

And right now, all she wanted was to feel anything other than the foolish heartbreak that raked at her body from the inside out.

Once again, she had underestimated how truly manipulative males could be. Lord Raff, in a dying testament to his ruthless cunning, had made sure to land his final blade as swiftly and succinctly as possible. Likewise, her father, knowing they were all to meet together at that hour in his receiving room, chose to read Raff's final words and have them available for Clara to discover, even though he most likely read the note when it had been delivered to him the prior morning before the last game.

And then there was Bronze, whose artfulness was perhaps the most beguiling of all. Every step he took was nothing short of extreme purpose, from saving her to fighting for her and then bedding her. The male had had a goal the entire time, one he'd wisely kept close to the vest while he played the other cards that were dealt.

Clara had been the only simpleton foolish enough to allow herself to get swept up in the machinations of the males around her. It was clear none of them had ever given credence to her own petty schemes.

But oh, it hurt, and only in the privacy of her mind could she admit that to herself and her wolf.

Because she was the queen now. Technically, part of the reigning monarchy, alongside Bronze. She'd won and gotten exactly what she sought to achieve.

The price, however, had been higher than she had been able to afford: her heart, her self-respect, and the respect of her people.

Sometime after Bronze left, Pascal and Broderick had searched her out. Broderick to ensure her the king was detained and the guard would see to her ruling, and Pascal to inform her that, under lycan law, she was now to decide the king's fate. Since her father, as the monarch, had openly threatened another member of the monarchy's life in the presence of witnesses, the law dictated that he may be stripped of his family ties and either exiled or killed for his crime.

It was a decision that, as both the victim of the attack and the sole remaining monarch save for her absent mate, fell squarely on her shoulders. So, yes, she'd gotten exactly what she'd wanted, hadn't she?

Clara picked up the long ivory comb from the top of her desk and ran her fingers across the teeth. Each time her skin snagged a bit, another tug was mirrored behind her breastbone. It had been barely twenty-four hours since Bronze's lips had pressed their sweet affection onto the bald side of her scalp the night they'd last been together, and she could still feel the ghost of it.

It was an affection she wished she could rip out of her memory, toss to the side, and refill the hole with something far more useful. Like the comb, she had no need for the reminder or him. Though she had to give him points for directness. Once she'd managed to piece the breadcrumbs of his deception together, at least he hadn't begged too harshly for her goodwill. He'd called for her understanding, but she had been fresh out of logic by that point.

So she'd shut him down. Shut all of it down. Her emotions, her duty, her capacity for clarity.

Especially her heart, absurd thing that it was. If she needed any more proof that her brain had not decided to accompany her on her journey, she need only look so far as the sun and moon cycles, for what female would anguish so sharply over a male she'd only known for a smattering of days? A week or so at best?

Clara gripped the comb, threw it into the top drawer, and slammed the thing shut. The bang was the closest thing to a curse she'd been able to muster since she'd locked herself in her room. It was the swear that broke the seal, apparently, for a proper curse echoed on its heels through the empty bedchamber with resounding purpose and struck Clara with its directness.

Her back stiffened as she absorbed the shock like a tuning fork.

She hardly needed the reminder that she was hollow, but it seemed the Moon Mother would never stop conspiring to make her aware of all she'd wrought upon herself.

Bronze, her soul bond, had made an oath to another, and it was one he held high above the vow he'd sworn to her. It didn't matter that his devotion to Polina wasn't of romantic affection. He'd taken an oath to another female, and up until today, he'd let that promise guide every step he took, despite his mark being branded upon *Clara's* skin.

Steps that had him walking all over her to fulfill his one supreme vow, regardless of the vows he'd given her.

Sisterly affection she could have forgiven and would have gladly done so, but not at the sake of her self-respect.

God, she wished she could scratch off the tattoo. Burn it. Score it from her skin with her fangs and claws. Anything so she wouldn't have to look at the permanent reminder of her ineptitude as a female for having ever trusted him.

A knock at the door had her pulling her sleeve over her wrist. "Yes?"

"Pascal and the other advisors await your judgment regarding the king, lady," Broderick called through the door, somehow sensing she wasn't yet ready to talk to anyone face to face.

Judgment. It was perhaps the ultimate insult, asking for her opinion and ruling on a matter of such grave importance after everyone in the kingdom had witnessed her profound failings.

Clara lifted her head and stared at her reflection in the

mirror. The headband had been swapped out for a more prominent headwrap, this one a deep fuchsia inlaid with navy forest-like embroidery. The whole thing was a cruel depiction of all she sought to hide: her image, her nature, her new status that *she'd* set out to obtain, despite the risks.

Strange how, when she started on her journey, she'd done so independently. Yes, she'd sought the aid of a few merchants to get her to the human lands, but it was *she* who actually intellectualized it all and *she* who, after some time in Bronze's company, thought he was different. That perhaps she hadn't needed to learn how to manipulate him to achieve the seat of the monarchy and help her people alongside him. And she'd been all too eager to drop that farce as soon as he'd begun to fight for her. Actually *fight* for her. Not win for the sake of winning, as most males did, but put his vote of confidence in her, all while protecting her and helping her parse out her father's treachery along the way.

So it was fitting how her journey ended where it had begun, in a sense.

As a lone wolf, though worse somehow. Patriarchal male-dominated lycan law still recognized Bronze as a successor to the throne by virtue of winning the Betrothal Games. She could at best serve alongside him, which had been part of their mutually beneficial arrangement, as it was the most she could ever hope for. Her desires for her people would be spoken and enacted through his position. As it stood right now, there was no law she could set forth without his say.

Turned out, the manipulations she'd sought to enact when she originally fled had worked far too well, especially when the universe saw fit to turn them on her.

What a cosmically cruel joke.

Her sallow reflection was a reminder of the toll it took to think oneself part of a devoted pair and what was left behind when one half chose to sever themselves from the whole.

But she'd not shed another tear. She couldn't afford to. Not when her wolf had yet to cease howling her anguish within. It was one thing to let your pain manifest physically but quite another when you had to hold it all together for the sake of the more primal part of you.

God, she wanted to fall apart. Just collapse on the floor and rail and kick and scream until her vocal cords were abused and swollen and she'd rubbed her skin raw trying to crawl out of it. To throw a tantrum like she'd never been permitted to show, even as a child, even when she grew into womanhood as the only arctic wolf lycan among her people and had no mother to explain why rules were meant for her but not others.

Why there was no such thing as a love match in lycan monarchies.

"Lady? Are you well?"

"Yes, Broderick. I'll be out momentarily and will meet you downstairs."

Clara lifted her chin and tried to focus on her father's situation. No, *her* situation. The one she'd been put in by that male and all the others who came after him. But her heart . . .

Was affection supposed to hurt this much? Was it supposed to ache with such physical suffering that would soon see her running to the bathroom again?

No, it wasn't. But betrayal and deception . . . now those things had no shortage of claws to strike with.

As she rose to the door, intending to find Broderick, she steeled her features from the decision she had come to regarding her father's future. Strange how, once she'd settled on the course of action, it hadn't filled her with the remorse she thought it might. *That* had been somewhat of an easy surprise.

What hadn't been easy was what came after.

Clara stepped from the room and nearly cowered beneath the weight of the final thought that would trail her every step of the way to the first floor.

In all the time spent in her brave warrior's presence, she'd never once noticed whether his angel's wings had been tipped with talons. Nor had she conceptualized how the very person she thought would be the key to her independence would instead trap her more tightly within a gilded prison.

A prison, as it turned out, that was of her own making.

CHAPTER 34

Bronze swallowed another mouthful of bourbon, not even allowing his flavor receptors to smell the roses as all that vanilla, oak, and caramel fire water traveled southward to his gut. There wasn't much in there to impress anyway, so why bother with the sensory introspection? It wasn't like the liquor had chased down a prime rib and wanted to talk about its feelings or anything.

Truth be told, Bronze wasn't feeling much these days, and that was by fucking design. The Vermont watering hole he'd been setting up shop at the past several weeks was everything he needed: the thing wasn't in Aurora, wasn't in New Hampshire, and wasn't anywhere near a certain mountain range that would have been far too easy for him to plow through just to locate a certain forested lycan property.

Besides, he knew better than to go after an animal that had taken a swing at him.

Even if the animal had no hope of truly harming him because he'd already ensured the worst of the damage and taken ownership of that shit like a flag drop on the lunar surface.

Bronze lowered the glass tumbler onto the mahogany bar,

not giving a rip if he lined up the condensation circles he'd already made. That was what the place got for offering up cocktail napkins instead of proper coasters. Besides, he'd picked the sports bar because it was so damn loud, he couldn't hear what the bartenders said half the time, let alone his own thoughts.

Which was just perfect, honestly. All he'd had to do was point at the bottle of Maker's Mark Private Selection on the wall, hold up two fingers, and voilà! He'd had himself a standing drink order that had been seeing him through a whole lot of sunsets he'd rather not see.

Oh, yeah, and bonus points for keeping this little spot secret from his brothers. Bronze had made the fatal mistake of hitting the den after Clara had ordered him gone and then had to explain the whole shitstorm that had swept in on the heels of his failures.

Yes, I won the games but lost Clara.

Yes, I had the relic but torched whatever was left of its magic.

Yes, we're still stuck here.

Yes, I lied to her and broke her heart.

Yes, she's my soul bond . . . and never wants to see me again.

'Kay, thanks. Bye.

Logically, none of this should have shocked him. Since he first signed up for the whole ride, he'd known his actions would put in place the very things that would ultimately have them go their separate ways. He just never thought his preferences had anything to do with it. But like he got to cop to that sort of excuse?

Deep down, he fucking knew. He'd always known. For how many years had his soul been stooped over, carrying around the weight of his oath? It wasn't until he plucked Clara from that river that he'd finally been able to stand up straight.

Above the bar, a TV far too large for its cheap-ass mounting bracket blared some halftime interview roundtable with announcers giving their two cents on things they'd never been good enough at for anyone to pay them two cents to begin with. It was mind-numbingly pointless, and yet pointless was right up Bronze's alley. He needed mind-numbing because he was that much of a coward.

Bronze took another sip and ran the cool glass along his jawline, chasing away an itch. He'd given up on the razor scene some time ago because he didn't want to be reminded of anything that would bring a blade to a hair follicle. Every time he'd tried to run through the trim job, images of Clara tied to a tree, gagged, with half her scalp shorn and the scent of her blood in the air nearly drove him over the edge.

God, the way she'd shut down on him after reading Raff's note. It was like every bit of her emotions had turned to ice and had then been locked solidly inside a glacier that had no chance of being penetrated until it destroyed every vessel that threatened to come in contact with it.

Bronze swallowed against the dryness in his throat, which was surprisingly at odds with how much liquored lubrication he'd been hammering. Was this what the mortals felt like when they got so drunk, even the rocks moved aside so there was never truly a bottom to hit?

Because he'd hit it, all right. Clara. His soul bond. His brave, beautiful mate who'd transformed herself into a formidable warrior for the sake of her people, had shrunk away from him after the stun of his lies.

And then, like any good predator, she'd attacked because he'd given her a reason not to trust him.

He'd hurt the one being for whom he'd merrily throw himself in front of a 777 just because the aircraft threatened to block out her favorite view of the sunset.

God, he'd throw himself off a bridge if he thought it would kill him.

Anything. He'd do fucking anything for her because he loved her. He didn't just love her with his whole chest or being but with the eternity of a life unending. There were no earths left with ends he would go to for the mere chance she would even look at him because he'd explored them all over the eons.

He just never knew why. Never knew that what he was truly searching and fighting for didn't require an oath. There was no blood sacrifice, no sworn commitment. Just a love he'd never had the stones to vocalize or earn in the way he needed to.

The fire burned hotter in his belly, though he wasn't sure whether it was the abundance of pissed-off stomach acid finally coming for him or the conceptualized truth staking its claim on a shoddy foundation.

Bronze dropped his head into his hands and held the thing like the bag of rocks it was. Fuck, everything hurt, and if he played his cards right, everything would hurt again tomorrow, too, and the day after that if he was *really* lucky.

Fortune favors the brave, apparently. Yay.

Just as he was beginning to consider the merits of anticipatory anxiety—because no one had to tell *him* he wasn't capable of bleeding before he was wounded, thank you very much—murmurs of conversation from that giant electric box on the wall started worming their way into his brain.

" . . . a great player on the field and off. We're joined now by Emmanuel Valdez's parents, Maria and Leo Valdez, to talk about their son's charity, Does the Buzz, which features professional athletes shaving their heads in solidarity with young children undergoing cancer therapy and helps raise money to cover the costs of their treatment. The program is truly unique because all the patients who are enrolled never see a bill. Their treatments are scheduled by the parents and children's doctors, but the bills for those treatments go straight to the charity to pay. No insurance approvals. No middlemen. Just one-way funded care, no questions asked. It began when Manny was in high school, and he had been diagnosed with thyroid cancer . . ."

A thousand and one stimuli vied for Bronze's attention in

that bar. Muscle bros hollering over at the dart board. A group of women at the table behind him celebrating someone's thirty-umpteenth birthday. Competing broadcasts from the three TVs all lined up next to each other on the wall in the dining room to his left.

But all that noise faded away as whatever was left of his woozy attention got ramrod straight, tucked in its shirt, and covertly swiped a tongue across its teeth. Tendrils of an idea began to form in his mind, and before any intrusive thoughts could rise up and remind him of how much of a piece of shit he was and how it would never work, he paid his tab and fled the bar. Once he found a dark corner of the parking lot, he unleashed his wings and headed east.

CHAPTER 35

The stifling sun sat high above the treetops bordering the lycan lands, and Clara had never been more grateful to be on the other side of the perimeter. Not that it was cooler or different in any way from how the oppressive sunlight leaked through the leaves where she was standing. When she was going to let her wolf out beyond the stronghold's borders for the first time since she'd been crowned queen, she figured it was best to trick her mind into thinking the experience was something significant.

Yesterday, on the morning of the summer solstice, her father's sentence had been carried out. To say there was some dissent with her ruling would have been like saying a bonfire had a bone to pick with the rain that was snuffing it out.

The tide her words had ushered in was inevitable, but she hadn't been prepared or particularly interested in the backlash that followed. Gasps and cries and groans had bubbled up around her declaration when she'd first voiced the intended repercussions for her father's attack on her life. That had been a week ago, after which she'd promptly fled the room because she only had so much interest in hearing her advisors' opinions.

Words like *unconventional* and *unprecedented* had floated along the stone walls, chasing her out of the great hall and constantly prodding her mind with doubts about how she wasn't equipped to rule the monarchy on her own.

As if she needed another reminder of just how horribly backward her life had become.

So, with a new fleet of guards at her command and no one on the premises to tell her otherwise, she decided that being *off-premises* sounded like a fine idea. Definitely the best she'd had in days.

Her wolf, at least, agreed with her. Besides, it would be the first time in her life she'd let her wolf run free beyond her father's borders.

Not the first time, Clara. You shifted in these woods once before.

And just like that, her throat tightened up again with the familiar remorse she'd toiled at choking down over the past few weeks. She'd done so well, working herself up to a full four hours of sleep each night instead of the one or two she'd managed in the early days following Bronze's betrayal.

God, she hated thinking of that word. *Betrayal.* Even its own letters seemed like daggers, with its towering T and under-handed Y. The bold B was the most ruthless of all, as it was a constant reminder of the male who'd stolen her heart, then struck it through with a blade so well concealed, even her wolf hadn't been able to sniff it out.

"Lady, do you wish to shift here? The guards will hang back," Broderick offered, his sandy blond hair and broad shoulders catching the sunlight on its way to the forest floor. He had escorted her to the perimeter with two other males, and while the rest of the guard followed Broderick's orders closely, he followed her exclusively. It was a protocol she appreciated, but one that had quickly advanced from endearing to over-whelming at times.

It was also not lost on her that part of his duties as the newly appointed chief of arms was accounting for the security of *both* monarchs. A hard thing to achieve when the queen had chased away the days-old king and not addressed his absence publicly yet.

There was no need. They all knew. Gossip wasn't exclusive to humans. If anything, it spread faster among the lycans, who had the benefit of keener senses on their side with which to grasp the whispers faster.

So, yes, everyone knew what had transpired between her and Bronze, and Broderick had been showing her immense kindness in not bringing up the subject. That courtesy wouldn't be afforded her for much longer, though. Soon she'd have to declare the facts of the matter and officially give voice as to why the rightful winner of the Betrothal Games, the champion *she'd* selected, had not shown his face in—

"Oh, Lord Bronze! I had not expected to see you today." Broderick stepped past Clara, casting a shadowy blur in her periphery that blocked out the approaching figure.

"Hey, my man."

That voice. By the Moon Mother, *that voice.*

A painful twitch pricked beneath her ribs at hearing the resonant baritone, and damn her foolish heart, the stimulus wasn't anything she could resist. Her head had already jerked up in response, swiveling back and forth in frustration to try and get a peek beyond the mountainous width of Broderick's back.

A slap, as if arms had been grasped, resounded off the tree trunks surrounding the males, but it was quickly muted. Had that been a . . . handshake?

Broderick's voice followed up the out-of-place greeting. "Pascal did not—"

"Actually," Bronze cut in, "you mind if I speak to Clara alone for a bit?"

And that was when Broderick stepped aside, and her jaw nearly hit the ground.

Gone were the magnificent waves of auburn hair that always dusted Bronze's shoulders and seemed to dance with enthusiasm every time the wind caught them. He'd shaved his head nearly to the root on the sides, while the top was fashioned into a neatly and only slightly thicker trimmed patch down the center. The high-and-tight appearance was so at odds with what she'd remembered of him, and yet her heart still clenched at the sheer brilliance of all he commanded. Ever so handsome, ever so domineering. And despite the painful nudge of his mark's heat radiating from her wrist—or perhaps because of it—he was still ever so hers.

The reminder stung almost as much as his betrayal.

Clara collapsed onto a nearby log, and, not trusting her legs or her wolf to carry her away quickly enough, protected herself in the only way she could: she turned away from him.

She couldn't look at him, not like this. He had no right, *no right* to walk back here, regardless of whatever claim fate dared to make of them. It was on the tip of her tongue to say so when more male murmurings rose up behind her, and Broderick's great hulking shadow glided past her in the exact opposite direction of who she considered the enemy.

"Where are you going? You're retreating *now?*" she asked, letting all the derision she'd silently worked up over the past few weeks pelt her new chief of arms in the back. "All because he showed up and the law dictates you must abide by his word over mine?"

"I *have* heard his words, lady," Broderick said with a sad smile over his shoulder. "I know you are hurting, but I do believe it's best if you hear his words, too."

"What the hell is that supposed to mean?"

The answer, when it came, only served to agitate her confusion even more.

"It means Broderick doesn't have to listen to me or any other male monarch anymore, not unless you expressly allow it. I've taken care of that problem."

Clara shook her head, still refusing to meet Bronze's eyes. "What are you talking about?"

A cylindrical leather-bound scroll of papers plunked down into the soft earth at her feet. "Read 'em."

Clara slammed her eyes shut and breathed through her nose, doing her best to calm the agitation of her wolf prowling around in her mind. "If you think, for one minute, you can just come back here, to *my* home, and act like what you said, what you *did* could be swept away with some sort of . . . what? An apology? A show of male affection to my guards? Then you're about to find out just how deadly my arctic wolf can truly be."

She let her fangs drop and angled her head in his direction, fully intending to display whatever force necessary to get rid of him so she could break down all over again in peace.

The sight of Bronze on his knees, however, stopped her short. His massive weight no longer stood strong and commanding as it had done in Broderick's presence. Instead, the great fallen angel had crumpled somehow, shoulders rounded, head lowered, mouth pulled down at the corners into an exhausted frown.

The subtle breeze around them fell silent, mirroring Clara's shock.

Where was the confidence and discipline that had always tightened Bronze's muscles? Gone, apparently, along with the fire she expected to see blazing in his eyes. Instead, a cold lifelessness stared back at her, causing her snarling lip to lower into a frown that had grown so familiar these past weeks.

"What is this?" she asked again, gesturing toward what he'd thrown at her, forcing the words out through a tight throat.

He dropped his eyes lower so they no longer captured hers and ducked his head. "Please read them."

Perhaps it was her curiosity or the fact that a stupidly foolish part of her still hoped this whole thing was just some nightmare and she'd wake up any minute with a truth that saw them happy and together. Whatever it was urged her to untie the leather cord around the papers and read them.

For the second time in as many weeks, words her eyes took in failed to make sense in the context of how they were written. It didn't matter how hard she furrowed her brow or how often she blinked and reread paragraphs. None of it made sense, nor did the eerie sensation of having his eyes on her as she pored over what had to be the biggest practical joke of all time.

"This isn't real," she said, shaking her head in disbelief. "This can't be real. How could you have done this?"

Bronze sat back on his heels and, despite the kneeling, exhibited every ounce of warrior's strength she'd known from him. Where her face was surely painted with all sorts of confusion and incredulity, his revealed only absolute certainty. Her heart pounded out a rhythm of chaos, while his stony jaw and stoic gaze never wavered.

His chest rose and fell with the steady power of a calm sea, all while the silence roared between them.

"Pascal drafted it, and among all the advisors as witnesses, I signed it into law this morning while you were out visiting some of the farmers on the northern edge of the property."

Clara's head spun, and she was once again grateful for the log supporting her. "I can't let you . . . Why would . . . To do this, to enact it into the official canon of lycan law . . . Bronze, *why* would you do something like this?"

"Because you are the queen your people have always deserved, and now you're the sole monarch of the northeastern lycans. It took some fancy legislative tap dances on Pascal's part in terms of the wording, and I probably owe the male an entire brewery's worth of craft beer as thanks, but as of today, your monarchy will be exclusively matriarchal. Any male you choose to take as a mate will be considered a consort. A member of the monarchy, yes, but in name only. He will not have any say regarding your official rule, laws, sentences, proceedings, nothing, unless you wish it."

Clara could only shake her head as the silent minutes she took to reread the documents stretched on into eternities.

It was all there. Everything he said, everything he'd promised to help her achieve at the start of their journey was now baked into the official constitution of her people.

"I will never," he ground out, the muscles of his jaw flexing, "outrun the nightmares of seeing the anguish on your face knowing that I was the bastard who put it there. They've haunted me at the beginning of every single sunset these last agonizing weeks, and I'll gladly bed down with those fuckers each night for the rest of my life if it means you'll never have to wonder again whether your wishes will be granted by the whims of a male. No middlemen. Not anymore. You're the smartest and most courageous being I've ever known, and I've been around the block a long damn time, Clara. It's time for your people to see the female I fell in love with and to start loving her as much as I do, too."

Clara frowned, hating that the words she'd once longed to hear now came shrouded with humiliation. Hot tears stung her eyes. "You can't say that, Bronze. Words on a page don't negate one's actions. You lied to me about your true emotions, about us, about *me*."

The dirt littering the short distance between them kicked up into the air, clouding her already misted vision. Bronze appeared before her, faster than she thought possible. He was still on his knees, with eyes speaking pleas no warrior had ever known. Then his arms were around her waist, and he cradled his head in her lap like a child begging for atonement. By the Moon Mother, he clung to her, grasping at the back of her blouse and stretching it until she felt it pulling at the tops of her shoulders. The strength she'd always known him to possess was now around her, bunching into the cruxes of his joints with the force of a desperation that shook his sturdy frame.

"I'll tell you what my true emotions have been, Clara." Bronze shifted against her and placed a small dagger with a black blade—not metallic—in her fist, curled her fingers around it before wrapping his around hers, and pointed the lethal tip at his heart. "And if any lying words fall free, I happily give you permission to take the rest of them. The prime mages granted me a big fat mouth for a reason, and it's long past time I put it to good use."

There wasn't a thing Clara could do but hold the male in her lap as he gave everything to her. It was like being strapped into those past-vertical dive coasters he'd told her the humans loved so much, with any objectionable screams being swallowed up by the force of the fall.

"You want to talk about emotions? Fine, let's do it. I can't control my first thought. My lizard brain spews up whatever it needs to in the moment, and I execute it based on habit and skill. There's no logic in it, only emotional reaction. But that second thought? And the third? And the millionth? I sure as shit can control those thoughts. *Those* are the ones that have carried me through these eternally long years, keeping my brothers safe and keeping my miserable ass alive until I found you. Since then, though, you have been my *every* thought. The first, second, millionth. All of them. Emotions have nothing to do with the way my brain and soul are wired when it comes to you, and it took me an embarrassingly long time to realize that. You're not my emotional security blanket, Clara. You're my survival and the truest reason for my existence."

His back expanded on a great breath, the muscles shifting beneath his shirt, and Clara couldn't help but lay the knife down and drift her fingers over his body to map the breadth of him. "Malik, Polina, they're memories, ghosts of a time when I thought my station meant more than what it does now. I think a part of me was still trying to cling to that, to them. But you are my present, my reality, my future. I was so wrapped up in my goddamn head that I couldn't see what my heart and a frickin' goddess were trying to show me all along."

Then he lifted his head, and Clara's breath caught at the earnestness that stared back at her. "There will never be enough sunrises for me to express how sorry I am, nor will there be enough sunsets for me to vow against the moon how ardently I love you. But I'll keep doing it, day after day, night after night, because you're the first whispered word of my heart each time I rise and the last thought of my soul before I sleep. I love you, Clara. I need you to know that and to know that I'll happily follow you wherever you lead because you're the strongest being I know, and this sentinel of the Empyrean recognizes nothing above the strength of his queen."

There were words she meant to say, she was sure of it. Really powerful, monarch-worthy words that would have the male before her cower in fear. But, well, he was already cowering, wasn't he? And there were entire summits one had to climb before they could truly ascend to the heights he'd already placed her at, weren't there?

The tears that spilled over her cheeks smoothed away her doubts and answered her questions. All except one.

Clara moved her hands over the sides of his shorn scalp, curling her fingers around the downy skin above his ears. "Why?"

He grabbed up her hands, kissing her palms first, then the tattoo on her wrist. "Because I support my queen, now and always."

The vastness of the forest fell away from her. The vibrant greens above and loamy soil below were nothing more than vague sensations as she flung herself at him. And with the reflexes of a true warrior, Bronze caught her with practiced precision and guided them both to the soft earth. She didn't care about crushing him or dousing the poor male in a pool of her tears. It was the least he deserved and nowhere near the most of what she hoped for him. Oh, Moon Mother, she was a mess as she kissed him soundly and, yes, emotionally. Tears fled from her cheeks to his, chasing down both the cause and the cure for her present state of turmoil. But it wasn't until those strong arms banded around her back and pulled the tension free from her taut muscles that the words of her heart were let loose and finally permitted to soar free.

"I don't know how or why any of this happened, but I don't really care. My wolf, a far less emotional creature than me, mind you, claimed you from the moment she first smelled you in the forest, before I'd even fully risen to consciousness. But love has a way of carving out the meat from the fat, and nothing would gladden my lycan heart more than to spend the rest of my days filled with you by my side as my soul bond. My mate. My love."

His eyes misted over, and he squeezed her close as he blinked away the emotion pooling there. But when he opened his eyes again, they'd taken on a darker hue. "And don't forget consort. I kind of like the way that sounds. Gives off a naughty vibe, don't you think?"

On any other day, Clara would have rolled her eyes and begged the Moon Mother for patience and understanding. On this day, however, she mentally closed the curtain on any and all intrusions from fates heretofore known and unknown and made it her personal mission to consort with her soulmate in as many ways as her heart and wolf could imagine.

EPILOGUE

I t only took her about three months, but Clara was finally able to hold a piece of paper without thinking the thing would bite her or bring the untimely downfall of her monarchy.

Turned out, what she currently held in her hands would bring the exact opposite to her people: a gigantic cash fall.

"This is the fourth contract with human business owners this month. If this keeps up, we'll be able to expand our holdings into the natural reserves north of Montreal. I know many of the lycans have wanted more secure land for their second homes, and this lumber contract with those new developers will ensure that."

Bronze lifted his bare arms high and swung his carbon-fiber ax into the tree stump he'd been hacking away at. The wood promptly fell to pieces beneath his strength.

Much like she had a habit of doing, but she'd never admit it to him lest he keep her in their bed for weeks and never get anything done.

"It seems those mortals have the right of it, too," he said, tossing the hunks of wood into the back of a pull cart and grabbing his discarded shirt to wipe the sweat from his face and neck. "Everyone else is building out those huge multifamily townhome monstrosities that nobody wants. These guys are at least building actual single-family homes with the whole back-yard and double-wide driveway large enough for a basketball hoop and shit. They'd be fools not to sign with you, especially given our access to top-quality lumber." Then he walked over to her and gave her the same two kisses he always did when he got that dreamy-eyed look that told her he was proud of her.

One on her mouth and one on the side of her bald scalp.

Well, technically, it was an undercut, according to Bronze.

Clara touched the area on her head where he'd kissed her and dragged her fingers through the short fall of hair that began an inch or so above her ear and swooped across the rest of her head before falling at her chin. The idea for the style had come to her after the heat of the summer made head wraps unbear-able. Wending her way in and out of Bronze's world, she'd seen females with all sorts of hairstyles. Some styled short in a pixie fashion, and, like hers, buzzed on the sides, except still worn long and wavy.

There was freedom in the way human women owned their styles, and in many ways, Clara wanted to immortalize her own freedom. So, she kept her hair trimmed close to her scalp, where it had been shorn during the games in testament to her reclama-tion of power and how she would always use it in defense of her people.

Plus, she kind of adored the feel of Bronze's goatee brushing along her scalp, and as it seemed a favorite site for him to adore, she saw no reason to change it.

The expansion of business for her people had been another feat that had not only thrilled her heart but challenged her mind and business acumen for the first time in her life. With Bronze's help and the guidance of Pascal and her other advisors, she'd been able to establish safe and secure ways for the lycans to not only engage with human businesses but aggressively pursue them.

Turned out, under Bronze's guidance, trade industries, architecture, agriculture, and tourism had been the largest boons her people had ever seen. With skills honed over centuries that the humans couldn't manage without expensive schooling and apprenticeships, the lycans had been able to compete and advance in arenas her father had long shunned for being too lowborn: carpentry, crafts, construction, lumber. As the queen's consort, Bronze had facilitated all the contracts, inspecting the working environments to ensure lycan compatibility with minimal long-term exposure to metal and electronics. Sure, computer and general office jobs were largely out of the question for her people, but they had no problem with that.

Especially when word had gotten around over the past three months about the quality of their products and services across the various companies the monarchy and many of the lycans now controlled and operated.

It was a mighty cash fall, indeed.

"Have you thought about him at all?" Bronze jumped up onto the back of the cart and drew her close to him, wrapping the delicious weight of his arms around her. "Your father?"

A heavy sigh threatened to drag her shoulders down, but Bronze's support and the earthy comfort of his skin buoyed her. It had been a long time since they'd spoken of her decision regarding her father's fate, but the more she aired it out, the less it weighed on her.

"I've thought about him more than he deserves, quite honestly. But it's getting easier. Every time I encounter one of his previous paradigms throughout the kingdom and alter it in some way, I wipe a bit more of him out of existence, and that's a great relief. Sometimes I wonder whether I made the right choice in exiling him to the western lycan territories instead of executing him outright, but then I remember the shock on his face when I declared his fate in front of his former advisors and guards and how rewarding the satisfaction was, as was expunging the first of his many corrupt edicts: no more executions."

"Poetic justice."

"I'll just go with justice for now. You're the one with all the flowery words."

"Damn right," he said, squeezing her tighter. "And I say what you did to that piece of shit was pure fucking poetry."

Her father hadn't been the only one in the stronghold who'd been stunned when she gave the order *not* to kill him for the witnessed attempt on her life. Oh, she'd been more than tempted to. Had almost done it, even. But every time she looked in the mirror, she couldn't stand the idea of a murderer looking back at her. That was what she would have become if she'd had him executed. A monarch no better than her father.

Besides, death was a coward's way out. If she truly wanted him to know the extent of the vengeance she wrought, what better way than to build up the monarchy according to her vision, instill the love of her people into every decision she made, and grow their commerce by fiftyfold, all while carving him out of the bloodline and banishing him to the very people who'd lost their beloved lycan leader to the king's own games?

The whole construct of capital punishment hadn't just needed an overhaul but a female's touch, as Bronze loved to point out to her.

She couldn't say she entirely disagreed.

Clara shifted in his arms and rested her chin on his chest, giving into her wolf's very insistent urge to rub up against him. "Let's not discuss him. He's not worth it. I'd rather focus on happier things. Speaking of which, will all of your brothers and their mates be joining us for dinner tonight?"

"Are you kidding me? They wouldn't miss it. Eun Hee is, and I say this with all the respect I have for my beloved queen, the single best hire you've asked for my input on. The female is a beast in the kitchen, and Iron's already looking forward to the lycan's japchae. It's those glassy noodles, man. Who knew they were made from sweet potato starch?"

"She is quite magical," Clara agreed but stumbled a beat before pressing him further about what she knew still weighed heavily on him. "Will Rhode be there this time?"

Bronze sighed deeply. "I don't think so."

"But he assured you he wasn't upset about the relic's power being spent."

"Yeah, well, he's a spy. It kind of goes without saying that deception is part of his game."

"Your brother would lie to you?"

Bronze twisted his mouth with careful consideration. "I think he's been through things none of us know about, and he may never reveal them to us. All we can do is be there for him and leave the door open for whenever he decides to walk through it."

"You truly are a magnificent male, Bronze," she said as she rose up to kiss him. "And to think I almost closed the door on you entirely."

"Nah. I would have muscled my way through it eventually."

"Oh yeah?" The corner of her brow hitched in a mock challenge. "What makes you so sure?"

"Because I've got stamina, princess." Dark promise flared brightly in his citrine eyes, and her stomach tumbled beneath the force of his words. "That and a shitload of motivation. And if it takes another eternity of swearing however many oaths I need to in order to prove how much I love you, well, I've got nothing but time."

As Bronze's mouth peppered her neck with sweet, tantalizing kisses, Clara smiled and sank into his embrace. An embrace that she had finally come to know and adore and would do so thoroughly for the rest of her days.

Life was a game, after all, and she had the best partner to play with.

THE SILENCE in the den's great hall was oppressive in its weight. Tall granite walls long ago carved into caverns were their own form of sentinels. Ironic, really, especially when Rhode was the only one left behind while the rest of the angels and their mates had gone to the lycan lands for dinner.

Even in solitude, in a place that had become as true of a home as he'd ever had, he couldn't escape his stone jailors.

Rhode leaned on his bo staff and covered his eyes against the shame that always flooded his system whenever his mind wandered to the abyss of all he'd lost. It had become a private collection of sorts, a book of memories one only took out when they wanted the reminders of how far they've fallen and had no interest in the ropes dangling around them, offering a way out.

His anger did not lie with Bronze or any of his brothers. After all, they had rescued him from Cyro's domain. Without their aid, well, he didn't want to think about what his existence would look like. There were rare lucid moments when he imagined that, had he not been saved, his life couldn't possibly have been worse than what he'd already endured.

Then again, he knew firsthand just how imaginative Cyro could be.

Rhode shook his head, banishing the thoughts away as was his practice, and calmed his breathing by choosing an object in the room to center himself around.

Big mistake. Huge. Because there wasn't a single item in the space that didn't remind him of his lesser seraphim status among a mansion of sentinels. The tapestries on the walls depicting images of mortal history he'd not seen, the small practice area's array of weapons he'd no experience with, even the modern machinery in the kitchen, none of which he found intuitive.

He had been a spy. A commander of a powerful legion of seraphim.

But never had he been a sentinel, no matter how thoroughly they'd welcomed him into their home and their hearts.

Rhode's heart clenched tighter at the distinction, at how much he'd lost and how far he had yet to go. Entire civilizations had passed him by. People. Languages. Species. All while he'd been rotting away as Cyro's captive, a plaything to the demon charmers and their toxic tortures and experiments.

The relic could have changed all of that, and in the quiet of the den, with all the sentinels enjoying one another's company at the lycan stronghold, Rhode allowed himself to sink into the remorse of yet another thing lost.

Lost to him but not entirely gone.

He lifted his head and let the conviction of the mountain infuse his emotions, fueling the intrepid rage that he only ever let simmer below the surface. None would be prepared for the danger should he finally let it burst free.

He loved the sentinels. He truly did, with all his being. They were as much brothers to him as any there were. But *he* was not a sentinel. Hell, he was barely an angel after what had been done to him.

But all that would soon change. Soon, he would have his vengeance, and absolutely nothing would withstand the power he'd bring down on the charmers when he found them.

"I will not stray," he whispered into the empty cavern of the great mountain.

There was still another half of the relic, and if Cyro hadn't used up its magic already, then Rhode still had a token to obtain. One final journey to ease his soul's pain.

There was no going back for him. Nothing would stand in his way of exacting his revenge and bringing down the ruler of the demon charmers once and for all. Not his brothers. Not his powers.

And especially not a woman.

RHODE MAY HAVE INADVERTENTLY GUIDED Bronze toward his soul bond, but that's the last thing on the sagely seraph's mind. In fact, the only thing that's been front and center for him lately is one eternally guiding truth: vengeance on all demonkind. Find out what happens when a demon female who's the only one of her kind, and also Rhode's greatest enemy, turns out to be his greatest salvation. Start reading *Angel's Vengeance!*

CAN WE KEEP IN TOUCH? Are you curious to see what happens when Clara volunteers to help out a friend and brings Bronze along? It's all fun and games until he's left standing in front of three high chairs. Find out what happens when one of the fiercest warriors of all time embarks on the most dangerous mission of all time: babysitting two-year-old lycan triplets. Claim your BONUS EPILOGUE when you sign up to my newsletter to see how our big-mouthed fallen angel handles his first babysitting adventure. Enjoy!

THANK you so much for reading *Angel's Conquest!* If you loved seeing Bronze and Clara's relationship grow, let your friends know. Help other readers fall in love with this couple, and all those hunky angels, by leaving a review.

SCAN THE QR code to start reading *Angel's Vengeance* and the BONUS EPILOGUE today!

ACKNOWLEDGMENTS

There are far too many Claras in the world and not nearly enough writers to tell all their stories. This was my attempt to start chipping away at that mountain, while also trying to build it back up stronger than ever.

I'll never forget Niecy Nash-Betts' Emmy Award acceptance speech, in which she proudly declares, "And you know who I want to thank? I want to thank me, for believing in me and doing what they said I could not do." That's the energy I always hope to carry into whatever endeavors may lie ahead, and that is why I write.

As always, a huge thank you to Ben, who fights alongside me so I can tell my stories.

ABOUT THE AUTHOR

Aimee Robinson is a lover of romance novels in all forms. Her absolute favorites, though, are the ones that offer a little bit of something *extra*: time travel, guardian angels, good old-fashioned meddlesome grandmothers with a supernatural secret to hide, you name it.

She believes romance novels should transport you from the humdrum to the swoonworthy, preferably while being curled up on the couch with chocolate and tea (or a martini . . . or both!). Aimee's overactive imagination lends itself to fun tales with emotional adventures, sexy snark, and happily ever afters.

When not writing or reading, Aimee enjoys spending time with her husband and keeping up with her two young sons.